"Don't look now, but I think we have some admirers," Lindsey whispered excitedly as they walked to the car.

"Where?" Crystal asked, her head spinning around as her eyes darted everywhere. "Tell me where!"

"Don't mind Crystal," Jade explained. "She's a little guy crazy."

"The house next door," Lindsey said. "I saw a guy peeking out of the window. I think he was checking us out!"

"Cute?" Crystal asked as she casually gazed over at the house.

"Not sure. I couldn't tell."

Crystal slid into the front seat next to Jade. "We'll have to introduce ourselves once we get back. After all, they're our neighbors."

Spring Fling

SABRINA JAMES

✿ ✿ ✿ ✿ ✿ Point ✿ ✿ ✿ ✿ ✿

Copyright © 2010 by John Scognamiglio.

All rights reserved. Published by Point, an imprint of
Scholastic Inc., *Publishers since 1920*.
SCHOLASTIC, POINT, and associated logos
are trademarks and/or registered trademarks
of Scholastic Inc.

No part of this publication may be reproduced, stored
in a retrieval system, or transmitted in any form or by
any means, electronic, mechanical, photocopying,
recording, or otherwise, without written permission of
the publisher. For information regarding permission,
write to: Scholastic Inc., Attention: Permissions
Department, 557 Broadway, New York, NY 10012.

Library of Congress Cataloging-in-Publication Data

James, Sabrina.
Spring fling / by Sabrina James.
p. cm.
Summary: Three groups of teenagers flirt, experiment
with their images, form new friendships, and hit the
beach while in Miami on spring break.
ISBN-13: 978-0-545-13603-7 (alk. paper)
ISBN-10: 0-545-13603-2 (alk. paper)
[1. Spring break — Fiction. 2. Dating (Social
customs) — Fiction. 3. Self-perception — Fiction.
4. Beaches — Fiction. 5. Miami (Fla.) —
Fiction.] I. Title.
PZ7.J154365Sp 2010
[Fic] — dc22   2009021126

12 11 10 9 8 7 6 5 4 3 2 1   10 11 12 13 14 15/0

Printed in the U.S.A.
First printing, February 2010

Acknowledgments

Most authors usually have one editor. This book was lucky enough to have three. First, special thanks to Abby McAden, who asked me to write the first North Ridge High novel, <u>Secret Santa</u>, and allows me to keep going back.

Thanks also to Morgan Matson, who worked with me on <u>Secret Santa</u>, <u>Be Mine</u>, and the outline for <u>Spring Fling</u>. And thanks to my new editor, Amanda Maciel, who helped make <u>Spring Fling</u> the best that it could be with her insightful comments.

Thanks also to my agent, Evan Marshall, and to all my family and friends.

Chapter One

"Where's my luggage?!"

Seventeen-year-old Danielle Hollis watched for the third time as the suitcases from American Airlines flight 647 from New York to Miami wound past her. Other travelers were snatching up their suitcases and carryalls, ready to start their vacations, but Danielle couldn't begin her own vacation because she was still waiting for her bags.

She took a deep breath, trying not to panic. Her luggage was going to eventually slide past her. It had to. She had packed more than just her clothes. She had also packed her SAT study guides, and she *needed* those books.

Looking around the brightly colored airport filled with travelers, Danielle once again wondered how she had wound up so many miles away from

1

home. She should have been sitting in the North Ridge High library, going over vocabulary words, instead of wondering where her suitcases were.

It had all started the month before when her older sister, Jade, a college sophomore, called one Sunday night in February during a blizzard. Classes had been canceled for the next day, and Danielle had invited her two best friends, Ava Romano and Lindsey Kennedy, to spend the night. They had been watching a marathon of *The Real World* on MTV when the phone rang. Danielle had been surprised to hear her sister's voice on the other end of the line. Usually the only time Jade called was when she needed their parents to send her more money. And they had just done that the previous week. Before Danielle could say anything, Jade got right to the point. Would Danielle and her friends like to come down to Miami during spring break?

"Why would we want to come to Miami for spring break?" Danielle had asked.

As soon as Ava and Lindsey heard the words *spring break*, they lost all interest in *The Real World* and rushed to Danielle's side, trying to hear Jade's side of the conversation.

"My friend Crystal's aunt owns this fab beach house and she invited us to come down for spring break. Three of our sorority sisters were going to

2

come, but now they can't make it, and I thought maybe you'd like to. Since I went away to college, we don't get to spend as much time together as we used to."

That was true. When Jade had gone off to Emory University in Atlanta, Danielle had been thrilled to *finally* have her own bedroom. She and Jade had always shared, and they were *complete* opposites. While Danielle was neat and organized, Jade was a complete slob. Her side of the bedroom always looked like her closet had exploded. There were usually piles of jeans, sweaters, skirts, and T-shirts — not to mention boxes of shoes! — scattered everywhere.

Those first few days, when Jade had left to start her freshman year, Danielle had loved having a bedroom all to herself. For the first time in years, everything was put away and in its place. But after the second week of having her own room, she realized something. She missed her sister, especially at night. Usually when they were getting ready to fall asleep, they'd talk to each other across the room and discuss their days. Sure, they kept in touch with texting and e-mail and phone calls, but it wasn't the same as actually having Jade a few feet away.

"You know I'd love to see you, but the SATs are in May. I have to study for them."

"You can study down here!" Jade had insisted.

Before Danielle could say anything else, Lindsey had snatched away the phone. After talking with Jade, Lindsey hung up and then filled Ava in on the conversation. It took some arm twisting, but Ava and Lindsey finally convinced Danielle that they *had to* go to Miami. After all, how could they say no to a free week in a luxurious beach house? With Ava and Lindsey standing by her side, happily jumping up and down and already making plans for their week, Danielle had called her sister back and said they would come to Miami.

Thoughts of Jade made Danielle check the time on her watch. It was two o'clock. Jade was going to be here any second and she *still* didn't have her luggage. Could her bags have slid by her and she didn't notice?

"Has anyone seen my bags?" Danielle asked. She expected Ava and Lindsey to answer, but they didn't. "Guys?" Still no answer.

Danielle turned around and realized why they weren't answering. Ava and Lindsey were too busy checking out all the cute guys milling around the airport.

Okay, she couldn't blame them. There was *lots* of eye candy. Tall guys. Short guys. Muscular guys. Guys with ponytails and guys with buzz cuts. She bet the beaches were going to be packed this week.

Danielle walked over to Ava and Lindsey, snapping her fingers in their faces. "Hello! Is anyone listening to me? I'm in the middle of a crisis and I could use some support."

Lindsey, a petite brunette, blinked, tearing her blue eyes away from a cute Jonas brother look-alike. "Sorry? I wasn't paying attention."

"Obviously."

"What's up?" Ava asked, tossing her long red curls over one shoulder.

"This doesn't make any sense," Danielle said. "We all checked in together, and you and Lindsey have your bags. Mine should have come out right after yours."

"Everything gets all mixed up when they toss the bags into the plane," Lindsey explained. "And other people are still waiting."

Danielle looked back at the luggage carousel. Yes, there were people still waiting, but not as many as before. She nervously chewed her lower lip. A thought had popped into her mind, but she didn't want to say it. If she did, she was afraid it would come true. "You don't think they forgot to put my bags on the plane, do you?" She didn't wait for Ava and Lindsey to answer. "I bet that's what happened!" Danielle marched over to the nearest customer service desk. "I'm going to complain!"

"Danielle, wait!" Lindsey cried out, a note of panic in her voice.

Danielle stopped and turned around. "What?"

Lindsey didn't say anything, but she didn't have to. She had a guilty expression on her face.

Danielle turned to Ava, who had the *exact* same guilty look on her face.

Danielle *knew* that look.

She had seen it many times before. It appeared whenever Ava and Lindsey teamed up to do something they felt they "needed" to do for Danielle.

Like the time last October when they told Parker Manning, North Ridge High's star quarterback, that Danielle had a crush on him.

Or the time sophomore year when they set her up on a blind date with Andrew Monahan.

Or when they were seven and they pushed her into the pool at the country club after she completed her swimming lessons because she was too afraid to jump into the water and start swimming.

Danielle marched back over to them. "What did you do?" she asked.

"We didn't do anything," Ava answered.

"Except maybe we forgot to check your bags," Lindsey said in a rush.

Danielle could feel her eyes popping out of her head. "What?! How could you forget to check my bags?"

"Because we didn't really forget," Ava added in her own rush of words. "We did it on purpose."

"You did it *on purpose*?" Danielle shrieked.

Lindsey hurried to explain. "You're supposed to be in Miami having fun! Not studying for the SATs. Your bags were filled with test guides. You hardly packed any cute clothes or beachy outfits!"

"When you went inside to get your e-ticket, we gave your bags back to your parents," Lindsey explained.

"My parents were in on this?"

"They wanted you to have a good time," Ava said. "They know how hard you've been studying."

"Because I have to ace my SAT in May!"

"You already aced the PSAT and you've been studying like crazy. You also took that prep class," Lindsey reminded her. "You're more than prepared, Danielle. You're *super* prepared."

Danielle sat down on a bench. "Okay, geniuses, you've succeeded with your plan. I'm not going to be able to study while we're down here. But what am I supposed to wear for the next week? I have no clothes, remember?"

"That's the best part!" Lindsey gushed, sitting next to Danielle. "As an early birthday present, we're taking you on a shopping spree! We're going to get you a whole new wardrobe. Your parents are chipping in, too!"

7

"Not only that," Ava added, sitting on the other side of Danielle, "but we're taking you to a salon for new hair and makeup."

"We're giving you a Spring Break Makeover!" Lindsey exclaimed.

Ava and Lindsey then stared at Danielle, almost holding their breath, as if waiting for her to start shrieking like a contestant on a game show.

"Am I supposed to be doing cartwheels or something?" she asked.

Lindsey sighed and rolled her eyes. "Come on, Danielle! Loosen up! A couple of days of relaxing isn't going to make you forget everything you've already learned. You're one of the smartest juniors at North Ridge High! Everyone knows you're going to get into whatever college you want."

"You're not mad at us, are you?" Ava asked.

"Of course I'm mad," Danielle grumbled. "But I'll get over it. I always do, don't I?" After all, they were her best friends. You couldn't stay mad at your best friends for very long, especially when their intentions were good.

"Hey! There's Jade!" Lindsey exclaimed, pointing a finger.

Danielle looked across the airport. There was no mistaking her older sister. Every guy in the airport had his eyes glued to her. Why wouldn't they? Jade was gorgeous.

8

Today she was wearing faded denim shorts and a white halter top decorated with tiny red hearts. She glowed with a fresh tan, and her long blond hair was slicked back in a ponytail. Crystal, whom Danielle had never met before, was just as gorgeous, with cocoa-colored skin and shoulder-length brown hair streaked with strands of red. She kind of resembled Tyra Banks from *America's Next Top Model*.

"Hey, y'all," Crystal greeted them, her voice oozing with a Southern accent. "Welcome to Miami."

"Okay, what's wrong?" Jade asked as she approached, giving Ava and Lindsey a quick kiss on the cheek before hugging Danielle. "You have a sour puss and I know that look." Jade checked her watch. "Are you mad? We're not that late. Like ten minutes."

"I'm not mad at you. I'm mad at them. You will not believe what they did to me!"

Jade took off her oversize sunglasses and perched them on top of her head. "If you're mad, it can only be something that they needed to do."

"How can you be taking their side when you haven't heard my side?"

"Because you always overreact."

"I do not!"

"You do, too!"

"No, I *don't*," Danielle insisted through gritted teeth.

Jade sighed. "Okay, you don't."

"Where are your bags?" Crystal asked.

"Back in New York," Danielle answered.

"Why are they in New York?" Jade asked, sounding puzzled.

"THAT'S what I'm so mad about!"

Danielle quickly updated Jade and Crystal on Ava and Lindsey's latest scheme.

"The worst part is that Mom and Dad were in on it with them!" Danielle finished.

"If you want my opinion," Crystal said, "I don't know why you're so mad. After all, you're getting a shopping spree! What's so bad about free clothes?"

"Can I give you some sisterly advice?" Jade offered.

"What?" Danielle asked.

"They did the right thing."

"Thank you, Jade!" Lindsey exclaimed.

"I *knew* you were going to take their side!" Danielle hissed.

"I'm not taking sides," Jade insisted. "You can't always be studying, Danielle. You need to give yourself some downtime. Otherwise you're going to burn yourself out. Why are you worrying about your SATs anyway? You're going to ace them and

10

get into any college you want. Besides, you're taking the exam twice, right? If you're not happy with your score from the May exam, you'll be taking it again in the fall. Forget about being Danielle the Bookworm. For the next couple of days, try being Danielle the Party Girl instead!"

Aren't you the party girl in this family? Danielle wanted to say. But she didn't. She could see there was no way she was going to win this argument.

"Well, let's head out to the car," Jade said, taking one of Ava's bags while Crystal reached for another.

"Need any help with those?" a deep voice asked.

Danielle turned around and saw two guys, wearing University of Miami T-shirts with cutoff sleeves, standing behind them.

Crystal gave them a warm smile. "Thanks, sugar. You're so thoughtful. Follow me."

"So what's the plan for this afternoon?" Lindsey asked as they headed for the parking garage.

"Why don't we go to the beach house first, drop off the bags, grab some lunch, and then head to the nearest mall so we can get my baby sister some new clothes," Jade suggested. "I'll even buy her some new things."

"Count me in!" Crystal called over her shoulder. "I never say no to shopping!"

"Okay with you, Danielle?" Jade asked. "Or would you rather do something else?"

"That sounds fine," Danielle said, pasting a smile on her face while secretly counting down the days until they left Miami.

When the girls got to the beach house, they met Crystal's aunt Sharla, who was on her way out the door. Sharla was in her early thirties and just as gorgeous as Crystal. She almost looked like her older sister.

"Feel free to make yourselves at home," she said after introducing herself. "I'm afraid the cupboards are a bit bare. I only opened the house yesterday and I haven't had a chance to go shopping."

"Don't worry, Aunt Sharla. We'll do it," Crystal offered. "We're heading out to the mall in a little bit and we'll stop at the supermarket."

"Great!" she said as she slid behind the steering wheel of her car, a vintage 1969 cherry red Mustang. "Have fun!"

"Your aunt is beautiful," Danielle said as they walked into the house.

"She used to be a model, but now she works as a photographer. She does a lot of traveling. There's a gallery in downtown Miami that shows her photos. That's why she's in town this week. She's getting ready to do a new show." Crystal turned to everyone. "Ready for the grand tour?"

The beach house was gorgeous. Walking around from room to room, Danielle felt like it was something out of a design magazine. The floors were blond wood and the furniture was all super comfy, in bright ocean colors with huge cushions and pillows. The walls were painted a sky blue, and the curtains and drapes were all sheer. Seashells were scattered everywhere, and there were tons of plants and bouquets of flowers. The whole interior of the house felt as if a little bit of the beach had been brought inside.

After the tour, the girls headed upstairs and divided themselves into bedrooms. Ava and Lindsey decided to share a room while Jade and Danielle took another and Crystal had her own. Once everyone had finished unpacking, they headed outside to go to the mall.

"Don't look now, but I think we have some admirers," Lindsey whispered excitedly as they walked to the car.

"Where?" Crystal asked, her head spinning around as her eyes darted everywhere. "Tell me where!"

"Don't mind Crystal," Jade explained. "She's a little guy crazy."

"The house next door," Lindsey said. "I saw a

guy peeking out of the window. I think he was checking us out!"

"Cute?" Crystal asked as she casually gazed over at the house.

"Not sure. I couldn't tell."

Crystal slid into the front seat next to Jade. "We'll have to introduce ourselves once we get back. After all, they're our neighbors."

As everyone got into the car, Danielle glanced over her shoulder, trying to see if anyone was still peeking out at them. She didn't see anything.

As she buckled up her seat belt, she listened to the conversation in the car. There was no mistaking the excitement in everyone's voices. They were all looking forward to having a good time this week. It got Danielle to thinking.

Maybe, just maybe, she would try to loosen up and have a good time, too.

Chapter Two

Cooper St. John was trying not to be seen as he stared out the window at his next-door neighbors. He'd push the drapes to one side, take a quick peek, and then let the drapes fall back into place, before doing it again.

A voice from the couch asked, "Who are you spying on?"

"I'm not spying on anyone," Cooper said as he walked over to the couch and plopped down next to his best friend, Ethan Moore.

"Uh-huh," Ethan answered, not lifting his eyes from the issue of *Sports Illustrated* in his hands.

Damian Marsala, who was sprawled across a brown leather armchair, playing a handheld video game, murmured, "Were you checking out girls? Maybe some *hot* girls?"

"Maybe I was," Cooper said.

Damian instantly pulled his eyes away from his video game. "How many were there?"

"Five."

Damian pumped a fist in the air. "Score! One for each of us! What did they look like? Details. I want details!"

"Have you decided which one you want?" Ethan asked, eyes still glued to his magazine.

"It doesn't matter which girl Coop wants, because they're all going to want him," Damian said. "They always do. That's one of the perks of growing up in the lap of luxury."

"Are you saying girls only like me for my family's money?"

Cooper's family's wealth was a sore point with him. It wasn't that he didn't like being rich. He did. It gave him lots of nice things. Vacations. Great seats at concerts and sporting events. An iPhone and an iPod. His own car and motorcycle. But sometimes . . . and he would *never* admit this to his friends . . . sometimes he did wonder if one of the reasons girls liked going out with him was because his family was so rich.

"Of course not!" Damian exclaimed, cutting into his thoughts. "You look like an Abercrombie & Fitch model and you dress like one, too. Based on that alone, you're a catch. But girls also like guys who can treat them like a princess, and you always treat your girlfriends like princesses."

"When he *has* a girlfriend!" Ethan cracked.

It was no secret that Cooper was a serial dater. His classmates at South Ridge High had nicknamed him Smooth Operator because he was always going from girl to girl to girl. He knew his friends thought he grew tired of the girls he dated, but that wasn't it. Whenever he dated a new girl, there was always a feeling of excitement. Maybe this girl was going to be *the one*. At first, things would be great. They'd go out, have a fun time, get to know each other.

But then . . .

Then something would happen that would make him wonder if the girl he was dating was really into *him*.

He wanted to be liked for who he was and *not* his family's money.

This winter, he'd been dating Sherry Mulligan. For Valentine's Day, he'd gotten her a small box of chocolates and a bouquet of daisies. When he showed up on her doorstep, there was no mistaking the disappointment on her face. She'd quickly covered it up, but instinctively he had *known*. She'd been expecting a bigger box of candy. A bigger bouquet of flowers. And when he plugged himself into the

17

South Ridge High gossip grapevine, he learned that Sherry had been expecting a dozen red roses and a five-pound box of Godiva chocolates.

He ended things with Sherry the weekend after Valentine's Day.

Then there was Lisa Lonigan. Last spring, he'd invited her to the sophomore prom. As the night of the dance approached, she asked him if he was going to rent a limo to take them. When he told her he wasn't, she pouted, saying that everyone else was going in a limo and it wasn't like he couldn't afford it!

Cooper stood Lisa up the night of the sophomore prom and went with another girl.

Another time, he was dating Hillary Benson. He'd taken her to a movie, and afterward he suggested they grab a quick bite. Everyone at South Ridge High usually went to the Burger Hut, a local diner, but that wasn't good enough for Hillary. She wanted to go to the North Ridge Country Club. When he explained that he wasn't a member, she seemed shocked.

"But your family is so rich!" she had exclaimed.

That had been his last date with Hillary.

He didn't know why, but he always seemed to go out with girls who wanted to date a rich guy. They might not be obvious about it at first, but eventually it came out. Just once, he'd like to go out with a girl who was into *him*. A girl who didn't know that his father was an international banker and his mother was a stock investor. A girl who didn't know they lived in the biggest house in their town — okay, it was a McMansion — and that they had four cars, a vacation house on Martha's Vineyard, and a ski house in Denver.

Sometimes he wished he could be someone else.

"How about we pay a visit to our next-door neighbors?" Damian suggested. "The sooner we get to know them, the better!"

"They're not home," Cooper said, picking up a basketball and spinning it on his finger. "They went out. I saw them getting into their car."

"Were they wearing bikinis?" Damian eagerly asked. "Maybe they were headed to the beach. We could track them down."

Cooper shook his head. "They weren't dressed for the beach. I guess we'll just have to wait for them to get back."

"Bummer," Damian said. "So which one are you going after?"

Cooper shrugged and stopped spinning the basketball. "I don't know. They were all pretty, but two of them seemed a little older. I think they're in college like Steve and Howie."

Cooper and his friends were sharing the beach

19

house with Damian's older brother, Steve, a college sophomore, as well as Damian and Steve's cousin, Howie, a freshman. They were still waiting for them to arrive from the airport. Once they showed up, they planned on heading to the local supermarket so they could stock up on groceries for the week.

"Well, Ethan and I will stand aside while you work your magic. We'll take the ones you don't want."

"You know, he really doesn't have an advantage," Ethan said, still glued to his magazine. "These girls don't know anything about Cooper. For all they know, he's just like us."

As soon as the words were out of Ethan's mouth, Cooper realized something. Ethan was right.

The girls next door *didn't* know who he was.

They knew nothing about him!

Only seconds ago, he had wished he could be someone else.

Now he had that chance!

"Let's prove it," Cooper said.

"Prove what?" Damian asked, picking up his video game and starting to play again.

"That I can get one of those girls to fall for me. And she'd be falling just for me."

"How?"

"By switching places."

"With who?"

"Ethan!"

"What?" Ethan exclaimed, finally pulling his eyes away from his magazine.

Cooper nodded. "For the next week, you'll be the rich guy and I'll be the poor guy."

"I'm not poor!" Ethan exclaimed.

"No," Damian agreed. "But you're not loaded the way he is."

"We'll switch places," Cooper exclaimed, getting excited by his idea. "I'll give you all my credit cards." He reached into the pocket of his jeans and dangled the keys of the Mercedes convertible he had driven them down in. "My car, too. While you're living it up, I'll just be the average guy next door."

"Let's really make this interesting," Damian said, tossing the video game back on the coffee table and rubbing his hands together. "Let's make it into a bet."

"A bet?" Cooper asked. "What kind of bet?"

"I don't think I'm going to like the sound of this," Ethan groaned. "Especially since it involves me!"

"You switch places and you each romance one of our next-door neighbors. Whoever gets kissed first wins."

"What does the winner get?" Cooper asked.

21

"Yeah," Ethan said sarcastically. "Mr. Money-bags is the guy who has everything, in case you've forgotten. I don't have much to offer."

"Let's see," Damian murmured as he thought about it. Then he snapped his fingers. "I've got it! If Ethan wins, he gets to drive Cooper's Mercedes for the rest of the school year. And if Cooper wins, then Ethan washes the Mercedes every week for the rest of the school year."

"Sounds fair to me," Cooper said.

"I don't know about this," Ethan said, rubbing a hand across the back of his neck. "What if they find out?"

"They're not going to find out," Damian said. "How would they? Unless you blab it to them! Besides, after this week, we're never going to see them again! We're on spring break! Romances start and end here. They don't come back home with you."

Cooper dangled his car keys again, waving them in front of Ethan's eyes like a hypnotist. "What do you say, Ethan? Are you up for it?"

Ethan was tempted.

Very tempted.

He wanted to say yes.

The words were on the tip of his tongue.

He was dying to get behind the wheel of Cooper's Mercedes. He'd been jealous ever since Coop had gotten the car for his sixteenth birthday last year. It wasn't an evil/bad jealousy but more a wistful *I wish my parents could afford to buy me a Mercedes for my birthday* envy. Ethan's own car was a 1996 Toyota that he'd inherited from his uncle. It needed a new paint job as well as an updated stereo system. It was definitely *not* a car that girls noticed. Unlike Cooper's. But Cooper didn't even need his car. Girls flocked to him.

It was as Damian said. Coop looked like he had stepped out of the pages of an Abercrombie & Fitch ad. He had straight dirty blond hair that was always falling across his forehead, ice blue eyes, and sculpted arms, legs, and abs. Not to mention his killer smile bracketed by two dimples.

Damian wasn't hard on the eyes either and always had plenty of girls to choose from, too. He was over six feet tall, muscular, with green eyes, jet-black hair, and a swarthy complexion that made it look like he was tan all year round.

And then there was Ethan.

The average guy.

His hair was always out of control. It was a springy mass of brown curls that never did what he wanted it to do. His eyes were a plain brown, and no matter how many hours he spent in the gym, he couldn't add any muscle. Whenever he was standing next to Cooper and Damian, he felt like a ninety-eight-pound weakling.

It wasn't that he didn't have dates. He did. But Cooper and Damian were *always* surrounded by girls. They were *pursued*.

Ethan had never been pursued, and sometimes he wondered what that would be like.

Maybe he could find out this week.

Washing Coop's car would be a small price to pay, even if he had the car only for spring break. He'd ask out one of the girls next door, just to make Cooper and Damian think he was taking the bet seriously, but he wouldn't make her think he was interested in anything long-term. First of all, he didn't like the idea of leading someone on. Second, he wanted to do his own thing this week. He didn't want to hang out with some girl he was never going to see again.

Besides, he was going to have all the perks of being Cooper St. John. That meant driving around Miami in a Mercedes, seeing how the other half lived.

And dated!

This was one bet he didn't mind losing.

What could possibly go wrong?

"You're on!" Ethan exclaimed, snatching the car keys out of Cooper's hands.

Chapter Three

"Stop staring at the clock! It's one minute later than the last time you checked the time."

At the sound of her family's live-in housekeeper's voice, Mindy Yee turned away from the clock.

"Where are they, Carmela? They should have been here thirty minutes ago."

Carmela shrugged as she walked into the living room with a tray of snacks. "Maybe their plane was delayed or they hit traffic on the way from the airport," she said as she began taking bowls off the tray and placing them on the coffee table. "Don't forget, it's the first day of spring break. The roads are going to be crazy."

There was no way Mindy could forget that today was the first day of spring break. It was because of spring break that she finally had a chance to become friends with the North Ridge High Princess Posse. Of course, no one called them that to their faces, but it was their nickname and everyone knew it.

The North Ridge High Princess Posse consisted of Wanda Wong, Lacey Ramirez, and Vivienne Oleson. They were pretty and popular and had ruled the North Ridge High social scene since freshman year.

And ever since freshman year, Mindy had wanted to be friends with them.

No, she wanted to be more than just friends.

She wanted to be a part of their group.

Because everyone at North Ridge High belonged to a group. Except her. There were the slackers, the rockers, the sci-fi nerds. Amber Davenport and Shawna Westin had ruled the school for a while, until Amber went off to boarding school and Shawna started spending all her time with her boyfriend, Connor. Claudia Monroe was another queen of the North Ridge High social scene, although she was no longer friends with Eden Atkins and Natalie Bauer, who used to hang out with her. Eden and Natalie now spent most of their time with Jennifer Harris and Violet Wagner. The four of them had bonded after the Valentine's Day contest for Most Romantic Couple. And then there were Noelle Kramer, Lily Norris, and Celia

Armstrong. They had been joined at the hip ever since the Secret Santa exchange in December.

It wasn't that people didn't know Mindy. They did because she was always throwing parties, and her guest list was always long. Mindy's motto was, the more, the merrier! But at the end of the night, when the party was over, she was usually all alone to clean up the mess. No one ever offered to stay and help.

There was also *another* reason everyone at North Ridge High knew her. . . .

And not a good one.

She was North Ridge High's queen of gossip.

Its very own Gossip Girl.

Only without the cloak of invisibility.

Was it her fault that she was always in the wrong place at the wrong time? Could she help it if she saw or overheard things that were supposed to be secret?

She knew the *right* thing to do was not to repeat the info she stumbled upon, but Mindy wanted people to like her. She needed a way to work her way into conversations. To get their attention.

So, whenever she saw or heard something she wasn't supposed to, she repeated it. She couldn't help herself. She liked being the one who knew something before everyone else, casually dropping clues and hints until her classmates were begging her to share what she knew. When she dropped her bombshells, she liked seeing the shocked expressions on the faces of her listeners. She liked hearing their gasps of surprise. For just a few minutes, *she* was the center of attention. *She* was the person everyone wanted to be with. It gave her hope that maybe — just maybe — this time she'd be able to form a friendship with someone. And once forming a friendship, she could stop gossiping. She wouldn't need to do it anymore because she'd be too busy being a friend.

Of course, that never happened. Once she shared what she knew, her listeners ran off to tell their friends.

Leaving her alone again.

Being a gossip backfired on her.

After all, friendship was about trust, and how could you trust someone who was a blabbermouth?

But there was a difference between gossiping and keeping secrets.

If she had a close friend and that friend told her something in confidence, she would never, ever repeat it.

Of course, no one had ever given her the chance to prove it.

Mindy knew gossiping was wrong and she didn't want to do it.

But after three years of being North Ridge High's queen of gossip, how could she stop?

It was her identity.

It was how people knew her.

It was all she had.

If she stopped gossiping, she'd be no one.

And that scared her.

She was the girl who had everything except what she wanted the most.

All she wanted was a friend.

Just one friend.

There were times when Mindy felt sorry for herself, and she knew she shouldn't. Her parents were rich and successful and gave her whatever she wanted. Within reason, of course! They owned a popular restaurant, House of Yee, in her hometown, and it looked like the restaurant might be going national. The whole reason behind the trip to Miami was to meet with potential investors. Because they were going to be busy during the day, her parents told her she could invite three friends to come along and they would pay for their plane tickets. Immediately, Mindy had invited Wanda, Lacey, and Vivienne.

She'd been nervous extending the invitation — what if they said no? — but they had instantly accepted when she called them, and Mindy had been thrilled. She finally had the chance she'd been waiting for and she wasn't going to blow it. Ever since freshman year, she'd tried to be friends with Wanda — she knew Wanda was the one she had to win over — but for some reason, Wanda resisted. Maybe it was because Wanda *knew* that Mindy wanted to be friends with her and she didn't want to give her what she wanted. There was no denying that Wanda could be mean. If you crossed her, watch out! Your social life at North Ridge High was over! But so far, Mindy hadn't done anything to get herself on Wanda's bad side. Then again, she wasn't exactly on Wanda's good side. That was why she was going to make sure this week was perfect so that when they returned to North Ridge High, she would be the newest member of the Princess Posse.

Mindy tore her eyes away from the clock and peered over Carmela's shoulder. "Did you get everything I asked for?"

Carmela pointed at the bowls. "Peeled baby carrots for Wanda, yellow M&M's for Lacey, and Pepperidge Farm cheddar Goldfish for Vivienne. And just so you know, I had to buy three bags of M&M's to pick out all the yellow ones to fill that one bowl. Why won't she eat the other colors? They all taste the same! I should know; I was busy popping them into my mouth!"

Mindy shrugged. "Lacey says the yellow ones taste the best. Are we all set with drinks?"

"The refrigerator is stocked with Diet Pepsi, Snapple peach lemonade, and Perrier."

"Thanks, Carmela."

"Stop worrying. You're going to have a great week."

Carmela Dellaguzzo had been the Yees' live-in housekeeper since Mindy was five years old. She was a fortysomething Italian woman from Brooklyn with a teased blond bouffant who always said what was on her mind. She had come along to Miami to prepare all their meals as well as act as unofficial chaperone when Mindy's parents weren't around.

"I don't know why you're so nervous," Carmela stated.

"I want these girls to like me. I want to be friends with them."

"Just be yourself," Carmela advised. "That's all you can do. And if they don't want to be friends with you, then they're crazy." Carmela tilted her head. "I think I hear a car coming."

Mindy raced to the window and saw a black limousine pulling into the driveway. When the limo stopped, the back door opened and Wanda stepped out, followed by Lacey and Vivienne.

Wanda was always first, front and center, with Lacey and Vivienne trailing behind her.

Mindy instantly noticed the way the girls were dressed, and panicked. Had she underdressed? All she was wearing was a pair of white shorts, flip-flops, and a violet tank top, her long dark hair pulled back in a ponytail. She hadn't gotten herself all glammed up the way the others had.

Wanda was wearing black leggings with knee-high black boots, a black V-neck T-shirt, and a short black leather motorcycle jacket with the collar turned up. She wore a heart-shaped pendant on a chain around her neck and oversize sunglasses. Tossed over one arm was a leopard-buckle satchel.

Vivienne was in gray skinny jeans with yellow high heels, a sleeveless white turtleneck, and gold cuff bracelets embellished with glittering white stones, while Lacey had on a simple pink shirt with a pink-and-white fringed skirt and high-heeled sandals. Vivienne looked like a California beach girl with her long blond hair and cornflower blue eyes, and Lacey resembled the actress who played Adrian on *The Secret Life of the American Teenager*. She had the exact same pouty lips and dark, sultry eyes.

Compared to the three of them, Mindy felt like a Fashion Don't. Well, it was too late to do anything about her outfit. She'd just have to make sure she found out what the girls were wearing the rest of the week and dress the way they did.

"Hi!" Mindy greeted them, waving a hand as she came out of the house.

Wanda breezed past Mindy without even a hello, Lacey and Vivienne following after her, while Carmela went to help the limo driver unload the trunk. Mindy hurried back inside and found Wanda taking off her sunglasses and perching them on top of her glossy black bob.

"Is this the place?" Wanda asked, her dark almond-shaped eyes traveling from room to room, her ruby red lips puckering up.

There was no mistaking the unspoken tone in Wanda's voice: *What a dump!*

"Yes, this is the house."

Mindy wanted to ask what was wrong with it. She thought the house was great. It was huge and airy, with tons of windows and ceiling fans that brought in the scent of the ocean. The furniture, while not exactly new, was comfy and perfect for a beach house. Brightly colored rag rugs covered the scuffed wood floors, and the walls were hung with paintings of beach scenes.

"I guess it'll have to do," Wanda said. "It's nowhere near as nice as the house I stayed at in the Hamptons last summer."

Mindy wondered what she was supposed to say to that. Apologize for having an inferior house?

"So, Mindy, what was up with our plane tickets?" Wanda asked.

"What do you mean?"

Wanda plopped herself down on the couch. "Did you know our seats were in *coach*?"

"Uh, I think I knew that," Mindy hesitantly answered. She had the feeling her answer was going to be wrong, although she didn't know why. She had flown down in coach, and her parents had bought everyone's tickets. So if she had flown coach, it only made sense that Wanda had, too.

"I *only* fly first-class," Wanda said. "*Never* coach."

"I didn't know that." How would she know that? She had never traveled before with Wanda, and when she had extended the invitation, Wanda hadn't said anything about needing to fly first-class. She wasn't a mind reader!

"You should have!" Wanda snapped. "You wouldn't believe how uncomfortable my seat was!"

Mindy's seat hadn't been uncomfortable and she'd flown down on the same airline as Wanda. She'd even taken a nap! She was about to tell that to Wanda when she saw the grim expression on her face and changed her mind.

Wanda was pissed.

Big-time.

Pissing off Wanda was the last thing Mindy wanted to do.

She was going to need to do damage control ASAP!

"I'm sure we can change the ticket when we fly home," she hurried to say.

"I assumed you would," Wanda stated.

"Yours, too," Mindy said to Lacey and Vivienne.

Vivienne, who was munching on some goldfish, waved a hand. "I'm fine with coach."

"Me, too," Lacey added.

Phew! Mindy thought in relief. At least they weren't mad at her. But Wanda was, and she needed to undo that.

"Why don't I show you guys upstairs so you can unpack and then we can go do something fun?" Mindy suggested.

Mindy brought the girls to the second floor and showed them to their rooms. Lacey and Vivienne were sharing a room filled with white wicker furniture and rose-patterned wallpaper, while Wanda had a room of her own. After sticking her head in the bedroom that Mindy showed her, Wanda asked to see where Mindy was staying.

Mindy brought Wanda to a bedroom at the back of the house. Mindy had chosen it because she loved the bed, a four-poster that was covered with mosquito netting. There was also a huge picture window that looked out onto the ocean.

"This bedroom is fab!" Wanda gushed, plopping down on the bed and stretching her arms out. "It reminds me of something out of Africa."

"I feel the exact same way," Mindy said.

"You wouldn't mind if we switched rooms, would you?" Wanda asked. "I'd love to sleep in here. It would be great to have the sound of the ocean in the background."

Mindy didn't know what to say. She had already unpacked and all her clothes were put away. Wanda's request had totally caught her off guard.

Carmela, who was out in the hallway with Lacey's and Vivienne's suitcases, stuck her head inside. "Mindy's already in this room."

"I'm sure Mindy doesn't mind switching, do you, Min?" Wanda asked with a sweet smile.

The smile might have been sweet, but Wanda's eyes were daring Mindy to disagree with her. Mindy gulped. She'd seen that look before. What usually happened afterward was *not* pretty.

"Of course not!" Mindy exclaimed, pasting a smile on her face. "Let me just get my stuff out of here and you can move right in."

"Great!" Wanda exclaimed, hopping off the bed. "I'll just go get my bags." As she walked out of the room, she ran a finger over the dresser and made a face. "Ugh!" She waved her dusty finger in Carmela's face. "You need to give this room a thorough cleaning. By the end of tonight would be great. I have allergies."

Out in the hallway, Carmela rolled her eyes at Mindy.

"I think I'm allergic to *her*!" Carmela grumbled.

"She's just cranky because she's been traveling."

"Uh-huh," Carmela said, a skeptical tone in her voice. "Something tells me I should have stayed in North Ridge. I can see that one is going to be a handful and it's only day one!"

"She's usually not this bad," Mindy reassured Carmela. "She'll mellow out."

I hope! Mindy thought.

Chapter Four

"Stop hiding in that dressing room and come out so we can see what you're wearing!" Jade shouted.

Danielle ignored her sister's order, staring at her image in a full-length mirror. Why had she allowed everyone to pick out the outfits she was trying on? She should have done it herself. These clothes were *so* not her.

"Danielle, I'm going to count to five and if you're not out by the time I'm finished, I'm going to come in there and drag you out," Jade warned.

"Okay, okay, I'm coming," Danielle said as she flung open the red curtains of the dressing room and walked through. "Satisfied?"

"Wow!" Lindsey exclaimed. "You look great!"

"I do not," Danielle insisted, a pout on her face. She felt like a Barbie doll being dressed up.

"You do!" Ava added. "We wouldn't say it if it wasn't true."

"Honey, you were made to wear a bikini!" Crystal raved. "And that red bikini was made for you! You're going to look even better in it once you have a tan."

"My little sister is all grown up!" Jade exclaimed. "I knew there was a body hidden underneath all the loose T-shirts and baggy jeans that you always wear. We're taking it! Add it to the pile."

Danielle stared at the growing stack of clothes. So far, everything she had tried on had gotten a thumbs-up from Ava, Lindsey, Jade, and Crystal. There were short skirts, camisole tops, and summery dresses all in styles and colors that she usually didn't wear.

"Don't I get a say in what we're buying?"

"No, because we're paying," Jade said. "You have to wear what we tell you."

"At least for this week," Lindsey added.

"But this isn't me!" Danielle said, pointing to the bikini she was wearing and then to the stack of clothes. "And neither are those!"

"That's the point of a makeover!" Ava explained. "You become someone else."

"It's just for a week," Lindsey reminded her. "When we get back home, you can go back to being yourself. But for the next few days, you don't have to be Danielle Hollis. You can be anyone you want!"

But what was so wrong with being Danielle Hollis? Danielle Hollis was the "smart" Hollis sister, while Jade was the "pretty" Hollis sister. It had been that way all their lives, and she was perfectly fine with that. Jade was the one with the active social life, always getting invited to parties. Jade was the one on the cheerleading squad and who had a constant parade of jock boyfriends. Jade was the one who was into shopping and clothes, who subscribed to *Vogue*, *Elle*, and *Cosmo*.

Danielle was the complete opposite. She wasn't the "ugly" sister — she'd gone on lots of dates but so far hadn't had a serious boyfriend — but she was the one who focused more attention on her schoolwork and grades. While she was straight A's, Jade had more a B average. Jade could be a straight-A student if she wanted to — Danielle had lost track of the number of times her parents had told Jade that she needed to apply herself — but having a good time mattered more to her sister.

And while Danielle's wardrobe wasn't as hideous as everyone else made it out to be, she wasn't obsessed with shopping. Sure, she dressed up on special occasions, but the rest of the time she went for comfort over style. She liked wearing loose

T-shirts and tops. She was more into flared jeans and bell-bottoms than skinny jeans. She hated high heels and was perfectly fine wearing sneakers, flip-flops, or ballet flats.

"You like the way you look," Jade whispered into Danielle's ear, coming up behind her. "You just don't want to say it."

Danielle hated to admit it, but a teeny tiny part of her *did* like the way she looked in the clothes she'd been modeling.

But would she have the courage to wear these outfits outside the store?

They just weren't her!

Jade was the one with the body that rocked. No matter what she wore, she looked like a knockout.

Jade pressed another pile of clothes into Danielle's hands. "Try these on next. And hurry! We don't want to be late for your appointment at the hair salon."

Danielle groaned. The hair salon! She'd forgotten all about phase two of Ava and Lindsey's evil plan. "I'm telling you right now, I don't want to cut my hair! I like it long!"

Jade pushed Danielle back in the direction of the dressing room. "You don't get a say in how your hair gets cut. Makeover day, remember? You have to leave yourself in the capable hands of experts. Us!"

Danielle shuddered, wondering how much worse her day could get.

It got worse as they were heading to the hair salon.

"Don't look now," Ava whispered as they were walking through the mall, "but Mindy Yee is heading our way."

"What's she doing in Miami?" Danielle groaned.

"Maybe she won't see us," Lindsey said.

"Mindy Yee has eyes in the back of her head," Ava said. "She sees everything."

"I don't believe it!" Mindy exclaimed, as she caught sight of Danielle, Ava, and Lindsey. She threw her arms open and gave them a hug. "It's a North Ridge High reunion."

"Hey, Mindy!" Danielle said, forcing herself to smile as she broke free of Mindy's hug.

"What are you guys doing down here?"

"Spending the week with Danielle's older sister and her best friend at a beach house," Ava explained.

"And doing a little spring break shopping," Lindsey said, holding up a shopping bag but pulling it away before Mindy could take a peek inside.

"That's what we were about to do. Do you girls know Wanda, Lacey, and Vivienne?"

"I know that Wanda Wong's initials stand for Wicked Witch," Ava whispered in Danielle's ear.

"Shhh!" Danielle scolded, trying not to laugh.

Jade and Crystal, who had been lagging behind Danielle, Ava, and Lindsey, caught up with them. "Crystal and I were just talking. After the hair salon, we're going to head over to the supermarket. We thought we'd barbecue tonight. Hot dogs, hamburgers, spareribs."

"Yum!" Lindsey exclaimed.

"Your friends are more than welcome to join us if they want," Jade offered, smiling at Mindy and the rest of the group.

"We're going to have plenty of food," Crystal added.

Danielle couldn't believe what she was hearing. The last person she wanted to hang out with was Mindy Yee! Not to mention the North Ridge High Princess Posse!

"Are there going to be any college guys there?" Wanda asked.

"Maybe," Crystal answered. "Jade and I are in a sorority, and we know a lot of fraternity brothers. Some of them are down for the week, so we're hoping to invite a few over. But you won't know unless you show up."

"We'll be there!" Wanda quickly answered.

"Great!" Jade gave Wanda directions to the

beach house. "We'll see you later." Then she grabbed Danielle by the arm. "We better hurry! We've got a hair appointment to keep!"

Mindy stared at Wanda in disbelief.

She couldn't believe what she had just heard.

Wanda was interested in college guys?

But Wanda had a boyfriend, the incredibly hot Rick Cho, who was a junior at North Ridge High.

Didn't she?

"Did you and Rick break up?" Mindy asked, wondering if they had ended things before Wanda flew down to Miami.

"Of course not!" Wanda snapped. "Why would you ask me that?"

Uh, because you were practically drooling at the thought of meeting some college guys tonight!

Mindy didn't know how to answer. She could tell she was on thin ice with Wanda. She didn't want to say something that would insult her and make it sound like she was accusing her of two-timing Rick. But if she *did* still have a boyfriend and she *was* interested in meeting other guys, well, wasn't that cheating?

"The day before classes ended, I overheard someone in the hallways say that you and Rick were

44

having problems," Mindy lied. "I guess I jumped to the wrong conclusion."

"It was probably some girl trying to cause problems so she could get her claws into Rick," Lacey said, staring at Mindy.

Don't look at me! Mindy wanted to shout. Rick might be hot, but she knew he was off-limits. Any girl who went after Wanda Wong's boyfriend would have to be crazy.

"Rick and I are still together," Wanda said. "But this week is spring break and I'm taking a little break from Rick. If you know what I mean."

Mindy knew *exactly* what she meant.

Wanda moved closer to Mindy, slipping her arm through hers as they started walking through the mall. Lacey and Vivienne followed behind them.

"Mindy, what happens in Miami stays in Miami," Wanda said. "I know how much you love sharing information, but I wouldn't want Rick finding out about this." She sunk her long bloodred nails into Mindy's arm. "We're friends, and friends keep secrets, right?"

Mindy tried not to flinch as Wanda's pointy nails dug into her skin. There was no mistaking the message she was sending. Blabbing equaled pain. Lots of it. And Mindy knew Wanda was queen when it came to emotional and physical torment if she was crossed. "We're friends," she echoed. "Friends always keep secrets. And it's like you said. This week is spring break. We can take a break from our regular lives and do anything we want. Anything!"

Wanda withdrew her nails from Mindy's arm and gave her a satisfied smile. "I knew I liked you."

Mindy smiled back, trying not to rub her arm. A little bit of pain was worth it if it meant she'd become a part of the Princess Posse.

Danielle was ready to explode.

"Why did you invite Mindy Yee over tonight?" she asked Jade as they waited to get checked into the hair salon.

Jade shrugged. "What's the big deal? She and her friends seemed nice."

"Nice?" Danielle gasped. "They're awful! Mindy Yee is the biggest gossip at North Ridge High. She'll probably be spying on us the entire night."

"If she does, she'll be bored out of her mind," Ava said. "We're not the wildest girls at North Ridge High."

Jade laughed. "What are you so afraid of? That you might cut loose and Mindy will get word back to the admissions offices of the colleges you're going to apply to?"

"Danielle cutting loose?" Lindsey sputtered. "That would be the scoop of the year!"

"Last time I checked, you were supposed to be my best friend," a surly Danielle told Lindsey.

"I'm only teasing!" Lindsey exclaimed.

Before Danielle could say anything else, she was taken into the back of the salon by a stylist named Giorgio. As soon as she sat down in his chair, Danielle told him what she did and didn't want done to her hair. When she finished, Giorgio held up a hand.

"*Bella ragazza*," he said in his Italian accent. "Giorgio is a genius with the scissors. Trust me when I say you will be *la bellezza* when I'm finished."

"Er, what did you just call me?"

Giorgio's blue eyes twinkled. "Beautiful girl," he explained as he walked her over to the shampoo area. "And when I finish, you'll be the most beautiful."

"Oh," Danielle said, blushing. Maybe this makeover business wasn't so bad after all. "Well, I guess I'll let you do your thing."

Two hours later, Danielle returned to the reception area of the salon.

"So?" she asked, trying to keep a satisfied smile off her face. "What do you think?"

Ava rubbed her eyes. "You look *amazing*!"

Lindsey happily clapped her hands. "Like Victoria Beckham!"

"That's definitely because of the haircut," Danielle said, swinging her head back and forth as her new short bob fell into place.

Giorgio had cut her shoulder-length brown hair to the back of her neck and added some highlights. It was now a warm honey color. She'd also gotten a spray-on tan, and a salon makeup artist had given her a whole new palette of colors to add to her face. Her green eyes were now highlighted with mascara, making her lashes lush and bold. Smoky eye shadow had been added to her lids, and a touch of blush had been brushed onto her cheeks. A dab of red lipstick was applied to her lips and made shiny with a finishing layer of lip gloss. Danielle didn't usually wear much makeup, so, hopefully, she'd be able to do just as good a job when she tried it herself.

When Giorgio had spun her chair around so she could see the finished results, Danielle's mouth had dropped open. She couldn't believe what she was seeing. She still looked like herself but a more groomed, sophisticated version.

"What happened to my little sister?" Jade squealed, giving Danielle a hug. "She's all grown up!"

"You can't leave here wearing the clothes you came in!" Crystal said, rummaging through their shopping bags. "A new you requires a new outfit. You have to change!"

Ten minutes later, Danielle was wearing a multi-colored print wraparound dress and high-heeled sandals (another purchase that had been forced on her). Although Danielle hated wearing heels, she did know how to walk in them, so at least she didn't fall on her face.

"Now you look sensational!" Ava gushed.

Crystal fanned herself with a hand. "Look out, Miami. Deeeelicious Danielle is on the loose!"

After they paid at the salon, they left the mall and headed out to the parking lot. As they walked through the mall, Danielle couldn't help but notice some guys looking their way. For Danielle, it was nothing new. She was used to it. That was always the case when she was with Jade.

But after a while, she noticed something.

Something different.

Today, instead of looking at *Jade* the way they always did, this time the guys were looking at *her*!

At first, she thought she was imagining it. So

she allowed Jade and Crystal to walk a little bit ahead of her and then followed after them. As she walked, she got the sense she was being watched.

When she peeked over her shoulder, there was no mistaking the smiles and winks being sent *her* way.

Danielle was floored.

And flattered!

This had never happened to her before.

At the same time, she also realized something.

Maybe this week, she'd get to see what it was like to be the pretty sister.

Chapter Five

Ethan had heard of empty calories, but this was ridiculous!

He stared into the shopping cart he was pushing. It was filled with every kind of junk food imaginable. Chips, sodas, cookies, candy. And the pile kept growing and growing.

After Steve and Howie had arrived from the airport, they'd decided to tackle their grocery shopping. Ethan was put in charge of pushing the cart while the rest of the guys threw what they wanted into it. But they weren't filling it with anything edible! Ethan loved junk food, but there was a limit to how much of it he could eat!

"Hey, guys, how about some fresh fruits and vegetables?" he suggested as Howie added three bags of Cool Ranch Doritos, two bags of barbecue Lay's, and a jar of salsa.

"Those are just for me," Howie said.

Howie was over six feet tall, with a blond buzz cut and lean swimmer's build. He was on the University of Delaware swim team and was constantly eating because of his training.

"A midnight snack?" Ethan joked.

"Probably!"

Ethan blinked at Howie in disbelief. "Are you serious?"

"I need the calories."

"How about some healthy calories?" Ethan suggested. "Filled with vitamins and minerals."

"Like Cheez Whiz!" Howie exclaimed, rushing down another aisle.

"Cheez Whiz is not real cheese!" Ethan called after him. "How about some meat? You know, hamburgers. Hot dogs? Chicken? I'd even settle for a can of tuna. Or Spam!"

"Spam's not a food," Damian said as he tossed a package of ice cream sandwiches into the cart.

"Then what is it?"

"I think maybe it was created for astronauts to eat in space."

"That's Tang! Spam is made from all the leftover parts of a pig that no one wants."

"Yuck!"

"How about you take over pushing for a while?" Ethan asked. The supermarket was crowded and he was getting tired of trying to steer their cart down the clogged aisles. It was like a racetrack, with shoppers veering to the left and right and not watching where they were going.

"Hey! Damian!" Cooper called from the end of the aisle. "Meet me in the soda section. I need help carrying some cases of root beer out to the car."

"Looks like you're still in the driver's seat," Damian said as he hurried off to join Cooper.

Ethan sighed and started to turn a corner with the shopping cart. As he did, he could see another shopping cart coming from around the other side. He tried to veer his cart to the right, but he wasn't quick enough, and the shopping cart coming into his aisle slammed into him.

"Oh!" a female voice cried out. "I'm so sorry!"

Ethan's mouth dropped open as the girl pushing the other shopping cart came into view.

She was a knockout!

"I'm usually not this clumsy," she explained, "but the store is so packed, it's hard to get around. I didn't break anything in your cart, did I?" She took a peek. "Something tells me this cart belongs to a houseful of guys," she teased. "Absolutely no healthy nutrients."

Voice! Voice! Ethan told himself. *Find your voice and say something before it's too late. Before she leaves and you lose your chance!*

53

"I guess we're lucky we weren't driving cars," she said. "Otherwise we'd have to exchange phone numbers."

There's your opening line! Tell her you still want her phone number. Unless that was her way of trying to get your number! Open your mouth. OPEN YOUR MOUTH!!!

"Are you okay?" the girl asked, her voice filled with concern. She stepped away from her cart and walked over to Ethan, putting a hand on his arm. "You're not saying anything. I didn't slam into you that hard, did I?"

Ethan shook his head, trying not to stare at the hand on his arm.

She was touching him. SHE WAS TOUCHING HIM!!!

Okay, it was time to take control. Otherwise she was going to think he was a freak, and girls as pretty as this one did *not* date freaks!

"I'm fine," Ethan said, finally finding his voice, although it sounded nervous. Ack! He took a deep breath and forced himself to calm down. "Just fine."

She sighed in relief. "That's good." She started to walk back to her shopping cart.

"But . . ." Ethan called out.

She turned around. "But?"

"I would like your phone number."

"Oh, you would, would you?" she asked. "How come?"

"In case I develop a case of whiplash and need to go to the doctor."

The girl walked back to him and folded her arms over her chest. "Whiplash, huh?"

Ethan nodded. "I'd need to tell the doctor where to send his bill."

"I don't know," she said. "Usually I don't give my phone number to the enemy."

Enemy? Ethan was confused. What was she talking about?

As if reading Ethan's mind, the girl pointed to his T-shirt. "You go to South Ridge High."

Ethan stared at the lettering on his shirt. "That's a problem?"

"It is if you go to North Ridge High."

Ethan blinked in disbelief. "You go to North Ridge High? We're from the same town?"

"Uh-huh."

"I can't believe it. Talk about a coincidence!"

Or maybe it was fate. Maybe he was meant to meet this girl today!

"How long have you lived in North Ridge?" he asked.

"All my life."

55

"Me, too! Where's your favorite place to hang out?"

"My two best friends are shopaholics, so we're at the mall at least three or four times a week. Afterward, we'll usually go to the Burger Hut. And we also like to go to Icing on the Cake."

Ethan couldn't believe it. "I'm always at the Burger Hut and Icing on the Cake. It's funny that we've never run into each other before today."

The girl shrugged. "I guess today is our lucky day."

Is it ever! Ethan thought.

"So, are you going to give me your phone number?" he asked.

"Only if you tell me your name."

D'oh! He hadn't even introduced himself. She must think he was an idiot!

"I'm Ethan," he said with an embarrassed grin.

"Hi, Ethan," she said with a smile. "I'm Danielle." She pulled out her cell phone. "If you give me your number, I'll call you."

Ethan did and Danielle dialed his number. When the phone rang, he let it go to voice mail. Then he pulled out his phone and saw that Danielle's number was on his Missed Calls screen.

"Got it!" he happily announced.

"So, Ethan, are you into the whole North Ridge High versus South Ridge High rivalry?" she asked.

"Sometimes I'll go to the games, but I'm not really a jock. You?"

"My older sister used to be a cheerleader, so we went to all the games. Family duty. But since she graduated, I haven't gone as much."

"You know what drives me crazy? Football games! They say there's five minutes left to a game, and that five minutes stretches out to twenty!"

"I know!"

"Are you spending the week down here?" Ethan asked, wondering if it was too soon to ask her if she wanted to go out. Maybe he should wait until later tonight. That way he could think about what he wanted to say. Maybe write it down on paper, so when he called her, he sounded smooth and confident.

"We leave next Saturday. How about you?"

"Same thing."

"Danielle!"

At the sound of her voice, Danielle turned around as two girls hurried toward her. One was a tiny brunette and the other was a tall redhead.

"What's taking you so long?" the brunette asked. "Jade and Crystal are waiting in line."

"You have two friends named after gemstones?" Ethan asked Danielle.

"Jade's my older sister, and Crystal is her best friend. And you're not the first person to say that to

57

me. Crystal says the reason they instantly bonded is because they're like the gems they're named after: beautiful and flawless!"

"Who's your new friend?" the redhead asked.

"I had a little bit of a shop-and-run accident and was talking to my victim," Danielle explained to the redhead before turning back to Ethan. "These are the shopaholics I was telling you about. Ava and Lindsey."

"Hi!"

"Hi!"

"Hi," Ethan said to both, trying not to squirm as Ava and Lindsey inspected him from head to toe. It was obvious they were both checking him out.

"Seems like you got a little sidetracked," Lindsey said, giving Danielle a knowing look.

"Why don't we take over and you can keep talking to Ethan," Ava suggested, moving behind the shopping cart.

"That's okay; we were just finishing up," Danielle said.

"Are you doing anything tonight, Ethan?" Ava asked.

"No plans so far. Why?"

"We're having a barbecue over at our place," Ava said. "You should come. Wouldn't it be great if Ethan came over, Danielle?"

Danielle, who seemed taken aback by Ava's sudden invitation, quickly nodded. "Definitely! You have to come!"

Ethan couldn't believe what he was hearing. Danielle wanted him to come over tonight! Okay, she had been caught off guard by Ava's invitation, but then she had extended one herself. If she didn't want him to come over, she wouldn't have done that. And she wouldn't have given him her phone number. Maybe tonight wasn't an *official* date, but it was a beginning! If they had a good time at the barbecue, maybe there would be a real date after tonight. Just the two of them.

"So, can you make it?" Ava asked.

"I'll be there," Ethan said.

"If you have any friends that are as cute as you, bring them, too!" Lindsey exclaimed.

"Here's our address," Ava said, reaching into her purse and scribbling it down on a piece of paper.

"See you later," Danielle said as she walked away with Ava and Lindsey, who were both whispering and giggling in her ear as they stared back at Ethan.

After the girls left, Ethan glanced down at the address Ava had written.

He blinked in disbelief and his stomach sank.

It couldn't be.

But it was.

The address was for the house next door to his.

Which meant Danielle was one of the girls Cooper saw leaving earlier that afternoon.

Suddenly he wished he hadn't agreed to that bet. . . .

Chapter Six

"What am I going to wear?" Danielle wailed as she paced from one end of her bedroom to the other.

Lindsey, who was lying across Danielle's bed, flipping through a copy of *Cosmo*, looked up at her. "What do you mean, what are you going to wear? We just came back from a major shopping spree! You've got a whole new wardrobe!"

"Why not wear what you've got on now?" Ava asked. She was sitting at a vanity table, trying on different pairs of earrings.

"He's already seen me in this!" Danielle exclaimed as she rummaged through the shopping bags cluttering the floor of her bedroom.

"And it got you results!" Lindsey reminded her.

Danielle abandoned the shopping bags and stared at her image in the full-length mirror hanging on the closed bedroom door. She still couldn't believe that the girl she was gazing at was herself. "That's the problem."

"What do you mean?" Lindsey asked, confusion in her voice.

Danielle turned around to face Lindsey and Ava. "Look at me! This isn't the *real* me. Do you think if Ethan had seen me this morning before I had this makeover, he would have been interested?"

Lindsey gasped. "Of course he would have."

Ava dropped the gold hoop earrings she had been about to put on. "How can you say such a thing!"

Because guys were *never* speechless around her. Guys always knew what to say to her. But Ethan hadn't. All he'd seen was a pretty girl and he'd been scared of her! For whatever reason, he thought she was unapproachable, and that was *so* not her.

Ethan hadn't been seeing the real Danielle.

He'd been seeing a different Danielle.

A Danielle who hadn't existed until that afternoon.

And it made her wonder.

Did she want to go out with a guy who cared more about a girl's looks than the girl herself?

"You're not giving this guy a chance," Lindsey said. "Okay, he liked what he saw. You can't hold that against him. Everything is based on appearance. It's what gets us to talk to people. We're attracted to them! After that, you get to know the person and you realize it's what's inside that counts."

"And not everything is always based on looks," Ava added. "Sometimes it's based on the way they dress or act. I once talked to a guy because he was wearing a Cookie Monster watch. I thought that meant he was quirky, and I was right!"

"I know why Danielle is freaking out and worrying about her clothes," Lindsey smugly stated.

"Why?" Ava asked.

"She likes him!"

"I do not!" Danielle quickly answered.

"You do, too!" Lindsey shot back. "If you didn't like him, you wouldn't have told him to come over tonight, right?"

"Right!" Ava added.

"Ava's the one who invited him over," Danielle corrected them.

"But you're the one who then told him he *had* to come," Ava reminded her.

"Don't deny it!" Lindsey added.

Danielle knew there was no winning when Ava and Lindsey ganged up against her. "Okay! Okay! I like him! I think he's cute and I want to look nice for him," she admitted. "But how can I top this outfit? It's like the *best* thing we bought."

Lindsey jumped off the bed and began emptying out the shopping bags. "You can't top it, but you *can* come up with something equally cute and fabulous. It's hidden somewhere in these bags. All we have to do is find it!"

Ava watched from the vanity as Lindsey started mixing and matching various pieces. When it came to clothes, Lindsey knew her stuff. She was one of the best-dressed girls at North Ridge High.

An hour later, Lindsey had worked her magic. Danielle was wearing a rainbow-colored one-shoulder tank top with a short, white pleated skirt. From her own wardrobe, Lindsey had chosen to wear a sleeveless, ruffled, violet silk chiffon top and skinny black jeans. Ava thought they both looked great.

"Ethan is going to be very happy when he sees you," Ava said.

"It doesn't look like I put a lot of effort into it, does it?" Danielle worriedly asked. "I don't want him to think I got dressed up for him."

"You look pretty but casual," Ava assured her.

"What are you going to wear tonight, Ava?"

64

Lindsey asked as she spritzed herself with some perfume.

Ava looked down at her cutoff denim shorts and SpongeBob SquarePants T-shirt. "I'm fine with what I've got on."

Lindsey's face fell. "No, no, no! You've been wearing the same clothes since this morning. They're all wrinkly. You need to change into something new!"

"Why?"

Lindsey stared knowingly at Ava. "You know why. Hopefully, Ethan is going to bring some cute guys with him tonight!"

"And?"

"And you've got to put yourself back out there. It's been over a month, Ava. Don't you think it's time to move on?"

"I really don't want to talk about this." There was a warning tone in Ava's voice, but Lindsey ignored it.

"You never want to talk about it! You're pretending like nothing has happened, when something major *did* happen."

"I'm not ready to start dating again."

"I bet Josh has started dating again."

Hearing her ex-boyfriend's name, Ava glared at Lindsey.

"What!" Lindsey exclaimed. "Don't give me the evil eye. You know you're thinking the exact same thing. Danielle, don't you think Josh is already dating?"

"Don't drag me into the middle of this!" Danielle stated. "You know talking about Josh is off-limits."

A frustrated Lindsey threw her hands up. "How is she supposed to move on if she *doesn't* talk about it! Are we never supposed to mention Josh's name again? Pretend like he doesn't exist?"

Ava knew that would be impossible. Josh O'Donnell had been her boyfriend for close to a year. They'd started dating last spring after accidentally running into each other in the hallway at school. Ava had been late for her first class and hadn't watched where she was going. She slammed into Josh, and her books went flying everywhere, including her sketchbook for art class. When he stopped to help her pick everything up, he noticed her sketches and told her how good he thought they were. A flattered Ava had blushed, collected her sketches, and then hurried off. When she slid into her seat in first period, she realized she hadn't thanked Josh for helping her.

After school, after asking a senior for directions, she found Josh at his locker and apologized for not thanking him that morning. Josh pretended his feelings were hurt and then told Ava she could make it up to him by going with him to the Burger Hut.

Ava said yes.

After that, they were joined at the hip, spending all their time together after school and on the weekends. Josh even took her as his date to the senior prom at the Waldorf Astoria in Manhattan. Most of the girls at the prom were seniors; Ava was one of the few underclassmen. The fact that Josh had wanted to take her made her feel special.

Over the summer, when they weren't working at their part-time jobs, they went to the beach and amusement parks. Josh loved all the daring rides and was always able to coax Ava into riding them, no matter how hard she protested. But then, that was always the way it was with Josh. He made her push herself and try things she wouldn't ordinarily do. Sometimes she liked it — like the time they went skydiving! — and sometimes she didn't — like the time they ate sushi. Blech!

Being with Josh was different from being with the other guys she had dated in the past. It could be because he was two years older and that made him more mature. More confident and self-assured. Ava really didn't know. All she knew was that she loved spending time with him.

Everything was perfect.

Until Josh had to leave to start his freshman year at Cornell.

Ava had known this day would be coming, but she hadn't expected it to come so fast.

The hardest thing Ava ever had to do was say good-bye to Josh when he left at the end of August. She'd wanted to cry but she didn't. Well, at least not in front of him. She knew how excited he was to be going off to college and she didn't want to spoil the experience for him. She didn't want him to think his girlfriend was falling to pieces. So she kept her tears bottled up and let them out in front of Danielle and Lindsey once Josh and his parents drove away.

Things only got harder when classes resumed at North Ridge High in September. Everywhere Ava looked, she had a memory of Josh. In the hallways. In the cafeteria. Outside the school. There were so many reminders of him! It only made her miss him that much more.

At first, Ava and Josh kept in touch by phone. As much as Ava wanted to call every day, she didn't. She knew college was different from high school and she didn't want to bother Josh.

In the beginning, Ava heard from Josh at least two or three times a week. He admitted to being homesick and feeling overwhelmed by his classes.

But little by little, he started to get into the swing of things and began making new friends. Now when Ava talked to him, he told her how much fun he was having, how great his classes were, and about all the cool people he was meeting. When Ava heard this, she was happy for Josh. Everything was finally falling into place for him.

But then she started hearing from him less and less.

At first she made excuses. After all, Josh was in the premed program and had a heavy class load. Some of his classes were also at night, so when he wasn't in class, she was. So she didn't call him as often as she used to. Instead, she sent him texts and e-mails.

But they went unanswered.

The few times they did get to talk, though, Ava noticed that Josh didn't mention how much he missed her. She still told him that she missed him, but he never said the words back. At least not as often as he used to.

It made Ava worry.

She didn't think Josh was cheating on her, but she did feel he was drifting further and further away from her.

She felt he wasn't making a place for her in his new world.

When Josh came home for Thanksgiving, they spent the entire weekend together, and it was like he had never gone away. They picked up right where they left off and had a great time, going to the movies, snuggling before the fire, baking cookies, and getting a head start on their Christmas shopping. The same thing happened over the Christmas holiday.

But when classes resumed in January, Ava stopped hearing from Josh again. And again, she made excuses for him because she knew he had finals coming up that month.

Valentine's Day was what pushed her over the edge. All week, five couples at North Ridge High had been competing in the Most Romantic Couple contest. Seeing them together made Ava realize that she didn't have a boyfriend who cared about her. If she did, he wouldn't be so out of touch. He would let her know that he cared about her and was thinking about her, even if he only sent her a one-word text. Ava's heart always pounded with excitement when her phone buzzed and she saw Josh's name pop up on the screen.

It wasn't just the Most Romantic Couple contest. Josh didn't send her a card for Valentine's Day. And he didn't even call to thank her for the card she'd sent him! When she called Josh the day after Valentine's Day, trying not to sound like a hysterical girlfriend, he apologized for forgetting and claimed he'd been too busy with his new class schedule. But Ava was finished with excuses. Josh knew how to make time for himself but not for her or their relationship. So she didn't say anything and decided it would be better to discuss their relationship with him when he came home for spring break.

That never happened.

And spring break was what ended things.

Originally, they were supposed to spend spring break together at home. They had discussed it at Christmas. But then Josh's fraternity brothers planned a trip to Cancun, and Josh decided to go with them. He didn't even ask Ava if it was okay! He just called a week after Valentine's Day and told her he was going, breaking their plans without even thinking of her feelings. Deciding to tell Josh what she was feeling, Ava told him that she felt their relationship was in trouble. That they were drifting apart from each other and they needed to spend time together to see if they could get things back on track.

"There's nothing wrong with our relationship," Josh had said. "Stop being so melodramatic."

"I'm not being melodramatic," Ava had calmly pointed out. "We made plans to spend spring break together and now we're not."

"Plans change," Josh shot back.

"But you didn't even ask me if it was okay!"

"Why should I?"

Ava couldn't believe what she was hearing. "Because I'm your girlfriend!"

"Not if you keep acting like this."

For Ava, that had been the last straw. She wouldn't allow Josh to talk to her like that. Maybe she should have given herself a day or two to cool off, but she had been angry. And she had wanted to show Josh that he couldn't take her for granted. So she instantly told him that if he went to Cancun, it was over between them.

"Then I guess it's over," Josh had said. "I'll send you a postcard from Cancun."

And then he had hung up on her.

At first, Ava had been in shock. She couldn't believe that her relationship with Josh had ended in less than five minutes. Then she had gotten angry. How could he just hang up on her? Hadn't the last ten months meant anything to him?

Instantly, Ava had called Danielle and Lindsey, asking them to come over to her house. She didn't tell them why, but they heard the urgency in her voice and raced right over. When they arrived, she lost it and turned into a blubbering mess, telling them that it was over between her and Josh. Both had been speechless when they heard the story and asked what they could do to help. Just listening was enough, Ava told them.

Then, when the chance to go to Miami for spring break came up a couple of days after her breakup with Josh, Ava jumped at it. The last place she wanted to be during spring break was in North Ridge. That was because she and Josh were supposed to have spent the week together at home, and she didn't want to be reminded of that.

"She hasn't even told anyone at school!" Lindsey exclaimed, cutting into Ava's thoughts. "Everyone thinks she and Josh are still a couple."

"Ava's breakup with Josh is her business," Danielle sternly said. "If she doesn't want to talk about it, then she doesn't have to."

Ava wasn't ready to discuss Josh with anyone else. It was still too fresh. Eventually, she'd have to tell her other friends at school, but for now, she was keeping quiet.

"All I'm saying is that sometimes talking about things helps." Lindsey went over to Ava and gave her a hug. "I know you're hurting. I just want to help take away the hurt."

When Lindsey said things like that, there was no way Ava could stay mad at her.

"I know you're only trying to help," Ava said. "I don't mean to be so crabby. I guess I'm still processing things. Trying to figure it all out. Josh was the first guy I was really serious about. Even though we never said the *L* word, I thought about it. That never happened to me before."

"Really?" Lindsey gasped, giving Ava another hug. "You never told me that!"

"It's going to take some time," Danielle said. "And you can take all the time you need. Right, Lindsey?"

"Absolutely. But won't you please, please, please change into another outfit? I want us to all look fabulous tonight, and I know you packed that cute denim skirt and yellow halter top that you bought on sale at American Eagle last week."

Ava threw up her hands. "I surrender."

"Go hurry up because Ethan — and his friends, I hope! — are going to be here soon!"

The doorbell rang as soon as the words were out of Lindsey's mouth.

"He's here!" Danielle squealed.

"Calm down," Lindsey said. "You're getting all flushed in the face."

"I can't help it," Danielle confessed. "I'm nervous."

"He's the one who should be nervous," Lindsey said. "He has to impress *you*, not the other way around."

"Don't be nervous," Ava said. "Just go with the flow. You don't have to fall in love with this guy. Have some fun. You can be anyone you want this week."

"That's right," Lindsey agreed. "Forget about being Danielle. This week you're Daring Dani!"

Daring Dani. Danielle mulled it over. She liked it!

Lindsey took Ava by one hand and Danielle by the other, pulling them out into the hallway. "Come on! Let's go get this party started!" Then Lindsey stopped in her tracks and pushed Ava in the direction of their bedroom. "But only after you change your outfit!"

Chapter Seven

"Which one are you interested in?" Cooper asked Ethan as they walked into the backyard, where the barbecue was taking place. They'd been let in by Crystal, who had gone off into the kitchen to get some sodas.

"Danielle," Ethan said.

"What's she look like?"

"She's a blonde."

Cooper's eyes traveled around the backyard and stopped when they came to a blonde in denim shorts lighting the barbecue. He whistled. "Foxy!"

"That's not her," Ethan said.

At the sound of Cooper's whistle, the girl at the barbecue turned around and gave them a smile. "Hi!" she said, walking over. "I'm Jade. You must be the guys that Ava and my sister invited." She waved to the picnic table, where there were bowls of pretzels, potato chips, and other munchies. "Make yourselves at home. We've got plenty of food."

"Thanks," Cooper said, reaching for a handful of potato chips.

At that moment, Steve and Howie arrived, and Jade went off to greet them. Ethan watched as Damian's brother instantly turned on the charm, making Jade laugh at something he said. Unlike Ethan, Steve always knew what to say to girls.

Ethan could feel his palms getting sweaty and wiped them on the sides of his shorts. He wanted to sniff his underarms to make sure his deodorant was working but thought that would be too gross. He was so nervous! He'd changed his clothes four times before deciding on a pair of khaki shorts and a white linen short-sleeve shirt with a pair of yellow Crocs.

"Calm down," Cooper said. "She's not going to bite you. Just be yourself."

"I'm *not* myself, remember?" Ethan said, bringing up their bet. "I'm you!"

"At least you'll be able to impress her."

"Yeah, but only for a week," Ethan shot back. "What happens when we get back home and I'm myself again? She lives in our town!"

"You're thinking beyond this week?"

"Yes. No. I don't know!" a flustered Ethan tried to explain.

Starting tomorrow, he was going to have a fancy car and money to spend, but that wasn't his life back home in North Ridge. How was he going to explain that to Danielle if he kept seeing her? Unless he *didn't* spend Cooper's money! Yes! Why hadn't he thought of that sooner! As for the car, he'd try to come up with some sort of logical explanation. Instantly, Ethan felt like a huge load had been lifted off him.

"Why are you thinking beyond the moment?" Damian declared, sticking his head between Ethan and Cooper and wrapping his arms around their shoulders. "For all you know, the two of you aren't going to click! Enjoy the perks!"

"He's right," Cooper agreed. "You worry too much."

"That's because I don't want to mess things up with her!"

"So which one is she?" Damian asked.

Ethan looked across the backyard and saw Danielle carrying a tray of hot dogs and hamburgers, with Ava and Lindsey by her side.

"There she is," Ethan pointed out. "The one in the middle."

"Wow!" Damian exclaimed. "She's hot."

"She's off-limits," Ethan reminded him. "Eyes back in your head, Wolfie. And stop drooling!"

"You want the brunette or redhead?" Damian asked Cooper.

"They're both cute, but I want to talk to the redhead," Cooper said.

"That's Ava," Ethan said. "Lindsey is the brunette."

"Hey, Ethan!" Danielle called out. "Want to help me barbecue?"

Ethan's entire face lit up with a smile as he abandoned Cooper and Damian and raced over to Danielle's side.

"We're staying for an hour and then we're out of here!" Wanda declared as they walked into the backyard. "I didn't come all the way down to Miami to hang out with girls from North Ridge High," she huffed. "Why did we even come tonight?" She didn't wait for an answer. "Danielle and her friends aren't exactly high on the social ladder at school. This barbecue is probably going to be a dud."

"Jade said college guys would be here," Mindy reminded her.

79

College guys who you're planning to cheat on Rick with!

"I'm not holding my breath," Wanda said. "Jade wasn't exactly Miss Popularity when she was at North Ridge High."

Actually, she had been, but Mindy wasn't about to correct Wanda.

"I'm sure this place is going to be packed with losers and they're going to be hanging all over us because we're so hot."

Jade and Crystal were pretty hot, too, maybe even hotter, but Mindy decided not to mention that, either.

"Who's the freak wearing the Crocs?" Wanda sneered.

Mindy noticed the guy in Crocs standing next to Danielle at the barbecue. What was wrong with Crocs? Mindy wore them when she was at home. They were extremely comfortable. From the look of distaste on Wanda's face, she decided not to mention owning a pair. Among other things. She was losing track of everything that Wanda hated. It had been that way the entire day. Wanda complained nonstop!

"Maybe we can go dancing later," Lacey suggested. "That would be fun."

Wanda checked the time on her cell phone. "We've got plenty of time to kill. I'm sure none of the clubs are going to start hopping until ten or eleven."

"We'd have to be home by midnight," Mindy said.

"Why?" Wanda asked.

"It's my curfew."

"You have a curfew?" Lacey asked in disbelief.

"Curfews were made to be broken!" Wanda declared.

"Not mine," Mindy said. Her parents were pretty laid-back, but the one thing they never budged on was her curfew. And her curfew applied to *everyone* in the house. But how was she going to tell that to Wanda?

"Well, while you're in bed, we'll be out on the dance floor!" Wanda exclaimed.

"If Mindy's curfew is midnight, then our curfew is midnight, too," Vivienne piped up. "Her parents are responsible for us this week and we have to follow their rules."

"That's true," Mindy said as she gave Vivienne a grateful smile for coming to her rescue.

Wanda rolled her eyes. "Is this entire week going to be boring?" she complained.

"We're going to have a great week!" Mindy vowed, hoping that some hot guys showed up tonight; otherwise Wanda wasn't going to let her hear the end of it even though it had been *her* idea to come to the barbecue. But of course she would forget that and blame Mindy. "And to commemorate the first day of spring break, let's take a picture." Mindy pulled out her camera. "Come on, everyone, stand together!"

"How does my hair look?" Wanda asked as she positioned herself between Lacey and Vivienne, forcing them into the background.

"Fabulous!" Mindy exclaimed as she took picture after picture.

After Mindy finished taking the last picture, she turned her camera off. She was slipping it into her purse when Wanda suddenly grabbed her by the arm, her nails once again sinking into her skin. Ouch! Was she going to need a skin graft by the end of the week? Then she panicked. Why was Wanda grabbing her arm? What was she upset about now?

"Who's that guy?" Wanda asked.

Mindy looked around the backyard. Guy? What guy was she talking about?

"He's gorgeous!" Lacey gasped.

"Talk about yummy!" Vivienne sighed.

Okay, had she suddenly gone blind? What guy were they all talking about and was he *that* good-looking?

Mindy took another look around the backyard and then she saw him, standing in a corner talking to Lindsey and sipping from a red plastic cup.

Okay, the girls were right.

He was gorgeous *and* yummy.

Tall, dark, and handsome also came to mind.

But there was something different about him, too.

Mindy couldn't put her finger on what it was.

Maybe it was his eyes.

They sparkled with mischief.

Or the way he smiled.

Cool and confident.

Whatever it was, Mindy liked it.

A lot.

As she was studying him, he tore his gaze away from Lindsey and stared across the backyard at her.

Then he waved his hand and started walking toward her.

"He's coming this way!" Vivienne squealed. She started rummaging through her purse for her compact. "I have to check my makeup!"

"He's heading toward Mindy!" Lacey exclaimed.

"Do you know him?" a stunned Wanda asked.

Mindy shook her head. "I've never seen him before in my life."

But as he got closer, Mindy doubted her words. There was something about this guy. Something familiar. But what? If she thought about it for a little bit, she was sure she'd come up with the answer. It was buried somewhere in her mind.

"Mindy Yee!" he exclaimed, giving her a hug and lifting her off her feet. "I haven't seen you in years."

A speechless Mindy wrapped her arms around him so she wouldn't fall to the ground. As she did, there was no mistaking the rock-hard muscles hidden under his T-shirt. Or the jealous looks the Princess Posse were sending her way.

"Hey! H-h-hi!" she sputtered as he put her back down. Obviously this guy knew her, but she had no idea who he was! "Long time, no see!"

"You don't remember me, do you?"

Mindy laughed nervously. "Of course I remember you!"

"Prove it," he dared. "What's my name?"

His name. Mindy's mind scrambled. What was his name?

"How about I give you a clue?"

Before Mindy could say anything, he leaned over and whispered into her ear. "You still owe me a kiss."

As soon as she heard those words, the memories came flooding back.

Damian Marsala was standing across from her.

They had gone to junior high together, but he didn't look like this back then!

The old Damian was short and chubby with braces on his teeth and pimples on his face. This Damian looked like he could star on a teen soap on the CW. And he knew it. He was well aware of the way the Princess Posse was checking him out and he was loving every minute of it. Who could blame him? Back in junior high, none of the girls had wanted anything to do with him, including Mindy. She hadn't laughed at Damian or teased him, but she never went out of her way to be friends with him.

In the spring of eighth grade, they'd had to work together on a project for science class. Damian was constantly slacking off, so Mindy told him if he did his fair share of the work, she'd give him a kiss on the last day of school. She figured if Damian told anyone about the kiss — and she was sure he would — it would be forgotten by the time classes resumed in September. It was the only thing she could think of that he might want. And cheek only! No lips! Damian agreed and they finished the project, which was a reproduction of the human digestive system, complete with sound and blinking lights. They got an A on it.

Unfortunately, Mindy was out sick the last day of school. Then her family went away for the summer, and that fall, she and Damian started their freshman year at different high schools. So Damian never got his kiss.

"We can discuss collecting later," Damian whispered, his breath blowing lightly against Mindy's earlobe and sending shivers down her spine. "I'm going to go get something to eat."

"How do you know him?" Wanda demanded as soon as Damian walked away.

"Tell us everything!" Lacey gushed.

"Did you used to date him?" Vivienne wanted to know. "Does he have a girlfriend?"

Mindy's head was spinning from all the questions being thrown her way. She didn't know whose question to answer first, so she played it safe and gave Wanda all her attention.

"We went to junior high together," she said. "His name is Damian Marsala. This is the first time I've seen him in years."

"He's from our town?" Vivienne gasped. "Where's he been hiding himself?"

"He goes to South Ridge High."

"If the guys at South Ridge High look like that, I'm transferring!" Lacey exclaimed.

"You're going to have to get his cell phone number so we can hang out with him this week," Wanda said.

"Go get something to eat!" Lacey urged, pushing Mindy in the direction Damian had headed. "And his digits!"

Mindy walked over to the barbecue. As she waited to be served, Vivienne came up behind her.

"Thanks for helping me out before," Mindy said. "You know, with that curfew stuff."

Vivienne shrugged. "Not a problem. Friends help each other out."

Were they friends? Mindy wondered. Wanda had said they were friends, but had she meant it? Now Vivienne was saying the same thing.

"If I can ever help you out, all you have to do is ask," Mindy said, wanting to show Vivienne she could count on her.

"Really?"

Mindy nodded.

Vivienne looked around, as if wanting to make sure she wasn't overheard. "Do you think you can get me a date with Damian?"

Mindy didn't know how to answer. She didn't want to make Vivienne mad. At the same time, she did want to prove she was a friend.

"I haven't seen Damian in three years," Mindy said. "I don't know anything about him. Hopefully, I'll be able to reconnect with him this week and I can feel him out. See if he's dating someone, and if he isn't, if he'd be interested in going out with you. Is that okay?"

Mindy held her breath, waiting for Vivienne's answer.

"That would be great! Thanks, Mindy." Vivienne peeked over her shoulder. "This is just between us, right?"

Mindy knew what she was asking. Vivienne was no dummy. She knew that Wanda and Lacey were also interested in Damian, and she didn't want them to know she was.

"Just between us," Mindy promised.

After getting a chicken breast, some salad, and a soda, Mindy found a seat on a chaise lounge next to the pool. As she sat down and started to eat, Lacey slid into the lounge chair next to her.

"You've got to help me, Mindy!"

"With what?"

"Wanda's setting her sights on Damian and it's not fair." Lacey pouted. "She already has Rick."

"What do you want me to do?"

"You've got to get me a date with Damian!"

Mindy almost choked on the soda she was sipping. "What?!"

Lacey nodded eagerly. "You're his friend. If you tell him how great I am and that he should ask me out, he'll listen to you."

"Damian and I aren't really friends," Mindy said, her mind scrambling for some sort of answer to get herself out of this mess.

"But *we're* friends, aren't we?"

There was only one answer that Mindy could give. And once she gave it, she was doomed.

"Of course we're friends!"

"Then you'll come through for me? You'll get me a date with Damian?"

"I can't promise a date with Damian," Mindy hesitantly said, watching as Lacey's face started to turn red with anger. "Wait! Let me explain." In a rush, Mindy told Lacey the same thing she had told Vivienne. Luckily, Lacey calmed down and was fine with Mindy's answer.

"If you come through for me, Mindy," she said, getting up from her chaise lounge, "I won't forget it."

After Lacey left, Mindy tried to keep eating, but she had lost her appetite. How was she going to get Damian to go out with both Vivienne and Lacey? And not have them find out about it?

"Mindy!"

Mindy turned to see that Wanda had slid into the chaise lounge where Lacey had been sitting.

"We need to talk."

"About?"

Wanda's red lips curled into a satisfied smile, and her dark almond-shaped eyes sparkled. "Damian!"

Mindy swallowed over the lump in her throat. She had a bad feeling about this. . . .

"What about him?" she asked, forcing the words out.

Please don't say what I think you're going to say. Please don't say what I think you're going to say.

"I want to go out with him."

She said it!

"And you're going to make it happen!"

Mindy knew there was no way she'd be able to tell Wanda what she'd told Vivienne and Lacey. No way. Wanda wanted a date with Damian, and she expected Mindy to deliver a date with Damian.

No matter what.

Mindy gave Wanda a huge smile. "Absolutely!"

After Wanda left, Mindy tried not to panic. She had to think of the positives and not the negatives. This was the opportunity she had been waiting for. If she came through on what she had promised, she would be *in* with the Princess Posse.

There was only one problem.

Wanda, Lacey, and Vivienne all wanted a date with Damian.

And Damian was only one guy!

How was she going to pull this off?

Unless . . .

Unless she did a group date. Yes! A group date. That way, they all got to spend time with Damian, and Damian got to know them. Hopefully, he'd click with one of the girls, and Mindy would be off the hook.

Mindy jumped off her chaise lounge and searched for Damian. Where was he?

"Looking for me?"

Mindy stared into the pool and saw Damian floating on his back, wearing only a pair of neon blue swim trunks.

He looked good without his T-shirt on.

Very good.

Mindy forced her eyes to move from his chest up to his face and found that equally distracting.

Focus. Must focus! My social life is at stake!

"Why don't you come out of the pool so we can talk?" she suggested.

Damian swam over to the side of the pool and pulled himself out, shaking himself off and scattering droplets of water everywhere.

"Ick!" Mindy screamed. "You're getting me all wet!"

"Stop being such a girl!" Damian teased, flicking some more water at her.

"I *am* a girl!"

"And a very pretty one," Damian said.

It was nice to hear the words, but Mindy wasn't gullible. She had a feeling that Damian was always saying things like that to girls. He was definitely a flirt. He knew what to say and do to make a girl feel special.

"Where've you been hiding all these years?" he asked. "North Ridge isn't such a huge town."

"Maybe I haven't been hiding. Maybe you've been too busy dating to think about some girl you went to junior high with."

Damian shrugged. "I do have a busy social life."

I'll bet, Mindy thought. Damian was probably South Ridge High's biggest heartbreaker.

"Are you doing anything tomorrow?" Mindy asked. "I thought if you didn't have plans, you might want to go to the beach."

"Just you and me?"

"And my friends."

Damian shook his head. "Two's company and five's a crowd."

"Come on!" Mindy pleaded. "It'll be fun." He had to say yes. If he didn't, she didn't know what she would do! "Please? I really would like to spend some time with you."

"I'll go to the beach with you and your friends tomorrow, but only if we can sneak off and spend some time alone," Damian shot back. "So we can catch up with each other."

Mindy knew if the other girls found out, they'd go ballistic. But that didn't mean they had to find out. . . .

And it wasn't like she and Damian would be going out on a *date*.

They would be two old friends getting together and catching up.

She didn't have anything to feel guilty about.

The words slipped out before she could stop them. "It's a deal!"

Danielle gazed longingly at the sparerib Ethan was gnawing on. It looked so yummy, slathered with barbecue sauce. Not to mention the corn on the cob oozing with melted butter on his plate.

"These ribs are delicious," Ethan said, licking his fingers. "Are you sure you don't want some?"

"I'm fine with my salad," Danielle said, holding up a forkful of tomatoes and greens.

She really did want some spareribs and corn on the cob, but she couldn't eat them tonight. They were too messy. She could wind up with corn stuck between her teeth or barbecue sauce smeared across her face. Hardly the look she wanted!

"Thanks for helping me barbecue," Danielle said.

"I'm pretty much a disaster in the kitchen," Ethan admitted. "But I'm good at barbecuing. All you do is light the charcoal and toss the meat on the grill and flip it over a couple of times."

Danielle gazed around the backyard. "I think everyone is having fun."

Including me, she wanted to say. Even though this wasn't an "official" date, they were having a really nice time. Of course, she'd had great first dates in the past and then disastrous second dates, so she wasn't feeling confident quite yet.

"This is so weird," Ethan said.

"What is?"

Ethan waved his sparerib in the air. "This. Not only are we all from the same town, but our beach houses are right next door to each other."

"Maybe it was fate."

"Fate?"

"Maybe we were destined to meet each other. It's like something out of a movie."

"So who's playing me and who's playing you?"

"I'm Anne Hathaway and you're Zac Efron."

Ethan made a face. "I can't stand *High School Musical*."

"Bite your tongue! That was my favorite movie when I was a tween."

94

"Are you a big moviegoer?"

"I love seeing movies on the big screen. Especially the ones with tons of special effects."

"Me, too!"

"I waited two hours in line to see the last *Star Trek* movie."

"Do you like going to the beach?" Ethan asked.

"I love the beach," Danielle said.

"Want to go tomorrow?"

"Sure!"

Date number two! Danielle happily thought. Hopefully, it wouldn't be a disaster.

"I see you're a ketchup girl," Cooper said.

Ava gazed up at Cooper. "Huh?"

Cooper pointed to her hot dog. "You put ketchup on it, not mustard." He held up his own hot dog, also covered in ketchup. "Just like me. Kids at school would always look at me like I was a freak when I put ketchup on my hot dog."

"Join the club."

"Is anyone sitting next to you?" Cooper asked, pointing to the spot next to Ava on the picnic bench.

"It's all yours."

"I'm Cooper," he said, putting his plate down and sliding next to her.

"Ava."

"Are you the matchmaker responsible for getting Ethan and Danielle together?"

Ava shook her head. "I can't take the credit for that. Danielle's skills with a supermarket cart are what did it."

Cooper couldn't figure out what it was, but there was something sad about Ava. And he wanted to take that sadness away. He could see it in her eyes. He tried talking to her, but every question he asked, she gave him a one-word answer. Finally, he gave up.

"It was nice *not* talking to you," he said after he finished eating.

"What?"

"You hardly talked to me. Did I do something to offend you? Because if I did, I'm sorry."

Ava sighed. "It's not you, it's me. I'm just in a funk. My boyfriend and I recently broke up. We were dating for a year. Just when I think I'm ready to move on, I find out I'm not."

"Oh," Cooper quietly said, feeling bad for criticizing Ava. "Well, if it's any consolation, I think he was a jerk for breaking up with you."

Ava gave Cooper a small smile. "Thanks. I think he's a jerk, too."

"You know what would cheer you up?"

"What?"

"A day at the beach. There's nothing like the feel of sand between your toes. Collecting seashells. Making sand castles. Swimming in chlorine-free water. I was thinking of going. Why don't you come with me?"

Ava shook her head. "Thanks for the invite, but I'm not ready to start dating again."

"Who said anything about a date? I just want to be friends. Nothing wrong with two friends hanging out together at the beach. Come on," Cooper urged. "You know you want to go. You didn't come all the way down to Miami to spend your time next to a swimming pool. You could have stayed home and gone to the North Ridge Country Club for that."

"Just friends?" Ava asked.

Cooper crossed his heart. "Just friends."

"What time did you want to go?"

"I'll pick you up at ten?"

"Okay."

Cooper didn't know why he did it, but he gave Ava a hug. Maybe it was because he felt she needed it. "I know you're still hurting. Trust me, I've been there. Eventually, the hurt goes away."

Just then, Mindy Yee popped up in front of them with her camera. "Say cheese!" she exclaimed.

Cooper blinked as the flash went off in his eyes.

Ava, however, had a completely different reaction.

She tore herself out of Cooper's hug and pushed herself into Mindy's face. "What do you think you're doing?" Ava didn't give Mindy a chance to answer. "Are you planning to send that photo to Josh? To tell him I'm cheating on him? Well, here's a news flash for you, Mindy. Josh and I are over! Didn't know that, did you? That's because I only told Danielle and Lindsey. I didn't tell anyone else. We broke up last month, so your big scoop is no scoop!"

At first, Mindy was speechless. But then she found her voice. "I wasn't going to e-mail a photo to Josh. I was only taking pictures of everyone at the barbecue. I've been doing it all night."

Lindsey, who was standing next to Mindy, nodded. "She has."

Mindy pulled up the photo she'd just taken and handed Ava her camera. "Here, delete it."

Ava shook her head. "No, that's okay."

"Then I'll delete it," Mindy said, pressing a button. She turned the camera around to show Ava the empty frame. "It's gone. Sorry I made you upset."

Then, before Ava could say anything else, Mindy left the barbecue.

★   ★   ★

Maybe I should have picked the brunette, Cooper thought.

Obviously, Ava was still hung up on her ex-boyfriend if she was freaking out over a picture of herself with another guy making its way to him. It also showed that she meant what she'd said. That she wasn't ready to start dating again. It hadn't been a line and she wasn't playing hard to get. She still had feelings for Josh.

It made Cooper like Ava even more because it showed that when she cared about someone, she *really* cared.

That was what he wanted in a girlfriend. He wanted someone to care about him the way Ava still cared for Josh. But unlike Josh, he wouldn't mess things up. He wouldn't throw away a girl as great as Ava.

Cooper never would have thought Ava could get so angry.

It intrigued him.

It made him want to learn more about her.

And he would.

Starting tomorrow.

But right now, he needed to make her feel better. He could see she was upset by her outburst.

"I can't believe I did that," she groaned to Cooper. "I *never* lose it like that."

"You made a mistake. It happens to everyone."

"It was more like a meltdown."

"You know what you need to feel better?"

"What?"

"Ice cream! And since you're a girl who likes ketchup on her hot dogs, I'm thinking you don't go for the same-old same-old when it comes to ice cream."

"So what do I go for?"

"You're not a vanilla with hot fudge girl, and I don't think you're a chocolate and hot fudge girl, either."

"Then what am I?"

"At first I was going to say caramel sauce, but I think you're more strawberry sauce. As for ice cream, this is going to be tricky. I think you like a little crunch with your ice cream, so I'm going to say either Rocky Road or chocolate chip."

"Close."

"What kind?"

"Cookies and Cream."

"I like Cookies and Cream, too!" Cooper exclaimed.

"Then what are you waiting for?" Ava pointed in the direction of the kitchen. "There's a gallon of Cookies and Cream ice cream in the freezer with our names on it!"

Chapter Eight

Danielle woke up to the sound of frying bacon. There was no mistaking the sizzling snap, crackle, and pop or the delicious smell wafting in the air. As Danielle inhaled, her stomach started grumbling. Suddenly, she was starving.

She jumped out of bed and threw on her robe, heading downstairs to the kitchen. She wondered if Sharla had decided to make breakfast for them and if she was taking requests. In addition to some crisp bacon, Danielle was craving a stack of blueberry pancakes.

As she neared the kitchen, Danielle could hear Lindsey screeching.

"What do you think you're doing? That's disgusting! Use a glass!"

Danielle pushed open the door to the kitchen

and found Howie standing in front of their refrigerator, guzzling from a container of orange juice.

Howie burped and handed the container of juice to Lindsey. "I don't know where the glasses are."

Lindsey shoved the container back at him. "Keep it! I wouldn't drink out of that if you paid me! You've gotten it all germy!"

"I'm cootie free," Howie said.

"What's going on?" Danielle asked.

"Our next-door neighbor thinks our kitchen is his own personal buffet!" Lindsey exclaimed. "He's eaten everything! All our eggs. A box of cereal. The potatoes and onions. An entire loaf of bread. And now he's getting ready to inhale the bacon!"

"Speaking of bacon," Howie said, walking around Lindsey and removing the bacon from the frying pan. He placed the strips on a paper-towel-covered plate so they could drain.

"That bacon is ours!" Lindsey cried, snatching the plate away from him. "We paid for it! If anyone is going to eat it, it's going to be me!"

Howie's face crumpled as he watched Lindsey shove the bacon into her mouth.

"How did you get in here?" Danielle asked.

"Crystal's aunt was leaving when I came over. I asked if I could borrow an egg, and she said to make myself at home and take whatever I needed."

"I'm sure she didn't mean that you could eat us out of house and home!" Lindsey told him between crunches of bacon.

"I'm in training. I need the calories," Howie said, staring longingly at the bacon Lindsey was eating. He tried to snatch a piece off the plate, and she slapped his hand away.

"Back off!"

"What's with the yelling?" a sleepy Ava asked, walking into the kitchen and rubbing her eyes. "I could hear you all the way upstairs."

"Our next-door neighbor thinks our kitchen is his own take-out diner," Lindsey said.

Ava walked over to the refrigerator and stuck her head inside. "What are we supposed to do for breakfast?"

Danielle shrugged. "I guess we could always grab some donuts."

"I'll go get them," Ava said, leaving the kitchen.

"I like chocolate glazed," Howie called out.

"You're not getting another bite out of us!" Lindsey ordered, pushing Howie in the direction of the back door. "Now, get out. Out!"

"Uh, Lindsey?" Danielle called out.

Lindsey ignored her, too busy slamming the back door after Howie and locking it.

"Linds?"

"What?"

"I think maybe you should have made Howie stay a little longer."

"Why?"

"Take a look around. Notice anything?"

The kitchen was a disaster area. There were eggshells, potato peelings, and onion wrappings scattered on top of the counter and on the floor, used pots and pans on the grease-splattered stove, and empty mixing bowls piled in the sink.

"He made a huge mess," Danielle said. "Now we're stuck cleaning it up."

Lindsey sighed. "I'll do it. You go get ready for your date with Ethan. That's more important."

"Are you sure?"

Lindsey shoved her out of the kitchen. "Go! I'll call you when Ava gets back with the donuts."

Donuts were the last thing on Danielle's mind. Now that Lindsey had reminded her of her date with Ethan, all thoughts of hunger were gone.

"I'll take four chocolate glazed, four jelly, and four apple cinnamon," Ava told the man behind the counter at Donut World.

"Anything else?"

"That's it."

As Ava was paying at the cash register, she saw

Mindy Yee walk over to the counter. Ava felt awful for the way she had snapped at her the night before. Talking about Josh with Cooper had stirred up all her hurt feelings. And since she couldn't take things out on Josh, she had aimed all her anger and resentment at the first person who had crossed her path.

Unfortunately, that person had been Mindy.

After Ava paid for her donuts, she went back to the counter.

"Hi."

A startled Mindy turned around. She seemed surprised that Ava was talking to her.

"Sorry for flipping out on you last night," Ava said. "I shouldn't have done that. I was wrong."

"Don't worry about it. I can't blame you. After all, my reputation speaks for itself!"

"Still, I should have given you the benefit of the doubt. I don't usually jump to conclusions like that. And I did remember seeing you taking pictures earlier in the night. I was mad, but I wasn't mad at you. I was mad at someone else."

"Josh?" Mindy asked.

Ava nodded. Since the secret was out, there was no reason not to talk about it, even if it was to North Ridge High's biggest gossip.

"Bad breakup?"

"Pretty bad. I'm still trying to deal with it."

"Give yourself some time."

Ava was surprised that Mindy wasn't bombarding her with questions. That was her usual style. Maybe her breakup with Josh wasn't juicy enough.

"Where's the rest of your crew?" Ava asked.

"Back at our beach house. Wanda was craving donuts, so here I am!"

Wanda couldn't get her own donuts? Ava had a feeling Wanda hadn't asked for the donuts but ordered Mindy to get them.

"You don't usually hang out with Wanda, Lacey, and Vivienne, do you?"

Mindy shook her head. "My parents are down here for business and they told me I could bring some friends, so I invited them."

Ava didn't think the Princess Posse was anyone's friends, but she didn't say that. Obviously, Mindy liked them or she wouldn't have asked them to come to Miami.

"Wanda seems like a handful."

"She's a perfectionist. She likes things a certain way."

"Nobody's perfect."

Mindy laughed. "Try telling that to Wanda!"

"So what are you doing today?"

"Heading to the beach. How about you?"

"Same thing."

"Maybe we'll run into each other," Mindy said before telling the counterman what kind of donuts she wanted.

"I'll keep an eye out for you," Ava promised. She held up her box of donuts. "I better get going. Danielle and Lindsey are waiting for breakfast. See you later."

Usually when Danielle went to the beach, she didn't put much thought into her appearance. She'd pull her hair into a ponytail and then toss a T-shirt and shorts over her swimsuit and that was it.

Today it was an entirely different game plan.

She couldn't look casual, but at the same time, she didn't want to look as if she had gotten dressed up. After all, she was going to the beach. Between the sun and sand and the wind, there was no way she could look perfect the entire day.

Ethan had seen her twice yesterday, and both times she had looked great.

She needed to look great again.

That meant wearing the red bikini.

Why not pull out her best swimsuit? Everyone had raved about it because they knew it would get results with the guys. So why not wear it for someone who was going to appreciate it?

Over the bikini, she added a white cotton jacket that had bell-shaped sleeves, and she decided to give herself some extra height by wearing sandals with cork wedge heels.

Her new haircut fell effortlessly into place, so she didn't have to worry about that. She dabbed a little mascara on her lashes, a touch of blush on her cheeks, and some lip gloss. She was good to go.

When Danielle walked downstairs, she found Ava and Lindsey in the kitchen munching on donuts. Ava held out the box. "Want one?"

Danielle shook her head. "I'm too nervous to eat."

"What did you decide to wear?" Lindsey asked.

Danielle loosened the belt of her jacket and opened it so Ava and Lindsey could see her red bikini.

"Ethan is going to love it!" Ava exclaimed.

"That's the plan," Danielle said.

Lindsey peeked into Danielle's tote bag. "Why do I see a copy of *Time* and *Newsweek* in there?"

"Because I'm going to read them. I like keeping up on current events."

"This is a vacation!" Lindsey stressed. "A vay cay!" She reached into the bag and pulled out the magazines.

"Hey! I want to read those."

Lindsey waved the magazines in Danielle's face.

"These are *not* suitable for vacation! You can read them on the plane ride home." Lindsey left the kitchen and returned with another stack of magazines, handing them to Danielle. "Today you're going to read these!"

Danielle flipped through the stack. "*People*? *National Enquirer*? *Us Weekly*? *In Touch*?! If Ethan sees me reading these, he's going to think I'm a mindless idiot."

"I don't think Ethan is going to be paying attention to what you're reading," Lindsey said. She waved a finger at Danielle's red bikini and then gave a snap. "His attention is going to be elsewhere." Lindsey peeked into Danielle's bag again. "You didn't pack that awful white sunblock that you always bring to the beach, did you?"

Danielle clutched her bag to her chest before Lindsey could reach into it. "I need to protect myself from the sun!"

"You'll look like Geekerella if you put that stuff all over your skin! I have this great sunblock with a high SPF that smells like coconut. Let me go get it."

"Hurry up!" Danielle called after her. "Ethan is going to be here soon."

Lindsey returned to the kitchen just as a car horn honked outside.

"There's Ethan!" Danielle exclaimed.

Lindsey tossed the sunblock into Danielle's tote bag. "Have a great time!"

Ethan sat behind the steering wheel of Cooper's red Mercedes convertible, the top down, waiting for Danielle to come outside. He ran his hand over the dashboard for the umpteenth time. He couldn't believe he was *finally* driving Cooper's car!

He was busy fiddling with the radio, trying to find a pop/rock station, when Danielle slid into the passenger seat and buckled up. "Wow! I can't believe this car! It's gorgeous! Is it yours? Was it a gift from your parents?"

Ethan abandoned the radio and pulled the car out onto the road, trying not to squirm. How did he answer Danielle's questions? He didn't want to lie to her. At the same time, he couldn't tell her the truth, because that would mean mentioning the bet, and he was sure she wouldn't be very happy about that!

He decided to fudge with the truth.

"The car came with the house." Which, in a way, it had since it was Cooper's car and Cooper was staying at the beach house. And if Ethan hadn't come to the beach house, well, he wouldn't be driving Cooper's car.

"Sweet," Danielle said. "So everyone in the house gets to drive it? Did you guys have to make up a schedule?"

Beads of sweat popped onto Ethan's forehead as a childhood phrase ran through his mind: *Liar, liar! Pants on fire!*

He stopped at a red light and gave Danielle a smile. "We couldn't agree to a schedule, so we drew straws to see who would have the car for the week and I won."

He *wasn't* lying. After all, he *had* won the car. In a way.

"That must have been your lucky day."

"It was the same day I met you," Ethan said. "So, yeah."

"Sweet-talker!"

Ethan pointed to the radio. "Why don't you find us some music to listen to?" he suggested, wanting to divert Danielle's attention before she could ask him any more questions about the car.

Cooper watched from the front porch as Ethan drove off. There had been no missing the smile on Ethan's face when he first saw Danielle. Cooper hoped they would have a good time at the beach.

"Looks like Ethan is getting a head start on the bet," Damian said, joining Cooper on the porch.

"I guess."

Damian wiped a peach on the front of his tank top and took a bite. "How about you? How are you going to impress Ava?"

"Who says I have to impress her?"

"You want her to like you, don't you? That means you have to impress her."

"No, it doesn't."

Damian took a bite of his peach, wiping a bit of juice off his chin. "Whatever. So how are you getting to the beach? You taking Ava by bus?"

"We're not taking the bus."

"Walking? It'll take you at least an hour."

"No."

"Then how are you taking her?"

"Follow me."

Cooper walked to the garage and lifted the door. "I found it last night."

Damian's mouth dropped open when he saw what was inside. "You can't be serious!"

"What's wrong?"

"You're really going to take Ava to the beach on *that*?"

"Why not?"

"Dude! It's like something from the last century! Your great-grandfather probably rode one of those things with your great-grandmother."

"I think it's kind of nostalgic. And girls love nostalgia."

"You better hope nostalgia helps you get that kiss, because that girl is still hung up on her ex."

Cooper slammed down the garage door. "Like I didn't know that."

"Just reminding you of the facts."

Cooper didn't want to think of Josh. He didn't want to think about the bet. All he wanted to think about was his day with Ava and having a good time.

He knew she wasn't interested in dating and he respected that.

But a small part of him was hoping that he could get her to change her mind.

Chapter Nine

The beach was packed. Everywhere Danielle looked, there were teenagers. A sea of colorful sheets with well-oiled sunbathers went on for miles. There were guys tossing Frisbees and footballs back and forth, and guys running in the surf with their dogs. Girls who weren't sunbathing were keeping themselves hidden under huge umbrellas while others were playing volleyball, laughing and shrieking as they tried to hit the ball over the net.

Of course there were couples. Some were holding hands, walking along the shore. Some were snuggled up against each other, laughing and whispering into each other's ears.

And naturally there were kissing couples.

"Guess we should have gotten here earlier," Ethan said.

"Now we know for tomorrow," Danielle said as they maneuvered their way through the hot sand. "Look! There's a spot!" She raced over to a patch of sand and threw down her tote bag, pulling out the striped sheet she had tossed inside. "Help me spread this out."

After the sheet was positioned, Ethan plopped himself down while Danielle remained standing.

"Aren't you going to sit?" he asked.

"Just let me take my jacket off," Danielle said, getting ready for her big reveal.

She unbelted her jacket and slid it off her shoulders, letting it fall to the sheet before turning around to face Ethan.

Success!

The expression on his face was what she had been hoping for. He was wowed by her bikini.

"You look amazing," he said.

Danielle tried not to blush. She wasn't used to getting compliments from guys. For years, she had always been good old Danielle, the girl whom guys would come to when they wanted to borrow her notes or needed help with an assignment. She wasn't the girl who usually turned heads.

"This old thing?" She laughed, trying to channel her older sister. Jade knew how to flirt with guys. "I was thinking of getting rid of it."

Ethan shook his head. "Keep it!"

"Well, if you like it so much, I will." Danielle sat next to him and reached into her tote bag. "Mind putting some suntan lotion on my back?"

Ethan squeezed a few globs onto her back and began rubbing it in. Instantly, she inhaled the scent of coconut as his hands traveled over her skin. She shivered and Ethan noticed.

"You okay?"

"The lotion is a little cold," she said.

That had to be it, right? It couldn't be because Ethan was touching her, could it? Although she had heard of some people having instant chemistry.

"Want me to do you?" she asked when he had finished.

"Okay."

Danielle rubbed some suntan lotion over Ethan's back and shoulders. She waited to see him shiver, but he didn't. So much for instant chemistry!

After they were both covered up, they lay down in the sun.

"How long to do you like to do this for?" Ethan asked.

"Not very long on the first day. I'm always afraid of burning. I try to tan in small doses."

Ethan looked at his watch. "What do you want to do after we finish tanning?"

"Toss a Frisbee?"

"I forgot to bring one."

"Make a sand castle?"

"And embarrass myself? My sand castles always come out lopsided."

"We could join a volleyball game."

Ethan flipped onto his side and propped his head up on a hand. "I know what we could do."

"What?"

"Go waterskiing!"

A startled Danielle sat up. "Waterskiing?" she nervously asked. "I don't know. I've never gone before. Is it safe?"

"There's nothing to be scared of," Ethan said. "I've gone lots of times. You'll be wearing a life jacket. And I'll walk you through it before you get on a pair of skis. Come on! It'll be fun!"

Danielle wanted to say no. At the same time, she also wanted to say yes. After all, this was her week to be different. Lindsey's words from the night before popped into her head: *You're Daring Dani!*

Daring Dani wouldn't be afraid to go waterskiing.

"Okay, I'll do it!" she exclaimed.

"Where did you find that?" Ava laughed as she walked out of her beach house.

"Our garage," Cooper said as he hit the kickstand on a bicycle built for two. "All I had to do was dust it off and put some air in the tires. Like it?"

Ava walked around the bike. "Don't tell me this is how we're getting to the beach?"

"Uh-huh."

"I hope you've got strong legs."

"Don't worry; I can do most of the pedaling."

"I'm going to hold you to it," Ava said, taking the seat behind Cooper.

As they headed in the direction of the beach, Ava asked herself what she was doing with Cooper when she still wasn't over her ex.

Last night, after the barbecue, all she could think about was Josh. The incident with Mindy made her realize that she didn't want Josh to think she had a new boyfriend. She still had feelings for him, and a small part of herself was hoping that he was going to ask her for another chance. If Mindy had sent that photo the way she thought she would, there wouldn't be another chance. Josh would think she had given up on him. But why was she thinking like that? *He* had given up on *her*. On *them*!

Why did she still have these feelings? Why was she hoping to save a relationship that was over? She should be putting Josh behind her and moving forward with someone new. Someone like Cooper. He was the complete package. Any girl would want to go out with him.

But not Ava.

If she went out on a date with him, she would feel guilty.

Like she was cheating on Josh.

Which was ridiculous!

It was over between them.

Over!

Cooper seemed like a great guy. And he said he was okay with just being friends. Why shouldn't she hang out with him?

Ava knew the real reason, but she didn't want to admit it to herself.

She was scared.

Scared of maybe falling for him and getting her heart broken again.

Cooper had been holding his breath when he showed Ava the bicycle built for two. Would she think he was crazy for suggesting they go to the beach that way? Would she ask him why he didn't have a car? Or worse, would she turn into a diva princess and insist that he find some other way to get them to the beach?

But then Ava had laughed, and it had been a *happy* laugh.

Hearing Ava laugh made Cooper happy. Very happy.

Because for the first time since he'd met her, Ava hadn't seemed sad.

For just a little while, it meant Ava had forgotten about Josh.

And that gave him hope.

So far, things were off to a great start.

Danielle was asking herself why she had opened her big mouth. She was on a pair of water skis, behind a motorboat, waiting for it to pull her into the ocean.

And she was petrified.

"Are you okay?" Ethan asked. "You seem a little pale."

"There aren't sharks in these waters, are there?" she blurted out.

"Huh?"

"Did you ever see *Jaws 2*? There's a scene in it where a girl is waterskiing and the vibration from the skis gets the attention of the shark and he bites down on her ski, pulls her into the water, and eats her!"

"I don't think you need to worry about becoming lunch for a shark," Ethan reassured her. "Are you sure you want to do this? If you're nervous or scared, it's no big deal. You don't have to if you don't want to."

Danielle shook her head resolutely. "No, I want to. I'm going to," she vowed, even though nervous butterflies were crashing around in her stomach. "What's the worst thing that can happen? I get all wet!"

"That's the spirit!" Ethan said as he went to sit next to the guy who would be driving the motorboat.

Danielle held on tightly to the line attached to the boat as it headed out into the water. As the boat picked up speed, she tried to remember everything Ethan had told her. She kept herself in a sitting position with her knees bent and her skis a couple of inches above the water. She didn't look down at her skis or up in the sky or around her. She just kept her eyes focused on the boat in front of her. As the boat drove farther out, it began to pull her onto the top of the water.

Danielle gasped.

She was doing it!

She was waterskiing!

Water splashed in her face, and the wind blew through her hair, but Danielle didn't care. She was loving every second of it.

But then, as the boat made a turn, she felt herself losing her balance.

Instantly, she remembered what Ethan told her to do if that happened. She let go of the rope attached to the boat so she wouldn't be dragged along. As soon as she did, she fell into the water, sinking under, but immediately popped back up.

"Are you okay?" Ethan asked as the boat pulled up next to her.

Danielle eagerly nodded as she pushed her wet hair out of her eyes. "Can we do it again?"

Ava watched as Cooper added another turret to the sand castle they were building along the shore of the beach. "You're really good at this," she said as she started digging a moat with a piece of driftwood.

Cooper waved his fingers. "I have magic hands."

Little kids who were building sand castles near them kept staring as Cooper added onto their castle.

"Want some help?" he asked them.

At their eager nods, he went over to offer his assistance. Ava couldn't help but notice how great he was with the kids, making them laugh and showing them how he molded the wet sand. He was the complete opposite of Josh, who called all little kids "brats" and refused to have anything to do with them, especially at Halloween, which was Ava's favorite holiday. She loved answering the doorbell with a bowl of candy in her hands and seeing how all the little kids had dressed up. They were always so adorable!

"I think you have a fan club," Ava said when Cooper rejoined her. "You're really good with kids. Do you have any brothers and sisters?"

"I'm an only child. How about you?"

"I have a younger sister, Carrie, who's a sophomore at North Ridge High."

"It must be nice having a sister."

"It is when we're not fighting with each other."

"Uh-oh," Cooper said, staring over Ava's shoulder. "I think we're about to have a natural disaster!"

Ava turned around and cried out as a big wave came in, splashing over them and washing away their sand castle.

"Yuck!" Ava exclaimed, staring at the wet sand covering her body from head to toe.

"Let's go in for a swim," Cooper suggested.

They jumped into the water to wash off all the wet sand and then floated on their backs, pointing out clouds in the sky and the shapes they resembled.

"I'm starting to wrinkle like a prune," Ava said, holding up a finger, after they'd been in the water for a while. "I'm going to head back to the sheet."

"I'll go with you," Cooper said, swimming after her.

When they got back onshore, Cooper took Ava's hand in his. Ava let him hold it for a little bit as they walked through the crowd, but then she pulled her hand away. If Cooper noticed, he didn't say anything. When they got back to their sheet, Ava started toweling herself off.

"Your back is getting red," Cooper pointed out, walking over with the sunblock. "Let me put some more on you."

"That's okay."

"You're telling me you'd rather take the risk of burning like a lobster?" Cooper waved his fingers. "Magic hands, remember?"

"I can do it myself," Ava insisted.

"Do you have elastic arms? There's no way you'll be able to reach the middle of your back."

"I can do it myself," Ava repeated as she squirted some sunblock onto her hands and began rubbing it onto her back and shoulders. "See?"

"I can see where you're *not* getting it."

"I'll be fine," Ava said, closing the bottle. "You know what? I'm hungry. Why don't I go to the concession stand and get us some lunch? My treat."

Before Cooper could say anything else, Ava grabbed her tote bag and hurried off.

Cooper watched as Ava headed to the concession stand.

Why wouldn't she give him a chance?

Even though he told her he was okay with just being friends, he wanted more than that. The more time he spent with her, the more he liked her.

The more he wanted to kiss her.

And it wasn't because of his bet with Ethan.

He wasn't even thinking of the bet. It was the last thing on his mind.

He wanted to kiss Ava because he liked her.

And the way a guy showed a girl he liked her was with a kiss.

But it was like she had this guard up and she was determined not to let anyone past it.

It was all her ex-boyfriend's fault.

He'd hurt Ava and because of the way he hurt her, she wasn't willing to trust another guy.

Cooper sighed, trying not to feel frustrated.

He reminded himself to be patient.

After all, it was only day one.

He still had the rest of the week.

And he didn't just have magic hands.

He had magic lips, too.

Chapter Ten

"Ready for some lunch?" Ethan asked Danielle after they had finished waterskiing.

"Want to grab a hot dog?" Danielle suggested.

Ethan shook his head. "We can do better than a hot dog," he said as they walked along the dock back to the beach. "Let's try this place."

Danielle gazed at the Ocean View, the restaurant Ethan was pointing to. "It looks kind of expensive."

"Don't worry about the price," Ethan said as he took Danielle by the hand and led her up to the restaurant's gold-encrusted glass doors. "It's my treat."

Ethan wanted to impress Danielle. So far, their date was going great and he wanted to keep it that way. Why not use Cooper's credit card again? He'd already used it to go waterskiing. Just one more time. After all, his intentions were good. He liked Danielle and wanted to show her that.

"Are you sure you want to eat here?" Danielle asked.

"Positive."

Ethan held the front door open for Danielle.

Cool air-conditioning wafted over them as they walked inside and a hostess instantly came over. "Welcome to the Ocean View."

They were shown to a table by the window and handed two menus written in calligraphy and printed on parchment paper. Ethan couldn't help but notice how fancy everything was. The tables were covered with white linen and there were multiple place settings, along with two sets of cut crystal glasses and silverware. There was also a bouquet of white tulips in a gold bowl on the center of every table.

"I don't know which is the right fork to use," Danielle whispered.

"I think you're supposed to start from the outside and work your way in. At least that's what they said on *Charm School*."

Danielle raised an eyebrow. "*Charm School*? You must be a reality TV watcher."

"I love it," Ethan said. "It's better than scripted TV because you never know what the people you're watching are going to do or say next."

"I'm addicted to *The Bachelor*," Danielle confessed.

"Why does every girl love *The Bachelor*?"

Danielle shrugged. "I don't know. We just do. Why do so many guys like WWE wrestling?"

"This guy doesn't," Ethan said. "WWE is *so* fake."

"What should we order?" Danielle asked. "There are too many choices."

"What looks good to you?"

Danielle's eyes glanced over the menu. "I'll probably get a burger."

"You can get a burger anywhere. Order something exotic. Something you wouldn't ordinarily eat."

"Like what?"

Ethan peeked at the menu again. "Oysters!"

Danielle made a face. "Gross!"

"What's wrong with oysters?"

"They're so slimy."

"I'm going to get some."

Danielle decided to order a crab salad, while Ethan went with the oysters and a lobster roll.

As they waited for their food, Ethan and Danielle talked about everything from movies and TV shows to books and music. They also both confessed to being nervous about their upcoming SAT exams.

"It boggles my mind that so much is riding on

that one test," Danielle said as she took a sip of lemonade.

"Well, it's not like *everything* is riding on it. Our school grades, extracurricular activities, and letters of reference also matter."

"I know, I know. But everyone is so focused on the SAT. It's like THE BIG TEST!"

"I'm sure you'll ace it."

"We'll see," Danielle murmured. "Once I get home, I need to hit the books again."

"No more talk about serious stuff!" Ethan insisted. "We're on spring break!"

Just then their waiter, a fiftysomething guy with a full head of silver hair, pouchy eyes, and a deep tan, arrived with their food. After serving Danielle, he placed a plate of oysters in front of Ethan.

"Sure you don't want one?" Ethan asked as he squeezed some fresh lemon and added a dash of Tabasco sauce to his oysters.

Danielle made a face. "They're all yours."

Ethan popped an oyster into his mouth. And almost spit it back out! Danielle was right. It was slimy!

"How's it taste?" Danielle asked.

Ethan forced himself to swallow.

He couldn't *not* eat it in front of Danielle.

"Delicious," he choked out.

She pointed to his plate. "You've got five more to go."

Lucky me, Ethan thought as he brought another shell to his lips. Somehow, he managed to swallow all six oysters. Ugh! At least his lobster roll was edible.

When it came to dessert, Danielle couldn't make up her mind. "I don't know if I want the chocolate mousse or the peach tart."

"How about you get the chocolate mousse and I'll get the peach tart and we'll share?"

"Great!"

Ethan had assumed they would each put part of the dessert on the other's plate, but Danielle had her own idea. He was caught totally off guard when she brought a spoonful of her mousse to his lips.

"Open up," she said.

Ethan had never had a girl feed him before. He opened his mouth, and Danielle slipped her spoon in.

"Good, huh?"

A speechless Ethan nodded. Then he gave Danielle a forkful of his peach tart.

"Yummy!" she exclaimed.

As Danielle licked a bit of whipped cream from the corner of her mouth, Ethan wondered what her lips would feel like pressed against his.

"Penny for your thoughts," Danielle said.

Yikes! He couldn't tell her what he was thinking. Ethan's mind scrambled. And then he remembered something.

"You mentioned wanting to go to the beach tomorrow. When we were looking for a spot to put down our sheet, remember?"

"Uh-huh," Danielle said around a mouthful of mousse.

"Still want to?"

Ethan held his breath while waiting for Danielle's answer.

"Sure."

Yes!!!

This day couldn't get any better.

"Your check," their waiter announced as he returned to the table with a leather billfold. Ethan reached into his wallet and pulled out one of the two credit cards Cooper had given him, handing it to the waiter, who disappeared.

Seconds later, their waiter returned.

"We have a problem," he said. "Your credit card has been declined."

"Declined?"

"That means it's no good."

"I know what it means!" Ethan testily snapped. He reached into his wallet and took out the other credit card. "Try this one."

The waiter left again and then came back. "Also

declined. Since your credit cards aren't working, you'll have to pay in cash."

How could Cooper's credit cards be declined? He hadn't had a problem when he used one to go waterskiing that morning. Had he hit Cooper's credit card limit? And of all days for it to happen, it had to be *today*?!

Ethan knew how much money he had in his wallet and it wasn't enough to pay the bill.

This day couldn't get any *worse*!

"I'll be right back," he told Danielle, as he stepped away from the table to use his cell phone.

Outside the restrooms, Ethan dialed Cooper's number. But Cooper didn't answer. Instead, the call went straight to voice mail.

"Coop!" Ethan hissed. "Where are you? I'm in the middle of a super-embarrassing situation and it's all your fault. Your credit cards are useless! Call me as soon as you get this message!"

After Ethan got off the phone, he returned to the table. There was only one thing he could do. As much as he didn't want to, he had no choice.

"Is everything okay?" Danielle asked.

"Danielle, I hate to ask, but could you help me pay the bill? There's a problem with my credit cards and I don't have enough cash on me."

Danielle reached into her tote bag. "You're welcome to whatever I have, but it's not a lot. I'm always afraid of losing my wallet when I go to the beach, so I never take a lot of money with me."

"Thanks," he said when Danielle gave him what she had.

"Are you ready to pay?" their waiter asked when he returned to the table.

"We don't have the full amount," Ethan said, handing over the billfold.

The waiter stared down at Ethan, making him feel like he was two inches tall. "Really?"

"But we can come back with the rest," Ethan promised, trying not to squirm in his seat. "Or we can call our friends and ask them to bring the difference."

"Stay right there," the waiter said as he left with the billfold. "I'm going to speak with the manager."

Five minutes later, he came back. "Follow me. Both of you."

"Where are we going?" Ethan asked.

He hadn't called the police, had he? Were they going to jail?

The waiter led them into the kitchen, where he pointed to a sink full of dirty dishes. "Roll up your sleeves and get to work. Once those dishes are washed and dried, your bill will be paid in full. And in the future, I strongly suggest you make sure you have enough money in your wallet before going to a restaurant that you can't afford!"

Ethan was mortified. Danielle probably thought she was on the date from hell. He turned to face her. "Danielle, I'm really, really, really sorry about this. All I wanted to do was take you to a nice lunch. I didn't know I was going to have a problem with my credit cards."

And when I get back to the beach house, Coop is going to have an even bigger problem! Like my hands around his neck!

"Don't worry about it. These things happen. I guess we shouldn't have ordered those two desserts, huh?"

"You're not mad?" Ethan asked in disbelief.

"What's the point of getting mad? It's not going to change the situation." She pointed to the pile of dishes they had to wash. "Let's just get this over with so we can go back to the beach!"

For a guy who hadn't wanted to go to the beach with four girls, Mindy noticed Damian didn't seem to be having a problem. Why would he? Wanda, Lacey, and Vivienne were fawning all over him. And he was loving it.

That morning at breakfast, when she'd returned with the donuts, Mindy had announced that Damian was meeting them at the beach. He'd called her on her cell while she was at Donut World and confirmed their plans. As soon as the words were out of her mouth, Wanda, Lacey, and Vivienne had raced back to their bedrooms to get ready.

"How come you're not rushing to make yourself gorgeous?" Carmela had asked as she started clearing the dining room table.

"Damian is off-limits to me," Mindy had answered.

"Do you want Damian to be off-limits?" Carmela had asked. "He must be something pretty special if those three are so excited."

"It doesn't matter what I want," Mindy had said. "Not that I want Damian! All that matters is what *they* want. And my making it happen!"

When they arrived at the beach, Damian had been waiting for them, sunning himself on a bench. He was wearing a tight white tank top and navy blue boxer-cut swim trunks. He'd slicked his dark hair back with gel, and mirrored sunglasses covered his eyes. He looked very cool and edgy.

He definitely knew how to give off a bad-boy vibe.

At the sight of Damian, Wanda had instantly rushed to his side and wrapped an arm around his, leading him through the crowded beach, while Vivienne and Lacey trailed behind, as always. Both

Vivienne and Lacey had shot Mindy looks of distress, and she knew she had to do *something* to make sure each girl had some private time with Damian.

Once they were settled on their sheets, Mindy had managed to get Vivienne and Damian to go searching for seashells together. Later, she had brought out the kite she had packed, and Damian and Lacey had gone off to fly it. Even Wanda had gotten some alone time with Damian when Mindy convinced Vivienne and Lacey to go with her for a swim.

Now Mindy was floating on her back, trying to figure out what her next step should be, when she heard a voice whisper in her ear.

"Your friends are all over me."

A startled Mindy turned her head to see Damian floating next to her.

"I guess they think you're a hottie," she said.

"And you don't?" Damian asked in a hurt tone.

"You know you're hot," Mindy scoffed. "You don't need me to tell you."

"When am I going to get some alone time with you? You promised if I hung out with your friends, I would, remember?"

If the words had come from any other guy, Mindy might have been flattered. But this was

Damian. He probably said them hundreds of times. Guys like Damian saw girls as conquests. Once they succeeded in getting what they wanted, they moved on to the next one.

"We're alone now," she said.

"Damian!" Wanda called out. "Damian! Where are you?"

"You were saying?" Damian pointed out.

"I'll go tell her where you are," Mindy said, swimming back to shore.

"You still owe me alone time," Damian called after her. "This didn't count!"

When Mindy emerged from the water, Wanda caught sight of her. But before Mindy could tell her where Damian was, Wanda started talking.

"There's something you need to know about me, Mindy. I *don't* like competition. *At all.* Damian doesn't need to be distracted by Lacey and Vivienne. I want a clear playing field. *All* his attention should be focused on *me.* Do something about it."

Talk about mission impossible! All three of them were interested in Damian. Hmmm. She probably shouldn't mention that she had just been swimming with Damian. That would probably be a big mistake.

Mindy's mind scrambled to find something to say. "But Damian will see how much hotter you are than them if they're still around." Then she went straight for Wanda's ego and laid it on thick. "Let's face it, Wanda, Lacey and Vivienne are no match for you. They just don't measure up and they never will. You're the best."

Wanda nodded with satisfaction. "That's true. But it's still not good enough."

"I'll work on getting you alone with him," Mindy said, although she had no idea how she was going to do it. "I promise."

"Good. Now, how about some lunch? I'm starving. And I'm sure everyone else is, too. Go get us some food."

"Whatever you want, Wanda," Mindy said, eager to make an escape. "Whatever you want."

Ava couldn't believe how rude she'd been to Cooper.

She was mortified!

All he'd done was offer to put some sunblock on her. Yet she was acting like he had wanted to have a make-out session. She needed to chill out!

Ava was so lost in her thoughts, she wasn't paying attention to where she was going and bumped into someone as she was climbing the steps to the boardwalk. It was Mindy, who was loaded down with five bags from the concession stand.

"You seem like you're a million miles away," Mindy said.

"Just thinking about something."

"Something or someone?" Mindy asked. "Josh?"

"Actually, I wasn't thinking of him."

"That's a sign of improvement!"

"I've still got a long way to go."

Ava stared at the bags Mindy was carrying. She could smell hamburgers and French fries. "You're not going to eat that all yourself, are you?"

"It's for Wanda and the girls. And Damian."

"Who's Damian?"

"This guy I used to go to junior high with. He was at the barbecue. He's staying in the beach house next to yours."

"He must be a friend of Cooper's."

"Was that the guy you were with last night?"

"I came to the beach with him today. We're just friends."

"I wasn't asking!" Mindy exclaimed.

"But you were wondering." Ava laughed.

"Maybe a little," Mindy admitted. "He's cute."

"So, are you dating Damian?"

"I'd be dead if I decided to date Damian."

"What do you mean?"

Mindy sighed. "Let me fill you in."

Ava listened as Mindy filled her in on the

139

Damian situation. When she was finished, Ava said, "I think you're going about this the wrong way."

"If you've got any advice, I'll take it. I'm desperate!"

"Why don't you talk to Damian? Maybe he can help you out. Each one of them wants to be alone with him, right? Well, maybe he can make it happen. All you have to worry about is this week. Once we get back home, it's out of your hands. Damian will be back at South Ridge High and we'll be at North Ridge. And Wanda will be busy with Rick!"

"Why didn't I think of that?" Mindy gasped. "Ava, you're a genius! Thank you, thank you, thank you! Maybe now I'll get to enjoy the rest of my spring break!"

Chapter Eleven

Danielle and Ethan were leaving the beach at the end of the day when a voice called out to her.

"You're the girl I've been waiting for!"

A guy with a brown buzz cut, wearing board shorts with a tropical pattern and a yellow T-shirt, jumped in front of her, waving a flyer. "You need to fill out one of these."

Danielle stared at the piece of paper. "Miss Spring Break?"

"You have to enter."

Danielle laughed. "Me? In a beauty pageant?"

"Why not?"

Danielle said the first thing that popped into her head. "I wouldn't win."

"All you have to do is look good in a swimsuit." The guy slid his sunglasses down his nose, and his green eyes moved from Danielle's red painted toes all the way up to her face. "And you look *very* good in a swimsuit."

Danielle blushed, glad she had tossed her cover-up jacket in her tote bag.

"I'm Rory," he said.

"Danielle. And this is Ethan."

Rory glanced at Ethan but focused his attention back on Danielle.

"I've got a good eye. You're the prettiest girl I've talked to today."

"I bet you've been saying that all day."

"Maybe I have," Rory coyly admitted. "But this time I mean it. You're a knockout."

Hearing those words, a tiny thrill went up Danielle's spine. It wasn't often that a guy flirted with her. And Rory was definitely flirting with her! Over the years, she'd been around enough guys who were interested in Jade to recognize the signs.

"Is there a Mr. Spring Break contest?" Danielle shot back. "Because if there is, you should definitely enter."

"Would I get your vote?" Rory asked.

"You wouldn't need my vote. You'd win first place."

"So would you. But if you didn't win, I'd make it up to you with a night out."

Okay, message received loud and clear! Rory wasn't just interested in having her enter the Miss Spring Break contest. He was interested in *her*!

Suddenly, Danielle realized that during her entire conversation with Rory, Ethan hadn't said anything. She turned to face him. "What do you think? Should I do it?"

Rory didn't give Ethan a chance to answer. "Of course you should do it! What's stopping you?"

Where to begin? What would her friends think? What would Jade say?

She wasn't a beauty contest girl.

Then again . . .

She *wasn't* the old Danielle.

This week she was a *new* Danielle.

And lots of guys had been checking her out today. She'd noticed the way their eyes were following her. Just like yesterday at the mall.

Maybe Rory was telling the truth and not just trying to get a date with her.

Maybe she *did* have a chance of winning the Miss Spring Break contest.

Maybe she *should* enter.

The old Danielle would have said no, but not this week.

This was her week to do the things she wouldn't ordinarily do!

What did she have to lose?

She reached into her tote bag and pulled out a pen, filling out the entry form. "I'm in!"

I'm not jealous.

I'm not jealous.

I'm not jealous.

Ethan kept repeating the words to himself, but they weren't sinking in.

Because he WAS jealous!!!

Ethan had eyes. He could tell that Rory liked Danielle, and he wanted to tell him to back off. But he couldn't. So far, Rory hadn't done anything wrong.

But in his gut, Ethan knew Rory wanted to make a move on Danielle.

And he probably would.

The only question was how and when.

Ethan sighed. How could he measure up to a guy like Rory? Even after a day at the beach, Rory was all shiny and polished, looking like a cover model. It was still a hot day and there wasn't a drop of sweat anywhere on him. And he smelled good, too!

Ethan, meanwhile, was a sticky, sandy, wrinkly mess who smelled like the ocean.

After Danielle finished filling out the entry form, Ethan put a possessive arm around her shoulders. "It's getting late. We better get going."

"Bye, Rory!"

"Bye, Danielle."

Ethan noticed that he didn't get a good-bye. That was fine. Let Rory underestimate him.

Ethan was a fighter.

The Miss Spring Break contest wasn't until the end of the week.

All he had to do was keep Danielle out of Rory's way until then.

As soon as Ava got home from the beach and jumped into the shower, she felt it. Her shoulders were burning. When she got out of the shower and checked them in the bathroom mirror, she could see they were red.

Well, she had no one to blame but herself. It served her right. Cooper had warned her, but she wouldn't let him put any sunblock on her.

After slipping on a peach halter top and a pair of white shorts, Ava headed downstairs. Everyone was still out except Sharla, who was in the laundry room, doing a load of wash. Ava had just settled on the couch and was aiming the remote control at the TV when the doorbell rang. She waited for Sharla to answer it, since it was her house, but when the bell rang again and Sharla didn't emerge from the laundry room, Ava got off the couch. When she opened the front door, she found Cooper on the other side, holding out a jar of aloe vera.

"I'm not the kind of guy that says, 'I told you so,'" he said, handing her the aloe vera. "But I thought you could use this."

Ava gave Cooper a smile. "Did I ever tell you that *stubborn* is my middle name?"

"I never would have guessed."

"Why don't you come in?"

Ava went back into the living room, with Cooper following after her. She sat down on the couch, turning her back to Cooper and tossing her red curls forward over one shoulder. "Mind putting some on my shoulders?" she asked.

"Sure," he said, taking the jar back from her and opening it up.

The aloe vera instantly cooled her stinging shoulders. "That feels *much* better."

"Maybe next time you'll listen to me."

"Sorry for being so weird today."

"You weren't that weird."

That was true. After they'd eaten lunch, they'd

gone back to making sand castles. Then they'd walked along the beach, collecting colorful stones and pebbles, done some swimming, and laid out in the sun until they finally decided to call it a day.

Ava turned her head to look over her shoulder. "How about if you let me make it up to you? Maybe we can do something tomorrow? I'll plan everything."

"I'd like that," Cooper said with a smile. "I'd like it a lot."

Baby steps, Cooper reminded himself. Baby steps.

He couldn't move too fast with Ava because if he did, he'd scare her off.

He was hoping that she would see him as boyfriend material, but if he pushed too hard, she might not even want him as a friend.

After lunch, he'd gone back to keeping things very low-key. Just two friends hanging out at the beach. He'd noticed Ava's shoulders getting red. As much as he'd wanted to say something, he didn't, biting his tongue because he didn't want Ava to think he was trying to make a move on her. Instead, he'd waited until they'd gotten home and then had come over with a jar of aloe vera. Just a concerned friend helping out another friend. There was nothing wrong with that.

And he *did* want to be friends with Ava, even though he was hoping for something more.

Maybe tomorrow would be a new beginning. They could start over. This time he wouldn't do anything that would scare Ava off.

Just friends.

Just friends.

But maybe, just maybe, more than friends . . .

"Where's Cooper?" Ethan asked.

Damian tore his eyes away from the big-screen TV showing *Family Guy* as Ethan walked into the living room. "He went next door to see Ava. Hey! How'd your day with Danielle go?"

"Don't ask."

"I guess that means you didn't get your kiss. If it's any consolation, Cooper struck out, too. I already grilled him. So much for being the Smooth Operator."

Ethan wished he'd never agreed to that stupid bet. If he hadn't, he wouldn't have taken Danielle out for a lunch he couldn't afford and they wouldn't have gotten stuck washing dirty dishes. What a way to make an impression on a girl he liked!

If Danielle gave him a second chance — and he wouldn't blame her if she didn't — he'd have to make sure everything he did was perfect.

Including their first kiss.

Because if he was lucky enough to kiss Danielle, he wanted it to be for real.

He didn't want it to be part of a bet.

But he couldn't tell that to Damian. Damian would call him a wuss and tease him nonstop.

At that moment, Cooper walked into the living room and Ethan forgot all about the bet.

"I'm going to kill you!" Ethan shouted.

Cooper held his hands up in surrender. "Chill out! What's wrong?"

"Didn't you get my voice-mail message?"

Cooper shook his head. "I forgot to take my phone to the beach. What's up?"

Ethan quickly filled Cooper in on his lunch fiasco at the Ocean View.

"No wonder Danielle didn't kiss you!" Damian howled with laughter, clutching his sides as he rolled back and forth on the couch. "You're lucky she didn't bop you over the head with a frying pan!"

"Oops!" Cooper exclaimed.

"Oops? *Oops?!* Is that all you can say?" Ethan demanded as he plopped down on the couch next to Damian. "Danielle was up to her elbows in greasy water, washing crusty dishes, and all you can say is *oops*?"

"My dad's been threatening to cut me off. Says I've been spending too much money. I didn't think he'd actually do it, but I guess he did. He must have called the credit card companies and lowered my spending limit."

"Lucky me!" Ethan fumed.

"I'm really sorry, Ethan," Cooper said. He pulled out his wallet and removed a wad of cash, holding it out. "This should cover you for the rest of the week. If you need more, let me know."

"I can't take your money."

"Why not? My credit cards are useless."

"Spending money I don't have is what got me into this mess."

"You don't have to spend it unless you want to."

"You might want to impress Danielle again." Damian snickered. "Only this time the right way and without dishpan hands!"

Ethan bopped Damian in the face with a throw pillow. "Har! Har!"

Damian snatched the pillow away from Ethan and bopped him back. "You can't be Mr. Moneybags without any money!"

"He's got a point," Cooper said.

"If you won't take it, I will," Damian said, reaching for the bills.

Ethan slapped away Damian's hand and took the money from Cooper. "I'll consider it an emergency fund."

"Was Danielle mad?" Cooper asked.

Ethan shrugged. "She said she wasn't, but who knows?"

"If she wasn't mad, what are you so upset about?"

"Oh, let's see, maybe I was embarrassed?!"

"Something else is bothering you," Cooper said. "I can tell. What is it?"

Ethan sighed. "When we left the beach, we ran into this guy handing out flyers. There's going to be a Miss Spring Break contest later in the week."

"Deets!" Damian exclaimed, sitting up. "I want deets!"

Ethan ignored him. "The guy handing out the flyers told Danielle she should enter and she did. He was flirting with her the entire time they were talking."

"So you're feeling a little threatened," Cooper said. "Like he was moving in on your turf."

"A little," Ethan admitted. "But it's not like they exchanged phone numbers or anything."

As soon as the words were out of Ethan's mouth, Damian smacked him on the top of his head.

"Ouch!" Ethan rubbed his head. "What did you do that for?"

"Duh!" Damian exclaimed. "If Danielle filled out an entry form, she must have put down some sort of contact info. An address. An e-mail. They didn't need to exchange phone numbers. If this guy wants to get in touch with her, he can."

Great.

Just great.

Those *so* weren't the words Ethan had wanted to hear.

Just when he thought his day couldn't get any worse, it did.

Chapter Twelve

Mindy hesitated before ringing the doorbell of Damian's beach house.

When Ava had suggested she talk to Damian, she thought the idea was great. Now she was having some doubts.

She and Damian weren't exactly friends. She could ask for his help, but that didn't mean he was going to give it.

And if he didn't . . .

No!

She couldn't think that way.

Damian *had to* help her.

He had to!

Mindy rang the doorbell and waited for someone to answer. When the front door opened, Damian was standing on the other side.

One day at the beach had darkened his already tan skin. He was wearing white jeans and a short-sleeve light blue pullover. The colors brought even more attention to his glowing tan. He looked even better than he had the day before.

How could that be possible?!

Damian pushed open the screen door. "Mindy? What are you doing here?" he asked, his voice filled with surprise.

"I wanted to talk to you."

Damian looked behind Mindy's shoulder. "Where's the rest of your posse?"

"Back at our beach house. I'm doing an after-dinner ice cream run."

"Did you stop by to ask me what I wanted?"

"Can I come inside?" Mindy asked.

"Sure," Damian said, continuing to hold the screen door open.

As Mindy walked past Damian, she could smell the cologne he was wearing. It was a clean, citrusy scent that she liked.

Damian hurried past her into the living room and cleared a pile of towels off the couch.

The beach house looked like a bunch of guys were staying in it. After one day, it was already a mess. There were newspapers and magazines scattered everywhere. Sneakers, socks, and sandals had been tossed in corners. T-shirts, shorts, and *even a wet bathing suit — ewwww!* — were scattered all over the floor.

An open pizza box was on the coffee table. "Want a slice?" Damian asked, holding out the box.

Cold pizza? Double ewwww!

"No, thanks," Mindy said as she sat in an over-size leather armchair.

"What'd you want to talk about?" Damian asked as he put the box of pizza back down and sat on the couch.

"Where are your roomies?"

"Out." Damian raised an eyebrow at Mindy. "We've got the whole place to ourselves. We can finally have some alone time."

Okay, it was time to burst that bubble. If Damian thought they were going to have some *alone* time, he was mistaken. "I don't plan on staying very long."

"Why don't you come sit next to me?" Damian suggested, patting the spot next to him on the couch.

Why did she suddenly feel like Little Red Riding Hood with the Big Bad Wolf?

Okay, she *did* look fierce. That was the point. She was no dummy. She had dressed for battle and was wearing a strapless blue-and-white-print sun-dress that hugged all her curves, along with thong sandals. She was almost positive that when it came to a pretty girl, Damian would have a hard time saying no.

And that was what she planned on.

"I'm fine here," she said, remaining in her seat.

"Don't you like me?" he asked, pretending to sound hurt. "I thought you liked me. If you liked me, you wouldn't be sitting so far away. You'd be sitting closer. Why don't you show me how much you like me, Mindy? Come sit next to me."

Oooh, he was good. Damian *so* knew how to turn on the charm.

"Of course I like you. And so do my friends. That's why I'm here," she said, getting to the point. "All three of them like you. They *really* like you. And I need you to help me out."

"How?"

"They all want to date you."

"Can't say that I blame them."

It was all Mindy could do not to roll her eyes. She hoped Damian was playing with her and not being serious. His ego couldn't be that out of control, could it?

"I was wondering if you could do me a favor," she said.

"What's the favor?"

"Could you go out with each one of them? Just

156

this week. When we get back home, you don't have to call them again. That is, unless you want to."

Mindy held her breath as she watched Damian think about it.

"Sure, I suppose so," he said.

Mindy exhaled. Phew! Success!

"But if I do," Damian continued, "what's in it for me?"

Mindy stared at Damian in disbelief. No! No! No! He couldn't do this to her!

"Obviously you're in some sort of bind; otherwise you wouldn't be here asking for my help, right?"

Mindy reluctantly nodded before filling Damian in on the North Ridge High Princess Posse and how she wanted to be part of their group. She was hoping if he knew the whole story, he'd take pity on her.

He didn't.

He settled back into the couch, crossing his arms behind his head. "So you need me. If I go out with them, they get what they want and you get what you want once we're back home. But what do I get?"

At that moment, Mindy's cell phone buzzed. She pulled it out and saw there was a text message from Wanda.

I WANT MY FROZEN YOGURT! NOW!!!
WHERE R U???

"I'll do anything you want if you go out with them," a desperate Mindy begged as she texted Wanda back and told her she was on her way home. "Anything!"

The second the words were out of her mouth, Mindy regretted them as Damian gave her a devilish smile.

"*Anything?*" he asked.

"Within reason!" she snapped back.

"I want the kiss you promised me three years ago."

That was it? Easy enough.

"Deal!" Mindy exclaimed, closing her eyes and puckering her lips as she waited for Damian to kiss her.

And waited.

And waited.

Finally, she opened an eye and saw Damian still sitting across from her on the couch.

"Aren't you going to kiss me?" she asked, opening both eyes.

Damian shook his head. "I'll collect my kiss when I'm good and ready. So be prepared! Because you're not going to know when it is!"

★　　★　　★

"Other than the screwup with Ethan's credit cards at the restaurant, it sounds like you had a nice day with him," Lindsey said as she dabbed a nail with nail polish remover on a cotton ball. "It was way better than my day at the beach with Jade and Crystal. All the guys were buzzing around them. You would have thought I was invisible!"

Danielle turned from the closet, where she was sorting through her new outfits. "Yeah, it was a nice day."

Lindsey turned to Ava, who was working on her own nails at the vanity table. "And it sounds like you had a nice day with Cooper."

"Cooper and I are *just* friends," Ava said.

"For now," Lindsey shot back.

"For always."

Lindsey sighed as she tossed a used cotton ball into the wastebasket. "But I thought you said you had a good time with him."

"I did!"

"So why not see if it develops into something more?"

"I *don't* want it to develop into something more."

"But you're not giving him a chance!"

"I'm still not over Josh," Ava said. "You know that!"

Lindsey held up her hands in surrender. "Okay, okay! I'm backing off! I know Josh is still a sensitive subject. All I'm saying is, try to be a little open-minded when it comes to Cooper. He seems like a nice guy. A lot of couples started out as friends first. Look at Noelle Kramer and Ryan Grant."

Ava shook a bottle of plum nail polish. "Cooper knows the deal and he's fine with it."

"Are you sure?"

"Yes."

Lindsey sighed again as she started giving herself a French manicure.

"I almost forgot!" Danielle exclaimed. "I didn't tell you the best part of my day. When Ethan and I were leaving the beach, we met this guy who was looking to sign up girls for the Miss Spring Break contest." Danielle paused, then shrieked, "I entered!"

Ava's mouth dropped open. "You did? Really?"

"Really! It's so not like me, but I'm *not* the old me, am I? I'm a new and improved Danielle! I do have to confess, though, that the guy handing out the flyers was kind of cute. And he made me feel *so* hot! I wanted to keep talking to him. I think he liked me."

"You can't be interested in another guy," Lindsey said. "You're going out with Ethan!"

"All we did was spend a day at the beach," Danielle said. "I wouldn't say we're going out with each other."

"You like him, don't you?" Lindsey asked.

"Yes," Danielle answered. "But I also liked Rory!"

From downstairs came the sound of the doorbell. Seconds later, Jade's voice called up to them. "Danielle! There's someone here to see you."

"I wonder who that could be," Danielle said.

"I bet it's Ethan!" Lindsey squealed excitedly. "He's probably come to ask you to take a moonlit walk on the beach."

When Danielle headed downstairs, she expected to find Ethan. Instead she was shocked to see Rory!

"What are you doing here?" she asked.

He held up her sunglasses. "These dropped out of your bag when you pulled out a pen to fill out the entry form. I figured you might need them tomorrow."

Danielle took the sunglasses out of his hand. "Why didn't you give them back to me then?"

Rory gave her a smug smile. "If I'd done that, I wouldn't be standing in front of you right now. So do I get a reward for bringing back your sunglasses?"

"What kind of reward?"

Rory shrugged. "I don't know. Surprise me."

Danielle remembered Lindsey's words. "How about a walk on the beach?"

"Perfect."

"Let me go get a jacket," Danielle said. "I'll be right back."

When Danielle headed back upstairs, she found Lindsey and Ava hovering over the banister.

"That's not Ethan!" Lindsey exclaimed.

"No, it's Rory!" Danielle stated as she hurried into her bedroom.

"The cutie from the Miss Spring Break contest?" Ava asked.

"The exact same one."

"Why are you going for a walk on the beach with him?" Lindsey asked.

Danielle tried on a denim jacket and then took it off. "Why not?"

"You're dating Ethan!"

"Ethan's a nice guy, but we're not dating."

"He bought you lunch! When a guy buys a girl lunch, it's a date!" Lindsey exclaimed.

"I paid for part of that lunch, remember?" Danielle reminded her.

"But he meant to pay for all of it!"

"Linds, this is spring break, remember? I'm

keeping my options open! The old Danielle might have said no to a walk on the beach with Rory, but the new Danielle isn't!" Danielle pulled out a violet sweater and wrapped it around her shoulders, tying the sleeves around her neck. "It's not like Ethan and I are a couple. Why should I just go out with one guy when I have another one interested in me?" Danielle didn't wait for an answer. "I'll see you guys later! Don't wait up for me."

"Guess who's taking me out later?" Wanda announced when Mindy arrived back at the beach house.

"Who?" Mindy asked as she handed out the containers of frozen yogurt and ice cream that she'd bought. From the glum expressions on Lacey's and Vivienne's faces, she had a pretty good idea who it was.

"Damian!"

"Really? That's great!" Mindy gushed, hoping she wasn't laying it on too thick.

After she'd made her deal with Damian, Mindy told him he needed to call Wanda immediately.

"Yeah, yeah, yeah," Damian had said as he walked her out the door. "Witchy Wanda will get my undivided love and devotion."

Mindy giggled. "Stop that!"

"Why? She *is* a witch. You were shaking in your sandals after she sent you that text. Are you sure you want to be friends with her?"

"Yes, I am," Mindy had answered as she slipped behind the steering wheel of the car her parents had rented for the week, to drive to the ice cream shop, feeling like a huge load had been lifted off her shoulders.

That was, until now, when she noticed the look of disgust on Wanda's face as she peeled the lid off her container of frozen yogurt and glared at Mindy.

"What's wrong?" Mindy asked, trying not to sound panicked, although she knew *something* was wrong. And it was probably her fault. Because who else's would it be?

Lacey and Vivienne peered into the container of frozen yogurt in Wanda's hand.

"Uh-oh," Lacey said.

Uh-oh? Mindy thought. *Uh-oh what?! Don't keep me in suspense. Tell me!*

"There are no sprinkles," Lacey said.

"Wanda *always* gets sprinkles on her fro-yo," Vivienne said.

"Always," Lacey repeated.

"I didn't know that," Mindy said. *No one told me when I was taking orders! Wanda said she wanted a frozen vanilla yogurt. That was it! She didn't mention sprinkles! And neither did you two! Am I supposed to be a mind reader?*

Mindy knew she couldn't say *any* of that.

"You should have asked," Wanda said, handing the container back to Mindy. "I can't eat this without sprinkles. And if I'm not having any, I can't see how the rest of you can enjoy yours."

Lacey instantly dropped the spoonful of strawberry frozen yogurt she'd been about to put into her mouth and closed her container, while Vivienne took a quick lick of her vanilla and chocolate swirl soft ice cream before doing the same.

"Not a problem," Mindy said, hearing Wanda's unspoken message. She knew Wanda was giving her a test and she was determined to pass it. "I'll just head back to the ice cream shop and have them add sprinkles."

"That's *so* sweet of you," Wanda said.

Of course, your yogurt will be melted by the time I get back there and I'll have to buy another one, but if it means staying on your good side, I'll do it.

"Does that mean we're allowed to eat ours?" Vivienne hopefully asked.

"If I were you, I'd skip dessert," Wanda stated. "You looked like you were busting out of your swimsuit today. You don't want the guys thinking you're a beached whale."

Mindy couldn't believe what she was hearing. That was so untrue! Vivienne didn't have an ounce of fat on her and she'd looked great in her swimsuit.

"Damian liked the way I looked," Vivienne said, as she reopened her ice cream and defiantly took a heaping spoonful.

"But *I'm* the one going out with Damian tonight, not you," Wanda shot back.

"Did you want chocolate sprinkles or rainbow sprinkles?" Mindy asked, trying to divert Wanda's attention. She didn't want to drive all the way to the ice cream shop, get the sprinkles, drive all the way back and find out she'd asked for the wrong ones, and then have to make a third trip.

"Rainbow," Wanda said.

Mindy nodded and grabbed her car keys, making a quick escape. A fight was brewing and she did *not* want to be around for it. As she walked outside, she ran into Carmela, who was emptying the kitchen trash can.

"Where are you off to?" Carmela asked.

Mindy explained the frozen yogurt situation. When she finished, Carmela stared at her in disbelief.

"She couldn't eat it without the sprinkles?"

"It's no big deal."

Carmela placed a hand on her hip. "Is kissing up to her worth it?"

"This week is a test," Mindy explained. "Wanda's trying to get me to prove myself to her. If I pass, I'm in!"

"Yeah, in with a bunch of mean girls!" Carmela shook her head. "I don't like them. They're not good enough for you. You deserve better friends." She threw up her hands. "But you're a big girl and you're capable of making your own decisions. I'm not going to tell you what to do."

"Isn't that what you're doing right now?"

Carmela didn't answer the question. "Listen, as long as you're heading back to the ice cream shop, get me a double scoop of Rocky Road."

"Double scoop of Rocky Road," Mindy repeated before heading back to the car.

"And, Mindy?" Carmela called out.

Mindy turned around. "What?"

"Don't forget to get me sprinkles!" Carmela teased.

Chapter Thirteen

"We've created a monster!" Lindsey exclaimed to Ava after Danielle had left the bedroom. "A monster!"

Ava laughed. "I think you're overreacting."

"Weren't you listening to a word she said? She's let this makeover go to her head!"

"She's only having a little fun. Would you rather she have her nose buried in an SAT study guide?"

"No, but I don't like the way she's juggling two guys!"

"She's not juggling two guys. She's only taking a walk on the beach with Rory. There's nothing wrong with that."

Lindsey peeked out the window and gasped. "There's a full moon. You know what walks on moonlit beaches lead to."

"What?"

"Kissing!" Lindsey exclaimed.

Ava laughed again. "You're such a drama queen!"

"And what about Ethan?"

"What about him?"

"This isn't fair to him!"

"Linds, you're overreacting. Danielle and Ethan aren't exclusive. They went out once. Once! You're being way too hard on Danielle. Cut her a little slack!"

Lindsey pinched two fingers together. "I'll give her this much and no more."

"She'll be back to her old self once we're home. Wait and see."

"She better," Lindsey said. "I don't think I like this new Danielle."

Jade's voice called out from downstairs. "Ava, you have a visitor."

Lindsey's eyes lit up. "I bet I know who it is! I bet I know who it is!"

"No hovering over the banister!" Ava warned.

"Of course not!" Lindsey promised as she followed Ava out of the bedroom. "I'm coming with you!"

At the foot of the staircase, Cooper was waiting. Ava wasn't surprised. She figured it was probably him, but what was he doing here? She watched as Lindsey gave him a big smile. "Hi, Cooper!"

"Hey, Lindsey."

"Hi, Coop," Ava said. "What's up?"

Cooper shrugged. "Not much. I was thinking of taking a walk on the beach and was wondering if you wanted to come along."

Ava shook her head. "Thanks, but I'm in for the night."

"Excuse us for a second," Lindsey said as she grabbed Ava by the arm and pulled her into the living room. "What are you doing?" she hissed when they were alone. "A cute guy asks you to go for a walk on the beach and you tell him you're in for the night?" Lindsey checked the time on her watch. "It's not even eight thirty! What are you, my grandmother?!"

"I'm tired. It's been a long day."

"You don't have to stay out all night! An hour, tops."

"It's a moonlit night," Ava pointed out. "Remember what you said?"

"So?"

"I don't want Cooper getting any ideas."

"You said you laid down the ground rules with him, right? Just friends."

"Yes."

"So, what are you worried about?" Lindsey's eyes widened with shock. "Unless . . ."

"Unless what?"

"Unless you don't trust yourself!" Lindsey squealed with excitement.

"That's not true," Ava quickly answered.

"Prove it! Go to the beach with Cooper."

"Fine. I will! Just to prove you wrong."

"We'll see," Lindsey smugly stated.

"Yes, we will!" Ava snapped back.

"Cooper!" Lindsey called out. "Good news! Ava's changed her mind."

"Sorry you didn't get your walk on the beach," Rory said as he strolled with Danielle along the local boardwalk, checking out the brightly lit booths and arcades.

"That's okay. Who knew it would be so cold?"

They'd tried walking along the beach, but there had been an icy breeze that kept blowing at them. It was so cold that at one point Danielle's teeth began chattering! Some couples were nestled in front of bonfires, but Rory and Danielle decided to give up on the beach and explore the boardwalk, where it was much warmer.

"You like cotton candy?" Rory asked as they passed a booth selling it.

"Love it!"

"Pick a color."

"Pink!"

"You're such a girl!"

Rory bought a stick of pink cotton candy and handed it to Danielle. She tore off a piece of the spun sugar and popped it into her mouth. Instantly, it melted. "Yum!" She held out the stick. "Want some?"

"I think I'll wait until you finish eating it."

"But it'll be all gone."

"Except for what's on your lips. I'll get a taste then."

Danielle's heart began pounding with excitement. *He wanted to kiss her!* "You think you're getting a kiss from me tonight?"

"That's usually what happens when a guy takes a girl home."

Danielle popped another piece of cotton candy into her mouth. "True. But sometimes a guy gets a kiss before that."

"Am I going to be that guy?" Rory asked, taking Danielle's hand in his as they continued walking.

"Maybe."

Danielle didn't know where this flirty side of herself had come from! She was never like this with guys!

Then again, she'd never been with a guy like Rory.

Being with Rory was different from being with the guys she usually went out with. Maybe it was because he was a senior and a year older. He just seemed more mature. More confident. He was brash and said *exactly* what was on his mind.

And there was no doubt in *her* mind that he liked her and wanted to kiss her!

Rory stopped walking and faced Danielle, looking into her eyes. "How long are you going to keep me in suspense?"

Before she could answer, she heard a shocked voice behind her.

"Danielle?"

She turned around and saw Ethan.

His eyes fell to her hand holding Rory's. Instantly, she dropped it, suddenly feeling guilty. Like she was cheating on him.

Maybe it was because of the stunned expression on his face.

He looked hurt. So hurt.

But why did he feel that way?

They'd only gone out once!

And she wasn't on a date with Rory, although she supposed it could look that way.

"What are you doing here?" he asked.

She could hear the unspoken part of his question: *with him.*

"Rory returned my sunglasses," she explained. "I dropped them this afternoon when I was filling out the entry form for the Miss Spring Break contest and he found them."

"Lucky you."

"When I dropped them off, I asked her if she wanted to go for a walk on the beach," Rory said, moving closer to Danielle as he wrapped an arm around her shoulders.

Okay, this was *not* good. With his arm around her shoulder, Rory was trying to make Ethan think they were together. A couple. They hadn't even kissed yet! Why were guys so possessive? Ethan had done the exact same thing with his arm that afternoon at the beach. Was it taught to them in PE class?

"Why don't you hang out with us?" she blurted as she slipped from under Rory's arm.

She didn't want Ethan's feelings to be hurt or have him think that she liked Rory more than she liked him. She hardly knew Rory! And she hardly knew Ethan! She was getting to know both of them, so why not do it at the same time?

"Ethan doesn't want to hang with us," Rory said. "I'm sure he's got other plans."

"Actually, I don't," Ethan told them with a smile. "I'd love to hang out with you!"

"It's freezing out here!" Ava exclaimed as they walked along the beach, listening to the sound of crashing waves.

"I'll start a bonfire," Cooper said as he began collecting pieces of driftwood. He took off his school letterman jacket and draped it over Ava's shoulders. She had on only a thin cotton sweater over her T-shirt and it wasn't doing much to keep her warm. "You can wear this until I get it started."

"But then you're going to be cold."

"That's okay."

Ten minutes later, Cooper and Ava were sitting together on a rock, staring into a blazing bonfire.

"Feeling warmer?" Cooper asked.

"Much," Ava said. "But you still look like you're cold." She lifted up one side of the jacket. "Come sit closer to me. We'll share."

"You sure? I wouldn't want you to think I was making a move."

"I'm making an exception this time."

"Okay if I put my arm around you and pull you close? Just for the body heat," he quickly explained.

"*Just* for the body heat," Ava stated.

Gazing into the flames as Cooper wrapped an arm around her, Ava couldn't help but think of another bonfire the summer before. She and Josh had gone to the beach with friends. At the end of the day, when everyone else went home, they decided to stay and watch the sunset. After the sun had disappeared, Josh suggested they stay a little longer. He built a bonfire and they sat next to each other, watching as the sky changed colors before turning dark and the stars came out.

The entire time, he'd held her hand, his fingers entwined with hers.

Then, when the bonfire died down, he had walked her to his car, still holding her hand, and driven her home. At the front door, he'd given her a long, slow kiss good night, holding her close.

Making her feel safe.

Making her feel special.

Making her feel loved.

With that kiss, Ava had realized, for the first time, that she was in love with Josh.

She'd almost said those three magic words — *I love you* — but had been afraid to. She'd never said them to a guy before. What if he didn't say them back to her?

So she decided not to say anything.

And it had still been the best day of her life.

"Okay, you're looking sad," Cooper said.

Ava shook her head. "Not sad. Maybe wistful."

"Are you thinking about Josh?"

"Yes," she admitted. "But it's a good memory. Not a bad one. It's just reminding me of what I had and lost."

"That's why it's important to make new memories," Cooper gently said.

"I know." Ava gave him a smile. "And I am."

Cooper tried not to get his hopes up.

Just because Ava said she was making new memories, it didn't mean she had changed the way she felt about him.

After all, *friends* shared memories.

But did friends sit this close to each other?

The setting was 100 percent romantic. A guy. A girl. A full moon. Cuddling together in front of a bonfire.

It would be so easy to kiss Ava right now.

To just lean his head down and press his lips against hers.

But he couldn't.

He wouldn't.

Even though he *so* wanted to.

If he kissed Ava, it would all be over between them. He could feel it in his gut.

177

Ava *trusted* him. She believed him when he said he was okay with just being friends, and he didn't want to destroy that trust.

So he wouldn't kiss her.

At least not tonight.

He didn't think Ava was testing him, but he could sense that she hadn't lowered her guard all the way.

And he wanted her to.

Because if she did, she might want to kiss him as much as he wanted to kiss her.

Danielle knew it was wrong having two guys fighting over her, but when was the last time this had ever happened?

Never!

Could she be blamed for enjoying it?

There was an unspoken competition going on between Ethan and Rory. Each was trying to outdo the other. If one of them offered to buy her something, say a pretzel or a bag of peanuts, the other instantly did the same. If she said she was cold, they both took off their jackets. If she needed change for an arcade game, they both gave her a handful of quarters.

They had both bought her some fudge, when

Ethan checked his watch. "It's getting late. Can I give you a ride back home?"

Danielle knew Rory was staying with his friends at a beach house in the opposite direction. It didn't make sense for him to go out of his way when she and Ethan were staying right next door to each other.

"Okay," she said. She gave Rory a quick hug good night. "I had a fun time."

"Guess I'll see you at the Miss Spring Break contest," he said.

It was on the tip of Danielle's tongue to tell Rory he could see her *before* the contest if he wanted, but she felt guilty saying the words in front of Ethan. It was exciting having two guys battling over her, but she didn't want to encourage their behavior. They both seemed like nice guys and she wasn't the kind of girl who played games. Besides, if Rory was really interested in her and wanted to see her again, well, he knew where she lived!

"Come on, Danielle," Ethan said, taking her by the hand and leading her away.

"Hey, Danielle!" Rory called out.

She turned around.

"I'll bring some cotton candy to the contest," he promised, giving her a wink.

Hearing those words, a chill shot up Danielle's spine.

He still wanted to kiss her!

Ethan was silent during the drive back home. Danielle tried making conversation, but she was doing all the talking. Finally, she gave up.

"Aren't you going to say anything?" she asked.

"What do you want me to say?"

"If you're angry, say it."

"I'm not angry."

"You're acting like you're angry."

"How am I doing that?"

"By giving me the silent treatment."

"What would I have to be angry about?"

"My going out with Rory. I could see it hurt you. I'm not blind."

Ethan shrugged. "We're not a couple. You can go out with anybody you want."

"It wasn't like it was a date," Danielle clarified. "I told you what happened."

"It looked like a date to me," Ethan said. "In fact, it looked like he was getting ready to kiss you!"

Danielle didn't want to hurt Ethan any more than he already was. Which meant a little white lie.

"He wasn't going to kiss me!" Okay, *maybe* he was, but there had been no lip action. And unless there was lip action, she was innocent! "You're imagining things."

Ethan pulled the Mercedes into the driveway of his beach house and put it into park. "Well, I wouldn't blame him for wanting to kiss you," he admitted. "You're very kissable."

"That's so sweet!" Danielle exclaimed. "Look, you and I spent one day together, Ethan. And we had a really nice time. If I hurt your feelings, I'm sorry. I think you're a great guy and I enjoyed spending time with you. Both at the beach and on the boardwalk."

"I've never been good with sharing," Ethan confessed as they got out of the car and he walked with Danielle to her front door. "It goes all the way back to my days in kindergarten, when Billy Barton ate his cookie before snack time and then wanted half of mine. Mrs. Winehauser said I should share, but that meant Billy would have eaten a whole cookie and half of mine! I didn't think that was very fair. I guess I wanted to have you all to myself tonight."

"If you want me all to yourself, we could go out tomorrow. We discussed the beach, remember?"

"What about Rory?"

"I don't have any plans with him," she said, as she reached into her shoulder bag for her house keys. "So do you still want to go out?"

Ethan's face lit up. "Absolutely!"

Danielle then waited for Ethan to take her into his arms.

She waited for his face to descend toward hers.

For his lips to touch her lips.

But none of that happened.

Instead, he gave her a quick hug and then pulled away, almost as if he had been scalded by touching her! What was up with that?!

"So we'll head to the beach tomorrow?" he asked.

"Okay," Danielle slowly answered, still feeling a bit confused.

"Same time as today?"

"Sure."

"Great!" Ethan headed back in the direction of the house next door. "See you in the morning."

A puzzled Danielle watched as he walked away. Okay, something weird was going on.

Why hadn't he kissed her?

She thought he liked her.

So why no kiss?

★   ★   ★

Why hadn't he kissed her?

Why?

Why?

Why?

He knew why.

Rory.

His instincts about that snake had been *so* right.

Rory was interested in Danielle and he had come *thisclose* to kissing her tonight.

Luckily, Ethan had prevented it from happening.

If anyone was going to kiss Danielle, it was going to be him! And when he kissed Danielle for the first time, he wanted the kiss to be perfect. He didn't want it to be because he was competing with another guy to get the first kiss. That was why he'd had to stop himself from kissing Danielle only seconds ago.

And speaking of competing . . .

There was still the bet with Cooper.

If he'd kissed Danielle, he would have won the bet.

But he wanted no strings attached to his first kiss with Danielle.

He wanted to kiss her because he liked her.

Not because of the bet.

And not because he was jealous of Rory and competing with him.

Ethan took a deep breath. Okay, tomorrow was another day. He was going to have Danielle all to himself and everything was going to be perfect. It already was, since there was no Rory.

But first he was going to find Cooper and tell him the bet was off.

Chapter Fourteen

"I need to buy lip gloss," Wanda announced the following morning as she walked into the dining room for breakfast.

"I thought you bought one right before we left," Lacey said as she filled a plate from the buffet on a sideboard and returned to her seat.

"I did."

"So why do you need another one?" Vivienne asked as she sprinkled some blueberries over her cornflakes.

Mindy watched as Wanda sat at the head of the table. The chair had been purposely left empty for her by Vivienne and Lacey. After all, where else would a queen sit but at the head of the table?

"I had to keep using it last night," Wanda said.

Mindy waited for Lacey or Vivienne to ask why

Wanda had to keep using her lip gloss, but neither one did. Lacey was too busy spreading strawberry jam on a piece of toast, and Vivienne was eating her cereal. Mindy knew it was killing them that Damian had taken Wanda out on a date. Both had gone to bed early so they wouldn't be awake when Wanda returned. Mindy had hidden herself in her bedroom, too, but heard Wanda come in at midnight. Now it looked like there was no escaping the details of last night.

Mindy asked the question that Lacey and Vivienne didn't want to hear the answer to. "Why did you have to keep reapplying your lip gloss?"

"Damian couldn't keep his lips to himself!" Wanda exclaimed. "He was kissing me nonstop. Every time I'd apply a fresh coat, he'd start kissing me again. It became like a game. Kiss. Reapply. Kiss. Reapply. I used up the whole tube!"

"That's not unusual for you, Wanda," Lacey said before taking a bite of her toast and loudly chewing.

Meow! Mindy couldn't believe what she'd just heard! Was Lacey dissing Wanda?! She whipped her head in Wanda's direction to see her reaction. There was no mistaking the anger on her face.

"Rick can't stop kissing you either," Lacey added. "Guys find you irresistible."

Phew! Mindy thought as she watched Wanda's anger quickly disappear. Crisis averted!

"Rick *is* a pretty good kisser," Wanda said.

Mindy wondered how Wanda could kiss another guy when she had Rick waiting for her at home. It just wasn't right! Didn't Wanda have feelings for Rick? How could she cheat on him? When you were with someone, you were supposed to be true to that person. If you weren't, then why stay in the relationship? Wanda hardly knew Damian, yet she'd had a kiss fest with him last night! Mindy couldn't even remember the last time she'd gotten a kiss. A real kiss. Moose Novak had kissed her under the mistletoe at the Secret Santa dance in December, but that didn't count. The kiss had been a freebie. And she also wasn't into Moose.

Sure, she'd gone out on dates and been kissed good night. Sometimes there was a second and third date, but then things fizzled out. She still hadn't found the guy that was right for her. Deep down, Mindy wanted a boyfriend. She wanted her own special someone. To spend time with. To laugh with. To kiss.

When she saw couples at school, like Noelle Kramer and Ryan Grant or Celia Armstrong and Froggy Keenan, she always found herself wishing she could have what they had.

Mindy sighed. Maybe someday she would.

Until then, she'd be watching Wanda juggle two guys.

At that moment, Carmela came out of the kitchen with a pitcher of orange juice and poured Wanda a glass.

"Is this OJ fresh-squeezed or from a container?" Wanda asked as Carmela handed her the glass.

"From a container."

Wanda shook her head and gave the glass back. "I only drink fresh-squeezed, Carmen."

"It's Carmela."

Wanda didn't apologize for calling Carmela by the wrong name. "And no pulp!"

Mindy jumped up from her seat and took Carmela by the arm — the arm that looked like it was getting ready to toss a glass of orange juice into Wanda's face. "Let me help you squeeze some oranges."

When they were alone in the kitchen, Carmela exploded. "That girl is a brat! I'd like to smash *her* to a pulp!"

Mindy began slicing some oranges. "Remember, she's a guest."

"A *rude* guest!" Carmela exclaimed.

"I know. And I'm sorry. Wanda says and does whatever she wants."

"That's because no one stands up to her," Carmela said.

Mindy started feeding oranges into the juicer. "Don't look at me!"

Carmela shook her head and started loading the dishwasher with the breakfast dishes that Mindy's parents had already used. They'd left early that morning for another business meeting before anyone was up.

When Mindy returned to the dining room with Wanda's glass of juice, she found her sitting alone.

"Where are Lacey and Vivienne?"

Wanda took a sip of juice, not bothering to thank Mindy. "I sent them upstairs to change."

"Why?"

"Did you see what they were wearing?"

Mindy had thought Vivienne and Lacey both looked nice. Vivienne had been wearing an orange one-piece swimsuit while Lacey had worn a pink two-piece bikini with a ruffled bottom.

"You should change, too," Wanda said as she popped a fresh strawberry into her mouth.

Mindy was wearing a pair of cutoff jean shorts with a long-sleeve white cotton shirt tied above her belly button and her hair in two pigtails. She thought the look was very mod country girl.

"Uh, sure," Mindy said as she collected the empty dishes on the table.

An eavesdropping Carmela was waiting for Mindy when she returned to the kitchen. "There's nothing wrong with what any of you are wearing. That Wanda knows you girls are competition. Heck, she's not even the prettiest. You are!"

A panicked Mindy dropped the dishes she was carrying onto the counter and clamped a hand over Carmela's mouth, petrified of Wanda overhearing. "Shhh! Don't say that!"

Carmela pushed away Mindy's hand. "Why not? It's the truth."

"Not in Wanda's world," Mindy said before hurrying up the kitchen stairs that led to the second floor. "*She's* the fairest one of all."

"Hmmmph! If you ask me, she's more like the wicked witch!"

When Danielle walked into the kitchen to get some breakfast, she found a plate of chicken bones on the table. There were also an empty bowl of potato salad, an empty bowl of baked beans, watermelon rinds, cherry pits, and the leftover crumbs of a chocolate cake.

Behind her, she could hear Lindsey and Ava approaching the kitchen.

"You really didn't have to do all that cooking," Ava said. "Cooper and I could have bought some sandwiches."

"I wanted to!" Lindsey said. "You know how much I love to cook. What else was I going to do last night? And I figured a picnic lunch would be fun. You could tell Cooper you made it yourself."

"Why would I want to do that?"

"Guys love girls who can cook!"

Danielle rushed out of the kitchen, blocking the door. "I don't think you're going to want to go in there," she said to Lindsey.

"Why not?"

"There's a little bit of a mess."

"What kind of mess?" Lindsey's eyes widened. "Not like yesterday morning?"

"Not exactly . . ."

"Then exactly like what?"

Lindsey didn't wait for Danielle to answer. Instead, she barged into the kitchen. And promptly shrieked.

"He ate everything I made for Ava's picnic! Everything! All the chicken I fried! The potato salad! The cake I made from scratch!" She stared at the remains of the eaten fruit. "He ate a *whole* watermelon and a pound of cherries!"

The back door opened and Howie walked in. "Did I leave my sunglasses here?"

"You! You!" Lindsey was so furious, she couldn't get the words out. She grabbed a pad of paper from the counter and scribbled on it. Then she ripped off a sheet and slammed it into Howie's chest.

"What's this?" he asked.

"What you owe us for the lunch you ate!" Lindsey ran over to the kitchen closet and pulled out a broom. She then lifted it over her head and charged toward Howie, who dropped the piece of paper and ran out the back door.

"Hey!" he yelped. "What's the big deal? Sharla had a flat tire this morning and I changed it for her. She wanted to pay me, but I told her she didn't have to. That I'd help myself to something in her refrigerator. She was cool with it."

"*Something!* Not *everything*!" Lindsey shouted from the back porch, shaking the broom at him as he ran back to his beach house.

"Don't worry about it, Linds," Ava said when she walked back inside.

"I wanted your date with Cooper to be perfect."

"It's not a date."

"Fine, it's not a date," Lindsey grumbled as she put the broom back in the closet. "How about you, Danielle? Any non-date dates today?"

"Ethan and I are going to the beach."

"What happened to Rory?" Ava asked.

Danielle shrugged. "Rory didn't ask me out."

"It's getting kind of overcast outside," Lindsey remarked as she tossed the plate of chicken bones into the garbage can. "Lots of dark clouds."

"If we don't go to the beach, we'll figure something out," Danielle said. "I'm not worried."

Ethan was worried. It looked like it was going to rain at any second and he didn't have a backup plan for his day with Danielle.

And then there was the bet.

It was still on.

Last night he'd gotten home before Cooper. He'd tried staying awake so he could talk to him about calling off the bet, but he'd fallen asleep. And then when he'd woken up this morning, Cooper was already out of the house. So he'd have to wait until later in the day to talk with him.

Ethan hopped into the Mercedes and drove to Danielle's house, honking the horn. Seconds later, she emerged from inside and raced to the curb.

"Hi!" she exclaimed.

Just the sound of her voice made him smile. "Hi!"

"It doesn't look like it's going to be a beach day," she said as she buckled her seat belt.

"Hopefully, it'll get sunny."

As Ethan drove, Danielle fiddled with the radio. They were waiting at a red light when Danielle held up a hand.

"Uh-oh. I think I just felt a drop of rain."

Ethan stared at the sky. Then he looked back down at the windshield, where three fat raindrops had splattered.

"We'd better put the top on," Danielle suggested.

Ethan pushed the button for the top of the Mercedes, but it wouldn't move.

"That's strange," he said, pressing the button again and waiting for the usual humming sound as it rose.

"Is it broken?" she asked.

"It worked fine yesterday."

As they waited for the top to unfurl, it started to rain.

Lightly at first.

But then the rain started coming down harder.

And harder.

Ethan and Danielle were getting soaked.

"It's not working," he said in a panic.

"What are we going to do?" Danielle asked as sheets of rain kept falling.

194

It was raining so heavily that Ethan could hardly see. He pulled the car over to the side of the road, under a row of trees, and pointed to an abandoned fruit stand. "Why don't we wait in there?"

Ethan parked the car and they jumped out, hurrying to the fruit stand, which smelled like rotting peaches. They found an empty box and used it to sit on, listening to the sound of falling rain. As they waited for the rain to end, Danielle reached into her tote bag, pulled out a towel, and wiped off her face. Then she handed the towel to Ethan. "Here, you could use this."

"Thanks." He dried his face. "Well, looks like I've given you another great date."

Danielle giggled. "The weather's not your fault."

"I feel like it is."

I feel like I'm jinxed! All I want is for our dates to be perfect. Instead, they're imperfect!

Danielle stared at the sky. "It has to stop eventually."

"And then what? The beach is going to be all wet. We're not going to be able to sit anywhere."

"Look!" Danielle pointed to the road. "A car's headed this way."

An emerald green Mustang pulled over and the

passenger window slid down as the driver leaned across the seat. "Need a lift?" he asked.

"Rory!" Danielle exclaimed.

Ethan groaned. Rory?! Great. Rory coming to the rescue. Just what he didn't need.

"The top of Ethan's car won't go up," Danielle explained.

"That's too bad."

He didn't sound like it was too bad, Ethan noted. It sounded like, *Well, what do you expect when you hang out with a loser?*

"And then it started to rain and it was coming down so hard, Ethan couldn't see the road. So he pulled over and we ran in here."

"I'd give you both a ride, but the trunk and backseat are filled with cases of soda and groceries. Friends and I are having a party tonight. I can only fit one person in the passenger seat."

Ethan knew which person that seat was meant for. And it wasn't him.

"I'm sure Ethan wouldn't mind my giving you a ride," Rory continued.

And let you drive off with Danielle? I don't think so!

"I could sit on Ethan's lap," Danielle suggested before Ethan could say anything. "That way you could drive the two of us."

Ethan knew there was *no way* Rory would go for that.

And he was right.

Rory instantly shot the idea down.

"It's against the law. Plus, I saw some cops on the side of the road as I was driving by. I don't want to risk getting a ticket."

Yeah, like he was *really* worried about being pulled over by a cop. He just wanted Danielle all to himself. As much as Ethan *didn't* want that to happen, he really didn't have much of a choice.

"Go with Rory," Ethan said. "I'll wait out the rain."

Ethan expected Danielle to leave. Why not? What girl in her right mind would want to be waiting out a rainstorm in a smelly, dilapidated fruit stand?

But she surprised him.

"I can't leave Ethan."

"Ethan's a big boy," Rory said. "I'm sure he can take care of himself. Right, Ethan?"

"Go," Ethan urged. "I'll be fine.

Danielle stubbornly shook her head. "I'm not leaving you."

Rory shrugged. "Then there's nothing I can do. I can only fit one more person. Hopefully, you won't be here all day. I'd love to stick around and chat, but I've gotta get this stuff home. See you around."

Ethan watched as the passenger window slid back up and Rory drove away. He couldn't believe how easily Rory had given up. Didn't he think Danielle was worth fighting for?

"Well, what should we do next?" Danielle asked.

Ethan caught sight of a sign across the road and pointed to it. "There's an indoor flea market up ahead. Want to check it out?"

"Why not? It's better than staying here."

It took Ethan and Danielle five minutes to race down the road to the indoor flea market. Once they got inside, they dried themselves off again and began exploring. The flea market was huge, with three floors.

"Where do you want to start?" Ethan asked.

"First floor, then second and third. Okay with you?"

"Sounds like a plan."

They went from stall to stall, checking out all the different items for sale. There were booths that sold nothing but glassware. Others selling china and dishes. There were stalls with stacks of old magazines, books, and newspapers. Others that had old toys and appliances, such as blenders and transistor radios. Another stall was filled with vintage clothing, while another had handmade jewelry.

"Are you having a good time?" Danielle asked after they had explored the first floor and were walking up the stairs to the second.

"Sure," Ethan said. "Why wouldn't I?"

"You've probably never bought anything used before."

"I love going to flea markets," Ethan said. "It's like going on a treasure hunt, only you don't have a map so you don't know what you're going to discover. My parents recently bought a dining room set and refinished it."

"Why would your parents need to buy old furniture?" Danielle asked, sounding perplexed. "Why wouldn't they buy it new?"

Ethan instantly realized his mistake. With "his" credit cards and the fancy restaurant he'd taken Danielle to yesterday, as well as staying at a beach house that "came with" a Mercedes convertible, she probably thought he was rich. And why wouldn't she? Cooper *was* rich. And he was pretending to be him.

"My parents are into antiques and they go to high-end flea markets," Ethan explained. "I guess you could call them auctions and not flea markets. There's a difference."

Danielle gave Ethan a strange look, but she didn't question what he told her. "If you say so."

Ethan nodded, glad that Danielle believed him but hating having to lie.

Chapter Fifteen

"You're all wet!" Ava exclaimed as Cooper hurried inside.

"In case you didn't notice, it's a downpour out there."

Ava poked him in the chest. "Ha! Ha! Very funny. I know it's raining." She handed him a towel. "Why didn't you use an umbrella?"

Cooper started drying himself off. "The house doesn't have one."

"That house of yours doesn't have a lot of things. No umbrellas. No food."

Cooper groaned. "Did Howie strike again?"

"Big-time. The picnic lunch that Lindsey made for us is now in Howie's stomach."

"What'd she make?"

"Fried chicken, potato salad, and a choco-late cake."

"Those are all my favorites."

"Talk to Howie."

Cooper held out a shopping bag. "Maybe this will make up for it."

Ava peeked into the bag. "What is it?"

"I thought it would be fun to make tacos for lunch. I went to the supermarket and bought all the fixings."

"Yum! Tacos are my favorite."

"Where is everyone?" Cooper asked as he handed the towel back to Ava. He followed after her to the laundry room, where she tossed the towel into the dryer.

"Danielle's with Ethan, and Lindsey went to the mall with Crystal and Jade," Ava said as she transferred a pile of wet clothing from the washer into the dryer and added a sheet of Bounce. "Sharla's out for the day."

"So we've got the whole place to ourselves?"

Ava turned the timer on the dryer. "Yes."

Ava wondered why Cooper wanted to know if they had the house to themselves. She hoped he wasn't planning to make a move on her. For most guys, a girl and an empty house equaled a make-out session. She'd been pretty up-front that she *wasn't* looking for romance. She knew most couples would be thrilled to have an empty house to themselves, but this *wasn't* a date. She and Cooper were friends. Nothing more.

Stop it, Ava! she scolded herself. Cooper agreed to be *just* friends. You're not that irresistible! Trust him!

"Hey, do you mind if I toss this in?" Cooper asked, pulling off his wet T-shirt.

Ava couldn't help but notice Cooper's defined muscles. It was obvious that he worked out. Ava threw the T-shirt into the dryer and then reached for an oversize white T-shirt from a basket of clean laundry. "You can wear this until yours is dry," she said, handing the T-shirt to him.

She didn't need to be staring at those muscles!

"Thanks." Cooper pulled the T-shirt over his head, using one hand to slick back his wet hair. "Unless it stops raining, it looks like we're house-bound. What do you want to do?"

"We could watch a movie."

They went into the living room and started flipping through Sharla's extensive collection of DVDs.

"What are you in the mood for?" Cooper asked. "Something funny? Something scary? Something classic?"

"You pick. I don't care."

Cooper pulled out a DVD called *Last Summer*

and handed it to Ava. "I haven't seen this. I heard it's good."

"This movie is *so* sad!"

Cooper put the DVD back with the others. "We can watch something else."

Ava snatched it back. "No! We have to watch it! It's good sad."

"Good sad?"

"You'll see," Ava said as she popped the disc into the DVD player and sat on the couch. Cooper took the seat next to her but left some space between them. Just enough if he wanted to *casually* reach out . . .

Ava stopped her overactive imagination. *He's not going to try to put his arm around you! Focus on the movie!*

The plot of *Last Summer* was centered around two high school sweethearts, Misty and Robbie, who are seniors and expect to go off to college together. But then Misty gets a fatal disease — it's never specified what she's dying of — and only has until the end of the summer to live. Misty and Robbie spend every second together until finally, on Labor Day weekend, Misty collapses on the beach and dies in Robbie's arms. Before she dies, Misty makes Robbie promise that he'll go to college and then medical school and one day find a cure for the disease that killed her. A sobbing Robbie, who begs Misty not to die, promises that he will. The movie then ends with an older Robbie playing on the beach with his daughter, Misty, while his wife, Sarah Jane (who was Misty's best friend), watches them.

As the movie played, Ava forgot that Cooper was sitting next to her. She became lost in the tragic love story of Misty and Robbie. No matter how many times Ava saw *Last Summer* — this would be her tenth time — she became engrossed even though she knew how it ended. Maybe that was because each time she watched it, a little part of her kept hoping Misty wouldn't die and that she and Robbie would be together forever.

"What did you think?" Ava asked when the end credits started rolling.

"What a chick flick!" Cooper exclaimed.

"Is that good or bad?"

Cooper hissed. "Bad! That movie was *so* cheesy!"

"Don't you have a heart?" Ava sniffed.

Cooper took a closer look at Ava. "Are you crying?"

"No, I'm not."

"Yes, you are." He pointed a finger. "Those are tears in your eyes."

Ava sniffed again, wiping them away. "Maybe I am. Just a little. It happens whenever I watch *Last Summer*. It's so sad."

"Are you sure it was just the movie?"

"What do you mean?"

"Maybe it has something to do with Josh?"

Ava was speechless. How did Cooper do it? He was like a mind reader! He always knew how to zero in on anything Josh-related.

"The first time I saw the movie was with Josh," she admitted. "And it made me realize how much I cared about him. Can you imagine loving someone with all your heart and not being able to save them? To watch helplessly as they're taken away from you?" Ava sighed. "I guess I identify with Robbie. He loved someone and then he lost that someone."

Cooper moved closer to Ava on the couch. "It's okay to be sad," he said. "But you can't live in the past. You have to move on. Robbie did!"

"I know." Ava rested her head against Cooper's shoulder. "It's just hard, you know? My heart says one thing and my head says another."

"Maybe your heart needs to be distracted," Cooper said as he pulled Ava into his arms and began to give her a kiss.

Ava knew she should tell Cooper to stop, but she

didn't. She didn't push him away. She didn't ask him what he was doing. She let him kiss her.

It was a very soft, very gentle kiss.

A caring kiss.

But it was still a kiss.

When he finished, he pulled away, sliding back to his side of the couch. "I'm sorry," he said. "I shouldn't have done that. It's just that you seemed so sad and I didn't want you to be sad anymore."

"That's okay," Ava said.

It was only a kiss.

Friends kissed all the time.

But they don't kiss each other on the lips! a little voice reminded Ava.

She jumped off the couch. "Why don't I make us some popcorn?" She didn't wait for an answer. "Be right back."

Stupid.

Stupid.

Stupid!

What had he been thinking, kissing Ava?

If he wanted to scare her off, he had done it. After all, she'd just gone running into the kitchen.

But he couldn't help himself.

She'd looked so sad and vulnerable.

So hurt.

He'd wanted to take away that hurt. He'd wanted to pull her into his arms and hold her close and tell her that everything was going to be okay. That she didn't have anything to worry about. No one was ever going to hurt her again because he was going to protect her.

Whatever progress he'd made was now gone.

He was back at square one.

Ava's guard was going to be up again.

The thing was, he'd been okay with just being friends.

But then he'd lost all control.

He could try explaining that to Ava, but would she believe him? Would she give him another chance?

He wished he had someone to discuss this with, but he couldn't tell the guys about the kiss.

If he did, he'd win the bet.

That stupid bet!

He needed to call it off ASAP because if Ava mentioned his kiss to her friends, there was the chance that one of them would mention it to his housemates. He was specifically thinking of Ava telling Danielle and then Danielle telling Ethan. If that were to happen, there was always the risk of the bet coming up, and that was the *last* thing he wanted to happen. He had kissed Ava because he *wanted* to. Not because of some bet. He wouldn't want her to think his kiss didn't mean anything, because it did.

Even though Ava was afraid of getting her heart broken again, he knew that she liked him. And it wasn't because he was the richest guy at South Ridge High. She liked him for who he was. She might not want to admit she liked him, but he could tell that she did.

That meant a lot to him.

And then there was their kiss.

Yes, she'd been freaked out and gone running into the kitchen. But she hadn't ended their kiss.

She hadn't pushed him away.

She'd let him kiss her.

That meant something, too.

He just needed to figure out what his next move was going to be.

In the kitchen, Ava found a bag of microwave popcorn. As she waited for it to pop, she ran her fingers over her lips, remembering Cooper's kiss.

It was so different from the kisses she'd gotten from Josh.

It had been softer.

Sweeter.

Gentler.

Only one word that could describe Cooper's kiss.
Nice.

Chills went up and down her spine.

As much as she hated to admit it, she'd liked Cooper's kiss.

She'd liked it a lot.

The microwave dinged and she pulled out the bag of popcorn. She opened the bag and emptied it into a glass bowl, adding a dab of butter and dash of salt, trying not to think of Cooper, but unable not to.

She'd told him she only wanted to be friends.

But she'd allowed him to kiss her.

Did that mean she wanted to be more than friends?

She didn't know!

"Is the popcorn ready?" Cooper called out.

"I'm on my way," Ava answered, deciding she wouldn't think about Cooper's kiss anymore. She was going to pretend it hadn't happened. "Let's watch another DVD. Something bloody and scary."

No more sad, romantic movies. They're too dangerous! They make you do things you shouldn't do!

★   ★   ★

"When is this rain going to stop?" Wanda asked as she stared out the living room window.

Mindy didn't know what to say. Wanda had been asking her the same question for the last hour. It wasn't like she had a direct line to Mother Nature!

"Are we going to hang around this house all day?" Wanda complained, pacing from one end of the living room to the other.

"We could play some board games," Mindy said.

Wanda yawned. "That's so junior high."

Vivienne looked up from the copy of *Seventeen* she was reading on the couch. "I love Scrabble!"

Wanda ignored her.

"Go to the movies?" Mindy asked.

Wanda stared at Mindy like she was crazy. "*Without* dates?"

"Wanda *never* pays when she goes to the movies," Vivienne said.

"And she *doesn't* watch the movie," Lacey whispered into Mindy's ear as she walked over to the CD player. "She goes through a lot of lip gloss that way, too."

Mindy didn't know what to suggest next. She knew she was the host, but Wanda was shooting down every idea she came up with.

"I can't believe this house doesn't have an indoor

pool!" Wanda exclaimed. "If it did, at least we'd be able to take a swim."

"We could go to the country club," Mindy said. "They have an indoor pool."

"I don't do crowds," Wanda stated. "Everyone is going to be at the country club today."

Mindy racked her brain trying to think of something — *anything* — that Wanda might like to do.

"Why don't we go to a spa?" she suggested. "We could get manis, pedis, and a full day of beauty treatments."

"That sounds like fun!" Lacey exclaimed.

Mindy held her breath, waiting for Wanda's answer.

Please say yes. Please, please, please say yes!

Wanda yawned. "Since there's nothing better to do, I guess so. Let me go upstairs and get my bag."

"Me, too," Lacey said as she hurried after Wanda.

"You guys go without me," Vivienne said, rubbing the sides of her head. "I'm going to stay home. I have a headache."

"Are you sure?" Mindy asked, sitting next to her. "Can I get you anything before we go?"

Vivienne looked around to make sure no one was around. "Now that you mention it, you could get me something."

212

"You name it!"

"I'm in the mood for something Italian."

"Pizza? Pasta?"

Vivienne shook her head. "I was thinking more like veal."

"Parmigiana?"

"Marsala."

Mindy's eyes widened. Vivienne *didn't* have a headache. She was just looking for a way to spend some time alone with Damian!

"Think you could help me?" Vivienne asked.

"Absolutely," Mindy said, pulling out her cell phone and dialing Damian's number.

Chapter Sixteen

Danielle and Lindsey were having a girls' night out with Jade and Crystal. That morning, before heading out to the mall, Jade had declared she wasn't spending enough time with Danielle and wanted to do something about it. So they made plans for that night. They were at a karaoke club called the Sing Along and were studying the song list. Ava was originally going to come, too, but changed her mind after dinner, saying she didn't feel like going out. When they'd left, she'd been nestled on the couch with a copy of Stephenie Meyer's latest novel.

"I want a diva song!" Crystal exclaimed. "Something by Mariah Carey or Beyoncé."

"I'm going to sing Cyndi Lauper's 'Girls Just Wanna Have Fun,'" Jade said.

"Good choice! Maybe after you sing it, we will," Crystal said. "Have you noticed those two guys in that corner booth checking us out?"

"Where?" Jade asked excitedly.

Crystal pulled Jade away from the table. "Come on! Let's go to the bathroom. We'll have to walk by them!"

"What about you, Danielle?" Lindsey asked after Jade and Crystal had left. "What are you going to sing? I can't make up my mind between Britney Spears's 'Toxic' and Christina Aguilera's 'Beautiful.'"

"No way am I getting up onstage!"

"Why not?"

"I'm not into embarrassing myself!"

"So you embarrass yourself. Big deal! We're on spring break! We don't know anyone here. Come on, Danielle. Cut loose! I thought you were going to be Daring Dani this week!"

Danielle gazed around the packed club. There were so many people. And they would all be looking at her once she got up onstage. Her stomach began doing nervous flip-flops at the thought. At the same time, the idea of pretending to be a pop star was kind of fun. Usually when she was home alone in her bedroom, she'd sing along with the radio or her iPod, using her hairbrush as a microphone.

"You can do it!" Lindsey urged, sensing her indecision.

"Let me take a look at the list," Danielle said.

Lindsey handed it over. As Danielle studied the songs, Lindsey asked, "Did Ava seem weird at dinner?"

"Weird? How?"

"She didn't talk very much. It was like she had something on her mind."

"Maybe she was thinking about Josh."

"Or maybe something happened when Cooper came over today."

Danielle glanced up from the song list. "What could have happened?"

"Maybe something romantic?"

Danielle shook her head. "She said she wasn't interested in Cooper."

"Saying is one thing. Doing is another!"

"You think they kissed?"

"They were at the house all by themselves," Lindsey pointed out. "And Cooper *is* a good-looking guy. Maybe Ava couldn't resist."

"I can't see her making the first move."

"I'm not saying she made the first move. Cooper probably did and now she's freaking out. I'm sure Cooper is an excellent kisser. She probably liked kissing him."

216

"If she wants to talk about it, she'll bring it up," Danielle said. "Let's not ask her any questions! If we do, she won't tell us anything. She's probably sorting through her feelings. It would be great, though, if she could forget about Josh and finally move on to a new guy."

"Speaking of guys, what's going on with Ethan? Did you have a good time with him today?"

"We had a blast," Danielle said, remembering their day at the indoor flea market. They'd gone from booth to booth, poking through what they liked to call "old junk" and pretending they were looking for hidden treasures. "He wanted to hang out tonight, but I told him I already had plans."

"Are things getting serious? Has he kissed you yet?"

"We've only gone out twice!"

Lindsey pounced. "You didn't answer my question. You're avoiding! That means he *did* kiss you."

"Sorry to disappoint you, Linds, but Ethan *hasn't* kissed me yet."

"You sound bummed about that."

"Not bummed. Confused," Danielle explained. "When he walked me to the front door last night, I expected him to kiss me good night, but he didn't. All I got was a hug."

"Maybe he's shy?"

"Maybe."

"Or maybe *you'll* have to make the first move!" Lindsey declared. "Remember, you're Daring Dani!"

"How about letting Daring Dani make it through tonight before you have her kissing guys!"

"Have you picked a song?" Lindsey asked.

"Kelly Clarkson's 'Since U Been Gone.' You?"

"Forget Britney and Christina. I'm going with Rihanna's 'Umbrella.'"

"I'll go put our names down," Danielle said.

After giving their names and song choices to the karaoke hostess, Danielle headed back to her table. As she was walking through the crowd, she bumped into a guy from behind.

"Sorry," she said.

"Not a problem," he said, turning around.

Danielle gasped. "Rory! What are you doing here?"

"Surprised to see me?"

The words slipped out before she could stop them. "I thought you were throwing a party tonight."

A party you didn't invite me to!

Rory instantly looked uncomfortable. "The party. Yeah. About that . . . I really wanted to invite you."

"But you didn't," Danielle pointed out.

So much for liking me!

"I didn't think your boyfriend would be too happy if I did."

"Boyfriend?" Danielle asked, her voice filled with confusion. "What boyfriend?"

"That guy you're always with."

"Ethan? He's not my boyfriend."

Rory's eyes lit up and he moved closer to Danielle, backing her up against a wall. "Guess I made a mistake."

Rory put his arms up, boxing Danielle between them and leaning his body toward her. Instantly, she knew he was getting ready to kiss her, but for some reason, the thought didn't excite her. After all, she hardly knew him! He was moving way too fast.

Danielle managed to duck underneath one of Rory's arms, putting some space between them. "So why aren't you at your party?"

"There wasn't anyone there who I wanted to hang out with." Rory moved closer to Danielle again. "But there is now."

Before Danielle could say anything, the karaoke hostess called out Rory's name. Rory waved to her and then took Danielle's hand in his. "Why don't you do a duet with me? We'll pick a song together."

"What were you going to sing on your own?"

"'Born to be Wild.'" Rory stared at Danielle, giving her a lopsided grin. "It's my motto."

Chills traveled down Danielle's spine.

It sounded like Rory was a bad boy.

And every girl knew how hard it was to say no to a bad boy. . . .

But she could handle Rory.

Hadn't she just avoided his kiss?

It wasn't that she didn't want him to kiss her. She just wanted to get to know him a little bit better first.

Obviously he wanted to kiss her.

Unlike Ethan, who *didn't*.

What was up with that?

"So, will you sing with me?" Rory asked again.

"Yes!" Danielle exclaimed. "I'd love to!"

Ethan was bored. When Damian, Steve, and Howie had suggested going to a karaoke club, he hadn't been excited by the idea. Who wanted to spend the night listening to lousy singers? And there was *no way* he would be getting up onstage. But he didn't have any other plans and he didn't want to stay home alone, so he'd come along. Cooper, whom he still hadn't seen today, had left them a note that afternoon, saying he was having dinner with his cousins who were also in Miami for the week.

"Hey, isn't that Danielle up onstage?" Damian asked, pointing a finger.

Ethan nearly choked on the soda he was drinking. "What did you say?" he asked between coughs.

"Look!"

Ethan looked. And saw that Damian was right. There, up on the stage, was Danielle.

"Who's the guy she's with?" Howie asked.

Guy?

What guy?

Ethan suddenly noticed a guy walking from the right side of the stage, holding a microphone out to Danielle. Ethan's eyes widened with shock.

It was Rory.

Rory!!!

What was he doing here? He was supposed to be having some sort of party tonight.

And how had Danielle hooked up with Rory? She'd told Ethan she was having a girls' night out.

"Guess who I found!" Steve exclaimed, returning to their table with Jade, Crystal, and Lindsey. "Our next-door neighbors!"

Ethan gave a sigh of relief. Not that he'd thought

Danielle had lied to him, but there had been a tiny seed of doubt in his mind when he saw her with Rory.

"Did you see who's up onstage?" Damian asked Jade.

Jade turned to the stage, and her mouth dropped open in shock. "It's my baby sister!" She gave a whoop. "Show them how it's done, Danielle!"

"You go, girl!" Crystal hooted.

"Way to go, Danielle!" Lindsey shouted before giving Howie the evil eye and pulling the bowl of peanuts on the table away from him so she could have some.

The music started and the song was "You're the One That I Want" from *Grease*.

A horrified Ethan watched as Rory and Danielle sang the words to each other and imitated the dance steps from the movie, trying not to crack each other up.

They were having a blast.

And there was nothing Ethan could do about it.

Nothing!

Rory was singing to his girl.

His Danielle.

Whoa!

Wait a minute.

Waitaminutewaitaminutewaitaminute!

His Danielle?

Did he think of Danielle as his girl?

The answer came immediately.

Yes, he did.

If anyone should be singing to her, it should be him!

Damian leaned close to Ethan, whispering in his ear. "That guy is making time with your girl. You're never going to get that kiss if you let him do that."

"She's not my girl," Ethan whispered back.

At least not yet.

But she would be!

Ethan rose from the table.

"Where are you going?" Damian asked.

"To sign myself up for a song."

There was no way he was letting Rory get the better of him. No way! Rory might have sung a duet with Danielle, but Ethan planned on singing a song just for her.

After that, he was going to kiss her, even though he still hadn't had a chance to tell Cooper the bet was off. He'd worry about that later.

Right now all he wanted to do was send a message to Rory to back off, and that was what he was going to do!

* * *

When Ethan got up onstage, he felt like everyone in the karaoke bar was staring at him. Of course, they weren't, but enough sets of eyes were on him that it made him nervous.

As a result, his voice cracked.

And he started sweating.

Unlike super-cool Rory, who had looked like a member of a boy band, Ethan felt like a messy slob while he stood behind the microphone and crooned Cheap Trick's "I Want You to Want Me."

But he managed to do it, singing the song from beginning to end.

There had been some boos from the audience, but he ignored them. Okay, he'd never make the cut on *American Idol*, but he didn't think his singing was *that* bad.

While he'd been onstage, he'd searched the crowded club for Danielle, wanting to make eye contact with her. He wanted her to know that the song he was singing was for her.

In the middle of the song, he found her and their eyes connected.

He gave her a smile, pointed a finger at her while he clutched the microphone, trying to channel his inner Jonas brother, and continued singing.

She'd smiled and waved at him until Rory walked in front of her and blocked Ethan's view.

Grrrr!

When the song was over, Ethan left the stage and started searching for Danielle, but he couldn't find her. She wasn't anywhere in the club.

Where could she have gone?

And then Ethan had a thought.

A horrible thought.

Could Danielle have already left the club?

And if she had already left . . .

Could Rory have driven her home?

If Rory had driven her home . . .

No, he didn't want to think about what would happen after that. Everyone knew what happened after a guy drove a girl home.

He kissed her good night.

Sometimes more than once!

Ethan couldn't get the image of Rory kissing Danielle out of his head. Ick! No! If anyone should be kissing Danielle, it should be him.

But there was nothing he could do to stop it. Danielle was gone.

Ethan sighed and headed back to his table.

As he wove his way through the club's patrons, he noticed someone and stopped in his tracks. He rubbed his eyes, unable to believe it.

Rory was *still* here!

He hadn't left.

That meant he *hadn't* taken Danielle home!

Just then, Ethan's cell phone buzzed. He pulled it out of his pocket and saw he had a text message from Danielle. It read:

```
Great song choice! Are u trying to tell
me something? ;) Sorry I had to leave.
Crystal wasn't feeling well and we had to
take her home. See u tomorrow.
```

The text put a smile on Ethan's face.

When Ethan got home, he found Cooper in the living room, watching the Cartoon Network. Damian, Steve, and Howie had already gone up to bed, so Ethan and Cooper were alone.

"How was your night with your cousins?" Ethan asked, plopping on the couch next to Cooper.

"Fine. They were filling me in about colleges."

"Can you believe that this time next year we'll be seniors?"

Cooper shook his head. "I can still remember my first day at South Ridge High. I was so nervous."

"You? Nervous? I don't believe it."

"Believe it. I thought everyone was going to see me as a spoiled rich kid."

"That's so not you."

"My friends know that," Cooper said. "But sometimes people jump to conclusions. I know that's going to happen when I go to college."

"College is still far away. I wouldn't worry about it now. We've got other problems."

Cooper raised an eyebrow. "*We?* And what problems are you talking about?"

Ethan got off the couch and stuck his head out in the hallway, wanting to make sure no one was around. "I wanted to talk to you about the bet," he whispered.

"What about it?"

"I want to call it off."

"You do? How come?"

"I'm falling for Danielle," Ethan confessed. "I like her a lot."

Cooper's face lit up with a smile. "Really? That's great!"

"So you're okay with calling the bet off?"

"I've been wanting to call it off since yesterday."

Ethan was surprised. "You have? How come?"

"You're not the only one who's fallen for someone."

"Ava?" Ethan asked.

"Yeah, but I don't know what's going to happen. Her ex-boyfriend really hurt her. She only wants to be friends with me."

"If anyone can make her fall in love again, it's you."

"I don't know." Now it was Cooper who left the couch and checked out the hallway. "If I tell you something, you have to promise not to tell Damian."

"Sure."

"Ava and I kissed today."

"What was it like?"

"Great. Well, I thought it was great. Ava didn't say much about it. She kind of pretended like it didn't happen."

"What's your next move going to be?"

"I don't know. I'm still trying to figure it out."

"Hey!" Ethan exclaimed. "I just realized something. Since you kissed Ava, you won the bet!"

Cooper rolled his eyes in exasperation. "Forget about the bet! It was over for me the second I met Ava. If I cared about winning, I would have been gloating about kissing her. Let's just keep all of this between us. If we say anything to Damian about calling off the bet, he's going to tease us nonstop and we won't hear the end of it until spring break is over."

"I won't say a word," Ethan promised. "My lips are sealed!"

Chapter Seventeen

The following morning, Danielle was in the shower when she heard a scream.

It wasn't a scared scream. It was more like an angry scream.

And it was coming from Lindsey.

Danielle sighed, quickly rinsing the shampoo out of her hair and getting out of the shower. She dried herself off with a towel and then wrapped one around her head, turban style, before slipping her feet into her pink fuzzy slippers and tossing on her white terry cloth robe.

Lindsey screamed again and Danielle hurried out of the bathroom and raced downstairs in the direction of the kitchen.

"What's wrong?" she asked as she stepped through the kitchen's swinging door.

"Yeah," Ava said with a yawn, walking in right after Danielle and rubbing her still sleepy eyes. "What's with all the screaming?"

"Mr. Munch Mouth strikes again!" a furious Lindsey exclaimed, shaking an empty box of cereal in the air and pointing to the messy counter and open cabinets. "He's inhaled everything! The fruit! The cookies! The granola bars! There's nothing for us to eat!"

"I'll make another donut run after I get dressed," Ava said.

"I don't want donuts for breakfast!" Lindsey shouted. "I want my Fruity Pebbles with sliced strawberries! And I want an English muffin with cream cheese and grape jelly. But I can't have any of those things because our next-door neighbor ate it all!"

Danielle yawned. "Maybe we should get a lock for the refrigerator."

"Or maybe we should ask Sharla to stop letting him help himself to our stuff," Ava suggested.

"That won't help," Lindsey grumbled. "He's got Sharla wrapped around his little finger. All he has to do is bat those baby blue eyes and she says yes to whatever he wants."

"How do you know he has baby blue eyes?" Danielle asked.

"He kept staring at me last night at the Sing Along when we were sitting with him and his cousins. His eyes were *glued* to me!"

"I didn't notice," Danielle said.

"Neither did I," Ava added.

"How could you not notice?" Lindsey asked.

"Really?" Danielle murmured. "I'll have to take a closer look next time I see him."

"Well, this is the last straw," Lindsey said as she threw the empty cereal box into the garbage and started cleaning the counter. "The last straw!"

"What are you going to do?" Danielle asked.

Lindsey gave an evil Bart Simpson chuckle. "Tomorrow morning I plan on leaving a little surprise for our next-door neighbor."

"Uh-oh," Ava said. "This doesn't sound good."

"When I'm through with Howie, he'll think twice before setting foot in this kitchen again!" Lindsey vowed.

An hour later, Danielle, Ava, and Lindsey were munching on jelly donuts when Jade and Crystal came in through the back door.

"Look at what we've got!" Jade announced, waving a bunch of blue tickets in the air.

"What are those?" Danielle asked.

"We're all going to an amusement park! Steve has a friend who gave him free passes! Come on! Go get your stuff," Jade urged as she left the kitchen. "We leave in fifteen minutes!"

"If Steve gave you the passes, does that mean he and the rest of the guys next door are going, too?" Ava asked.

"Of course!" Crystal exclaimed as she followed after Jade. "We're going to hang out together."

"Oh, no, you don't!" Lindsey exclaimed, cutting Ava off before she could say anything. "You're not staying home. You're coming with us. Don't think I don't know what's going on."

Ava took another bite of her jelly donut. "What's going on?"

"You're trying to avoid Cooper!"

Ava laughed. "Avoid Cooper? Why would I do that?"

"Because something happened yesterday afternoon," Lindsey said. "Something you're not telling us."

"Nothing happened."

"Something happened," Lindsey repeated. "I can always tell when you're holding back." Lindsey turned to Danielle. "Isn't she holding back?"

"Linds," Danielle warned. "We already discussed this. If Ava has anything to tell us, she'll do it when she's ready."

"She's never going to be ready!" Lindsey exclaimed. "Ava, we're your friends. We want to help you. That's what we're here for."

Ava took the last bite of her jelly donut and wiped her lips on a napkin. "If I tell you what happened yesterday afternoon, you have to promise you're not going to overreact," she said to Lindsey. "Promise?"

"Promise!"

"Cooper kissed me."

Lindsey squealed with excitement, happily clapping her hands. "Yes! I knew that's what happened. I knew it! I knew it! I knew it!" Lindsey pulled her chair closer to Ava. "So, what was it like? Is he a good kisser? Did you kiss more than once?"

"Linds!!!" Ava wailed.

"What?" Lindsey protested. "I'm not overreacting. I'm just so excited for you!"

"Did you like the kiss?" Danielle asked. "Is that the problem?"

"The kiss was nice," Ava admitted. "And it only happened once."

"But you want it to happen again!" Lindsey exclaimed. "Admit it!"

"I don't know what I want," Ava moaned, putting her head down on the table. "I'm so confused. That's why I think maybe it's better if I stay home."

"By yourself? No way! You need to be out having a good time. You need to distract yourself."

"Isn't that going to be a little hard to do with Cooper along?" Ava asked, lifting her head up.

"We don't have to hang out with him," Lindsey said. "We can go off on our own."

"But won't he think I'm avoiding him?"

"How did you leave things with him yesterday?" Danielle asked.

"We pretended like the kiss never happened."

"So you keep pretending," Danielle said.

"Keep pretending?" Lindsey made a face at Danielle. "I disagree!" She turned back to Ava. "Obviously there's an attraction; otherwise Cooper wouldn't have kissed you and you wouldn't be so torn up about it. I say go with the flow! Just hang out with him and have a good time. If another kiss is meant to happen, then it'll happen. And that will mean that there's something growing between the two of you!"

Danielle sighed. "I hate to admit it, Ava, but Lindsey is right. I say follow her advice. All we're doing is going to an amusement park, and we'll be on rides most of the time. It's not like you two are going to be alone. You're going to be surrounded by tons of people."

Ava thought about Danielle's words. "I guess you're right," she slowly agreed.

"So you'll come?" Lindsey asked.

"I'll come," Ava said. "After all, it's an amusement park. We'll be on rides. Nothing romantic can possibly happen there."

"How about we take a ride in the Tunnel of Love?" Cooper suggested.

Ava stared at Cooper in disbelief. "You're kidding, right?"

Once they'd arrived at the amusement park, everyone had broken into groups. Ethan and Danielle had gone off together, while Steve, Howie, Crystal, and Jade made up their own little quartet. Damian had invited Mindy, Wanda, Vivienne, and Lacey, so he was with them. Ava had been hoping to explore the park with Lindsey, but she had mysteriously disappeared, leaving her alone with Cooper.

Ava was going to kill Danielle and Lindsey the next time she saw them!

"You told me you don't like crazy rides," Cooper said. "The Tunnel of Love is one of the safest, quietest, most boring rides in the amusement park."

"It's also the most romantic," she shot back.

"Only if you make it romantic. Otherwise you're just sitting in a boat in the dark."

"How do I know you don't have an ulterior motive?"

"What could that motive be?"

"Maybe you want to kiss me again."

Cooper thought about it. "Maybe I do. I'm not going to lie. Would that be so bad?"

Ava thought of yesterday's kiss. It hadn't been bad. It had been nice. But she didn't want to fall in love again! Falling in love hurt too much. She was through with guys! At least for now.

"I told you, I'm not ready to date again."

"Then I won't kiss you. I promise."

Ava hesitated.

"What's the matter? Don't you trust me?" Cooper leaned close and whispered in Ava's ear. "Or is it that you don't trust yourself?" Ava could feel the heat of Cooper's body and smell the clean scent of his soap. Josh used to smell the same way, and the scent brought back old memories. Memories of being held. And kissed. Maybe she *wasn't* through with guys. Suddenly, she wanted to wrap her arms around Cooper's neck and snuggle against him. "Maybe I'm the one who needs to be worried about being kissed?" he asked. "Is that what you're afraid of? That once we're alone in the dark, you won't be able to control yourself?"

"Me? Afraid?" Ava snapped. "I'll show you who's afraid." She stepped up to the ticket window and slapped her money down on the counter. "Two for the Tunnel of Love!"

★ ★ ★

"What kind of rides do you like to go on?" Ethan asked Danielle.

Whenever Danielle went to an amusement park, she usually stuck to the safe rides. Like the carousel, the bumper cars, the water float. She never went on roller coasters or rides that spun you around or shook you upside down.

But that was the *old* Danielle.

This week she was Daring Dani and that meant shaking things up!

"I'll go on anything," she said.

Ethan's eyes lit up. "Great! This park has some really wild roller coasters. One's a runaway train, another is a roller coaster in the dark, and there's another one that goes backward! And there's this one ride called the Big Drop. It's like you're in an elevator that's plunging to the ground after the cables have been cut."

Danielle gulped, hoping all the blood hadn't drained from her face. "Sounds awesome!"

Ethan took Danielle by the hand and pulled her in the direction of the first roller coaster. "Let's go!"

Danielle screamed her lungs out as they went from roller coaster to roller coaster, clutching on to Ethan's arm and squeezing her eyes shut during every ride.

"Are you sure you're okay?" Ethan always asked. "You're not just going on these rides for me, are you? You seem really scared."

"Being scared is part of the fun!"

And it was true. Before each roller coaster took its first big plunge, she got a rush of adrenaline as she felt herself falling, the car she was in twisting and turning, before finally coming to a safe stop.

"What's next?" she asked as they got off the runaway train.

"Want to try the Big Drop?"

"Sure."

"It's all the way on the other side of the park. We could take a cable car or we could walk."

"Let's walk," Danielle said. "That way we can grab a bite along the way."

"I wonder what's going on here," Ethan said as they passed a booth that had a long line in front of it.

"Let's check it out," Danielle suggested.

As they got closer to the front of the line, which consisted only of guys, Danielle could see it was a kissing booth. But there was no one standing behind the counter.

"Hey!" a familiar voice called out. "Are you opening up for business?"

Standing at the front of the line was Rory.

"Me?" a shocked Danielle laughed, pointing a finger at herself. "No!"

"Why not?"

"Who'd pay to kiss me?"

Rory reached into his plaid shorts and pulled out a bunch of dollar bills, putting them down on the counter. Then he slid his mirrored sunglasses down the front of his nose and stared at Danielle over the lenses. "I would." He turned to the guys standing behind him. "And I bet they would, too! Wouldn't you, guys?"

All the guys reached into their pockets, pulling out dollars and waving them in the air as they whistled at Danielle.

"Your fans have spoken!" Rory exclaimed. "Besides, it's for charity!"

"It is?"

"For orphans," Rory added. "You can't say no to the orphans!"

Danielle stared at the line of guys. There were so many of them! Would she really be able to kiss all of them? Well, it wasn't like she was going to be *kissing* them the way a girl kissed her boyfriend. All she'd have to do was give them a quick peck on the lips. That was all. She could handle that.

Danielle turned to Ethan. "How can I say no when it's for a good cause?"

Rory turned to face the line of guys. "Pucker up, guys!" he called out. "She's going to do it!"

Ethan couldn't believe Danielle was going to do it.

Yes, it was for a good cause, but the idea of some other guy kissing Danielle was driving him crazy!

Not to mention that *Rory* would also be kissing her!

Rory!!!

No way was he going to let that happen!

But what could he do to stop it? Danielle was walking into the kissing booth, and Rory was already waiting at the counter.

Unless . . .

Ethan reached into his wallet and slapped five dollars down on the counter.

"Five dollars gives me five kisses!" he proclaimed, shoving Rory to one side and leaning over the counter to take Danielle into his arms.

Ethan then kissed Danielle with everything he had.

If she was going to be kissing other guys, he wanted to give her a kiss that she would compare all those other kisses to.

No matter who kissed her, he wanted his kiss to be a kiss that she wouldn't forget.

Danielle's head was swooning. She had never been kissed like this before! Never!

A second ago, she had been expecting to kiss Rory, and the next thing she knew, Ethan was pulling her into his arms.

His kiss was incredible.

Indescribable.

She couldn't put it any other way.

And she didn't want to stop kissing him!

"That's one," Ethan said, breaking the kiss.

"Now for two," Danielle said as she pulled him back into her arms for a second kiss. Would it be just as wonderful as the first?

It was!

At that moment, the girl who was supposed to be staffing the kissing booth showed up. She was a brunette who was over six feet tall and looked like a Brazilian supermodel. Danielle had no doubt she'd be doing a brisk business.

"I'll take over now," she said. "Thanks for covering for me." She faced Ethan. "How many kisses did you want to buy?"

"Sorry, but the only kisses I'm interested in are hers," Ethan said.

"And I owe him three more," Danielle said. "So

241

until he gets his money's worth, I suggest you wait outside."

Danielle then leaned across the counter to give Ethan his third kiss. As she did, she whispered, "You know, once we're finished here, if you want some more kisses, I'll give them to you for free!"

Chapter Eighteen

Even though Ava had agreed to a ride through the Tunnel of Love, Cooper could see she wasn't happy about it.

"This seat is tight," Ava complained as they were strapped in. She was trying to sit as far away from him as she could, but it was impossible. They were pressed right against each other.

"And that's my fault?" Cooper asked, trying not to sound frustrated. "I didn't know the seat was going to be so small."

"I didn't say it was your fault."

"You didn't have to say it with words. Your tone says it all."

"Are you two sure you're on the right ride?" the attendant who was strapping them in asked. She was the same age as Cooper and Ava, wearing a red

T-shirt and white shorts. Her long brown hair was pulled into a ponytail and she had a pair of sunglasses perched on top of her head. A name tag on her chest said VANESSA. "You're both sitting so stiffly. Loosen up! Put your arms around each other. Snuggle! This is the Tunnel of Love, not the Tunnel of Death!"

"She thinks I'm going to try to kiss her," Cooper explained.

"I didn't say that!" Ava protested.

"And she doesn't want me to," he continued.

"Are you nuts?" Vanessa asked Ava. "He's adorable! If I was taking a ride in the dark with him, I'd want him kissing me!" Vanessa gave Cooper a smile. "I get off work at six."

"I'll remember that," Cooper said, wondering if he could play the jealousy card with Ava.

"She gets off at six," Ava repeated as the car they were sitting in started to head toward the opening of the Tunnel of Love. "You should go out with her."

Cooper sighed. Forget about the jealousy card. "I don't want to go out with her."

"Why not? She's pretty. And you heard her. She'd want you to kiss her."

"Yes, she's pretty. But there's more to a girl than just the way she looks. There's what's inside, too. I don't know anything about her."

"That's why you go on a date. To get to know the person."

"And I don't want to kiss her!" Cooper already knew the person he wanted to kiss, but he had promised Ava he wouldn't kiss her again.

"Why are you making this so hard?" he asked as their boat slipped into the darkness of the tunnel and started to go around a curve decorated with strands of twinkling white lights. "Why can't you forget about Josh? At least for this week?"

"Everyone thinks it's so easy to forget about Josh, but it isn't!" Ava snapped. "We went out for a year! I had feelings for him. Just because you break up with someone, it doesn't mean those feelings end. They're still there. Eventually, they start to fade, but it doesn't happen overnight. As much as I hate to admit it, I still have feelings for Josh and I don't know when they're going to go away."

"But I don't think you're even trying to get over him! If you were, you would be having a good time this week instead of constantly thinking about him."

"Don't tell me how I should feel! You don't know what I'm going through."

"And you don't know what *I'm* going through!" Cooper shot back as the boat they were in came to a stop in front of a waterfall. "I like you, Ava. A lot. But I don't know if you like me. I think you do,

245

but you're not giving me a chance. And that's not fair."

Ava was silent. "You're right," she finally said. "I'm not giving you a chance. I'm sorry."

"You don't have to be sorry. Maybe just a little more open-minded?"

"This hasn't been easy for me," Ava admitted. "I'm still sorting things out."

"I'm *not* Josh," Cooper said. "Remember that, okay?"

Ava nodded. Then she asked, "Why aren't we moving? Is the ride broken?"

"I think not moving is part of the ride," Cooper said.

"Part of the ride?"

"Listen."

Ava tilted her head and heard the sound of couples kissing.

"How long do we have to listen to that?" she groaned.

Cooper shrugged. "Five minutes? Ten? I don't know."

"What are we supposed to do until then?"

"We could make ourselves a little more comfortable," Cooper said. "Is it okay if I put my arm around you? And you could put yours around me. It might give us some wiggle room. And don't

246

worry! I'm not going to hug you or kiss you or do anything affectionate."

"I didn't say anything," Ava said as she slipped her arm around Cooper's back.

"You didn't have to. I'm a mind reader."

"Really? So what am I thinking?"

Cooper gazed down at Ava. He stared into her blue eyes, glittering in the darkness. It would be so easy to kiss her. All he had to do was lean forward and press his lips against hers. But he couldn't. He'd promised.

But he *really* wanted to kiss her!

"That I'm a nice guy," he said, tearing his eyes away so he would no longer be tempted. "And maybe, just maybe, we'll kiss again before spring break ends. Am I right?"

Ava nestled herself against Cooper's chest and he placed an arm around her, holding his breath as he waited for her answer.

"Maybe," Ava whispered. "Maybe."

Cooper smiled in the darkness. Yes! It was exactly the answer he had been hoping for.

Mindy couldn't remember the last time she had been to an amusement park. Maybe junior high? She'd forgotten how much fun they could be! Since they'd arrived, she had gone on a ton of rides, eaten a lot of junk food, and was now playing the ringtoss, trying to win a stuffed pink rabbit. Unfortunately, her rings weren't getting anywhere near the top of the milk bottle they had to fall over. It was frustrating! She really wanted to win that stuffed rabbit. It was so cute!

"I'll take another three," she told the guy in the booth, handing him her money.

"Need a little help?"

Mindy whirled around. "Damian! What are you doing here?" She was surprised to see him all alone. When they'd first arrived at the park, Wanda had instantly slipped her arm through his, steering him in the direction she wanted to go, while Lacey and Vivienne trailed behind. Mindy had started to follow after them, but then remembered Wanda's orders from yesterday afternoon and decided to explore the park on her own.

When they'd gotten back from the spa, Damian had still been at the house. At the sight of him, Mindy had panicked. *What was he still doing there?* Wanda wasn't supposed to know that he'd been spending time with Vivienne! At the sight of Damian, Wanda had smiled, but then her smile had turned into a frown when she realized Damian and Vivienne had been alone. Of course, she didn't know *how long* — three hours and forty-five minutes, to be precise! — and that bugged her. Luckily, Damian had waved the amusement park passes he'd brought over. And Vivienne had kept her mouth shut. Crisis averted!

"My brother, Steve, got these from a friend," he said. "I thought you might want to come with us tomorrow."

"I'd love to," Wanda instantly answered, snatching the passes out of Damian's hand as she gave him a sweet smile.

"We'd *all* love to," Lacey said as she removed three passes from Wanda's hand, keeping one for herself and handing one to Vivienne and one to Mindy. Obviously, Lacey did *not* trust Wanda to distribute the rest of the passes! "That was so sweet of you to think of us."

"Great! We'll touch base tomorrow morning."

After Damian left, Wanda tried to convince Lacey and Vivienne that they should stay home, but they refused to change their minds. Wanda didn't say anything to Mindy, but maybe that was because she knew Mindy didn't dare cross her. If Wanda wanted her to stay home, she'd stay home!

"Why would he have brought four passes if he was *only* inviting you?" Lacey asked. "That doesn't make sense."

"He was being nice. He didn't *expect* you to take them!" Wanda pointed out.

"But we did," Vivienne said. "And he didn't say anything. That means he's cool with us coming along. If it was a problem, he would have said something. Right, Mindy?"

Mindy suddenly felt like a huge spotlight had been aimed at her. *Don't drag me into this!* she wanted to scream. But they had. And now she needed not only to show that she was loyal to Wanda, but at the same time not piss off Lacey and Vivienne.

"He probably figured we'd do it like a class trip," she said. "You know, everyone arrives together but goes off on their own once we get to the park. Then we all meet up at the end of the day."

"Exactly," Wanda agreed. "Damian will spend the day with *me* while everyone else goes off on their own."

And that was exactly what Mindy had done.

Until now.

"Where's Wanda?" she asked, searching behind Damian for a glimpse of her. If she was headed this way, Mindy did *not* want to be alone with Damian.

"I don't know and I don't care! We got separated after we got off the roller coaster and I decided to take a break from her."

Mindy decided to tease Damian for a little bit. "Maybe she went off to reapply her lip gloss. Or buy another one. I hear you helped her go through one the other night."

"Huh?"

"Should we start calling you the Kissing Bandit? The name kind of fits."

Damian stared at Mindy in confusion. "What are you talking about?"

"Don't play dumb! Wanda told us all about her excessive lip-gloss use during your first date. She had to keep reapplying because you kept kissing it off."

"What?!" Damian exclaimed, outrage on his face. "That's a lie! I never kissed her. Not once!"

"You didn't?" Mindy didn't know why, but the fact that Damian *hadn't* kissed Wanda made her feel . . . happy. "That's not what she says."

"Do you believe everything that girl tells you?"

"Usually. Why else would she lie?"

Damian gave Mindy a *duh* expression. "To make the rest of you jealous?"

"That is Wanda's style," Mindy admitted.

"My kisses are reserved for one girl and one girl only," Damian said. "You!"

Hearing those words, Mindy felt a thrill.

Until she remembered how dangerous they were.

Even though they'd made a deal for a kiss, Damian wasn't supposed to be kissing her.

She looked around in panic. "Shhh! Don't say that!"

"Why not?"

"It will make Wanda mad! The only girl you're supposed to be interested in is her."

"Yeah, well, she makes that a little difficult. She's too clingy. Too possessive. Vivienne's kind of cool. We spent most of yesterday afternoon playing with your Wii." Damian nodded at the ringtoss. "What are you up to?"

"Trying to win a stuffed rabbit." Mindy tossed her remaining rings. And missed. "Shoot!"

"Try again?" the guy in the booth asked.

Mindy shook her head. "Based on how much I've already spent, I could buy my own rabbit. Looks like it's game over for me."

"Let me try," Damian offered. "I bet I could do it."

"It's not that easy."

"We'll see," Damian said, handing the guy some money and getting ready to toss his first ring.

Mindy's mouth dropped open as she watched Damian toss all three rings over the milk bottle.

"We have a winner!" the guy in the booth announced.

"Which rabbit did you want?" Damian asked.

"The pink one."

The guy in the booth handed the pink rabbit to Damian, who gave it to Mindy. "All yours."

"Thanks."

"What are you going to name it?"

"B.W."

"B.W.?"

"Short for Bunny Wabbit."

Damian rolled his eyes. "Why do girls always resort to baby talk? Why can't his name be Bunny Rabbit?"

"Because he doesn't look like a Bunny Rabbit. He looks like a Bunny Wabbit!"

"Uh-oh!" Damian yelped, grabbing Mindy by the arm and pulling her behind him. "Wanda is headed our way."

"Did she see us together?" Mindy gasped.

"No, but it's only a matter of time. Come on," he said, pushing her toward the line for the Ferris wheel. "We're going for a ride!"

Within minutes, Mindy and Damian were in an enclosed car heading for the top of the Ferris wheel.

"We can't hide up here all day," Mindy said when the car stopped, swinging in the breeze.

"Why not? It's so quiet up here. Peaceful. It's like we're the only two people in the world."

"Bite your tongue!"

"You wouldn't want to be all alone with me?" Damian moved closer to Mindy, pressing her into the corner of the car. "What's the matter? Afraid you wouldn't be able to control yourself?"

Mindy wondered if Damian was about to collect the kiss that she owed him. Her heart began racing as she imagined what it would be like to kiss him. He was probably a very good kisser.

But she wasn't ready to be kissed! She was all hot and sweaty from going from ride to ride. She looked a mess! Damian couldn't kiss her now! She had to stop him!

"Down, boy!" she exclaimed, bopping Damian on the nose with B.W. "Your charm might work on the girls at South Ridge High, but I'm immune to it!"

Damian gave Mindy a sly smile. "Uh-huh." He folded his arms over his chest and slid back into his corner of the car. "That kiss is coming. Soon. Very soon. And you're looking forward to it. Otherwise you wouldn't have freaked out the way you just did."

"I didn't freak out," Mindy said, trying to sound calm, even though nervous butterflies were fluttering through her stomach. She *did* want Damian to kiss her. But she didn't want him to know that!

"So tell me about life at North Ridge High. You must be Miss Popularity."

Mindy laughed. "More like Miss Unpopularity."

"I don't believe that."

"Why not?"

"Why wouldn't people like you?"

"I have this little problem called gossiping."

Damian shrugged. "Nobody's perfect."

"I'm trying to change."

"And you think hanging out with Wanda and her friends is going to do that?"

"I already told you. They're the most popular girls at North Ridge High. If I become friends with them, then *I'm* popular."

"And that matters to you?"

"Yes, it does! Don't you understand? This is my chance to change things, and I'm going to change them! I want to have friends. I want people to like me!"

"I'll do whatever I can to help you," Damian promised. "You can count on me."

"Not if Wanda catches us together!" Mindy warned. "We can't go sneaking off by ourselves anymore!"

The Ferris wheel started to move and their car headed back toward the ground. Mindy stuck her head out, wanting to make sure Wanda wasn't anywhere in sight. "You get out first and then I'll follow you."

When their car landed back on the ground, Damian opened the door. But before leaving, he glanced back over his shoulder at Mindy. "In case you didn't know it, you *do* have a friend. Me."

Then he gave her a wink and left her alone with B.W.

Chapter Nineteen

Danielle was brushing her teeth when she heard a scream.

"Not again," she groaned, spitting out toothpaste and wiping her mouth on a towel before leaving the bathroom.

Out in the hallway, she ran into Ava, who was heading downstairs. "Does she always have to scream?"

"That didn't sound like Lindsey screaming," Ava said. "It sounded like a guy!"

Danielle listened to another scream. "You're right. And Lindsey did say she was going to leave a surprise for Howie this morning."

"I think he found it!"

As they approached the kitchen, they could hear the screams getting louder and louder.

It was definitely a guy.

They walked into the kitchen and gasped.

"What happened to you?" Ava laughed, clutching a hand over her open mouth.

Howie was covered from head to toe in some sort of sticky substance, with white feathers stuck all over him.

"Your crazy friend rigged a bucket of maple syrup and feathers over the back door!" Howie screeched. "That's what happened!"

"Would you like some pancakes to go with that syrup?" Lindsey asked, turning from the stove with a spatula and a plate of pancakes.

"Look at what you did to me!" Howie complained, waving his arms in the air.

Danielle giggled. With the way he was covered with feathers and waving his arms, Howie resembled a giant chicken.

"What *I* did?" Lindsey snapped. "I was only protecting what was ours. You've been sneaking into our kitchen all week, eating all our food and not even saying thank you!"

"Sharla said I could!"

Lindsey waved her spatula in Howie's face. "That doesn't mean you can just help yourself to whatever you want! You ate the picnic lunch I made for Cooper and Ava the other day and didn't even say you were sorry. I slaved all night over a hot stove because I wanted their picnic to be special. But you ruined it!"

"It was delicious," Howie said.

"You're just saying that so I won't be mad at you!" Lindsey fumed.

Howie crossed his heart. "Best fried chicken I ever had."

"It's my grandmother's secret recipe," Lindsey grudgingly admitted.

"I liked the cake, too."

"I made it from scratch."

"I could tell. It didn't taste like it came out of a box."

"What's going on here?" Ava whispered to Danielle.

"I'm not sure, but I think Howie's flirting with Lindsey!"

"Is it working?"

"I don't think so," Danielle said as Lindsey continued to glare at Howie, who kept sweet-talking her.

Just then, Ava's cell phone rang and she answered it.

"Hello!"

"Hi, it's Mindy!"

"Hey, Mindy, what's up?"

"I'm having a pool party today and I wanted to invite you and the girls."

"Sounds like fun. What time?"

"Swing by at around twelve."

"We'll be there," Ava said. "Any new developments with Project Damian?"

"I can't talk right now," Mindy whispered. "I'll fill you in when I see you."

"Okay. See you later."

"Bye!"

"Who was that?" Danielle asked when Ava got off the phone.

"Mindy Yee. She invited us over for a pool party."

"We're going, too!" Howie exclaimed. "Mindy called to invite Damian and told him to bring us along."

"Then I guess you better start cleaning yourself up!" Lindsey told him. "Maybe you can get one of your housemates to pluck you. Because I don't think Mindy's going to want feathers in her pool!"

"Who were you on the phone with?" Wanda asked as she walked out to the pool and lay down on a lounge chair.

Mindy wasn't sure if it was her imagination, but

ever since yesterday afternoon, when she'd been alone with Damian, she felt like Wanda was watching her every move. It was almost as if Wanda had some sort of radar and suspected that Mindy was interested in Damian, which was so *not* the case. Damian was a friend and *only* a friend. She had to stop being so paranoid!

"Ava."

"Why were you talking to her?"

"I invited her to our pool party."

Wanda made a face as she lathered her arms with suntan lotion. "Why did you do that?"

"She and her friends had us over for that barbecue the other night. I thought it would be nice to invite them over."

"That party was a snooze fest!"

What did Wanda expect her to do? Uninvite them? And did she forget that she had met Damian at that snooze fest? Apparently! "Well, they're coming over."

"You invited Damian, didn't you?"

"Yes."

"And he's coming?"

"He said he was."

"I don't want it to look like I'm chasing after him."

But you are! You are chasing after him!

And Damian seemed to know that. Which was why he was keeping his distance from Wanda. Mindy didn't know if he was doing it because he knew it would drive Wanda crazy or if he just wanted his own personal space, but Wanda was *not* happy that Damian wasn't at her beck and call. Of course, Damian *shouldn't* be at Wanda's beck and call. She already had a boyfriend! But Rick didn't exist this week. At least not in Wanda's world.

"Isn't today a great day?" Lacey asked, joining Wanda and Mindy by the pool. She sat down on the chaise lounge next to Mindy, stretching herself out in the sun.

"Why are you in such a good mood?" Wanda grumbled.

Mindy knew why. Damian had spent some time alone with Lacey yesterday afternoon. He'd gone on a couple of rides with her and even won her a stuffed teddy bear in one of the arcades. Lacey had told her all the details when they'd gotten home last night.

So far, Damian had come through for her, spending time alone with Wanda, Vivienne, and Lacey.

That meant that she was eventually going to have to settle her debt with him.

The only question was when?

When was he going to collect his kiss?

"Why not?" Lacey answered with a smile. "The weather is gorgeous, we're still in Miami, and delicious Damian is coming over today!"

"Delicious Damian is coming over to see *me*," Wanda reminded Lacey. "Not you."

Lacey made a face at Wanda. "Don't worry! I'm only going to look, not touch! You know, you should learn to share. What's going to happen once we get back home? You can't juggle two boyfriends."

Wanda gave Lacey a coy smile. "Says who?"

"I'd like to see that," Lacey scoffed.

"You will!" Wanda confidently answered.

"Think she can do it, Mindy?" Lacey asked.

Mindy didn't know how to answer. Wanda juggling two boyfriends? That could only mean one thing. Disaster!

"Guess we'll have to wait until we get home," Mindy said.

"I guess so," Lacey said, giving Mindy a secret smile that *instantly* made her nervous.

Lacey was up to something, but what?

Ava was the first one ready to leave for Mindy's pool party. While Danielle, Lindsey, Jade, and Crystal were still getting into their swimsuits, she was sitting on the steps of the front porch, flipping through a tiny photo album filled with pictures of her and Josh. Each one brought back a memory of a happier time.

And reminded her that those happy times were over.

Why are you torturing yourself this way? It's over with Josh! Over! Throw out these photos! You need to put the past behind you and move on!

When she heard footsteps on the walkway, she looked up and saw Cooper with his hands behind his back.

"What are you hiding?" she asked him.

"Just a little something I whipped up," he said, presenting Ava with a bouquet of flowers made from colored tissue paper. "They last longer this way."

"They're so pretty!" Ava exclaimed, putting down the photo album and taking the bouquet from Cooper.

Cooper sat on the steps next to Ava, pressing his knee against hers. "What were you looking at?"

"Nothing special," she said, pressing back with her knee.

"Mind if I take a look?" Cooper asked, reaching for the album.

Ava shrugged. Unless she snatched the album

away from Cooper, she really didn't have much of a choice. "If you want."

She watched as Cooper flipped through a few pages. From the frown on his face, he didn't seem too happy.

"I'm guessing this guy is Josh?" he asked.

"It's Josh."

Cooper flipped through the rest of the pages, then handed the album back to Ava and rose from the steps. "I'm going to go find Ethan. See if he's ready to go. I'll see you at Mindy's." He started walking away.

"Cooper! Wait!" she cried, throwing down the bouquet and jumping up off the steps. She could see he was angry, maybe even a little hurt, but he wasn't going to say anything. He probably wanted to leave so he could cool off. That was just the way he was. He didn't want to make her feel bad or put any pressure on her.

"I didn't thank you for the flowers," she said.

He turned around. "You don't have to," he said stiffly.

"I know. But I want to."

Ava closed the distance between herself and Cooper. Then, before she lost her nerve, she wrapped her arms around his neck, pulled his face close to hers, and kissed him.

She didn't know what she was doing.

This was all so wrong.

But if it was wrong, why did it feel so right?

Danielle watched from behind the screen door with wide eyes.

Ava was kissing Cooper.

Ava had made the first move!

She was shocked.

Shocked!

But also thrilled!

It looked like her best friend was finally over Josh!

Cooper couldn't believe what was happening.

Ava was kissing him.

She was kissing him!!!

Only seconds ago she had been flipping through a photo album filled with pictures of her ex-boyfriend. Seeing those photos, he had finally decided to give up. Game over. Josh had too strong a hold on Ava for Cooper to even have a chance.

But then Ava had surprised him.

She had kissed him.

Was *still* kissing him!

He never thought this day would arrive. Yesterday, after the Tunnel of Love, he and Ava had spent the rest of the day going on rides and avoiding all talk of romance. They didn't discuss dating or kissing or ex-boyfriends. They just had a good time. And when they'd gotten home, he'd walked Ava to her front door and given her a hug good night. Like a brother would give his sister. He hadn't even thought of kissing her.

Ava broke their kiss. "I shouldn't have done that," she instantly apologized, her forehead pressed against his as she stared down at the ground.

"But you did," Cooper said, unable to keep from smiling.

"It was wrong." Ava went back to the steps and sat down, running her fingers through her curls. "Wrong!"

Cooper followed after Ava and sat next to her, taking her hand in his and giving it a gentle squeeze. "Why was it wrong?"

"You're a great guy, Cooper, but I don't know what I feel for you. And until I do, I shouldn't be kissing you!"

"Maybe this will help you change your mind," he whispered.

And then, before Ava could say another word,

Cooper pulled her into his arms and gave her a kiss of his own.

At first, Cooper was doing all the kissing, but then Ava lost herself in the moment, allowing herself to kiss him again as she wrapped her arms around him and pulled him close.

Danielle didn't want to spoil the moment — it was so romantic! — but she could hear Lindsey, Jade, and Crystal getting ready to head downstairs. She figured the last thing Ava would want was an audience, so she clomped her feet on the floor and started to open the porch door. At the sound of the noise she was making, Ava and Cooper pulled away from each other.

"We're almost ready to go," Danielle announced as she walked outside. "Oh!" She pretended to sound surprised. "Hi, Cooper! I didn't know you were out here."

"Hey, Danielle," he greeted as he jumped to his feet.

"You coming to Mindy's?" she asked.

"Ethan and I are going to drive over together."

"We'll see you there."

"See you there," he said as he waved good-bye.

"Pretty flowers," Danielle said, picking up the bouquet on the steps. "Where'd you get them?"

"You know where I got them," Ava said. "I saw you hiding in the doorway. Real subtle, Danielle!"

"I didn't want to spoil things!"

"How much did you see?"

Danielle made kissing noises. "Only the juicy parts!"

Ava groaned.

"What's wrong?" Danielle asked.

"Cooper!"

"He likes you."

"You think I don't know that?"

"And from what I just saw, I think you like him, too, right?"

"Right," Ava slowly answered.

"So what are you going to do about it?"

Ava sighed. "I don't know. I feel like I'm sending him mixed signals. Kiss me! Don't kiss me! I need to make up my mind about what I want and then stick to it!"

Danielle picked up the photo album on the steps. "Why don't we start by throwing this away?"

Ava snatched the album away from Danielle. "I can't! I'm not ready!" She tossed the photo album back into her shoulder bag. "Let's not talk about me. Let's talk about you and Ethan. Are the two of you officially a couple?"

"We're hardly a couple," Danielle said. "We haven't been dating for even a week."

"You did lock lips with him yesterday."

"That was for charity."

"I thought you wanted to kiss him again?"

"I did! I do! But after the kissing booth, we ran into Steve and Howie, and they spent the rest of the day with us. We could hardly kiss in front of them. And then they rode home with us. I didn't even get a kiss good night!"

"Poor Danielle," Ava teased, making kissing sounds of her own. "Not getting her daily dose of kisses. I guess you'll have to make up for it today."

"You bet I will!" Danielle vowed.

Chapter Twenty

"Your party seems to be off to a nice start," Carmela said as she took a tray of mini pizzas out of the oven.

Mindy peeked out into the backyard. Ethan, Cooper, and Damian had just arrived and were taking off their T-shirts, getting ready to jump into the pool. Naturally, Wanda, Lacey, and Vivienne had rushed over to Damian and surrounded him. The poor guy! She was surprised he could even breathe!

"Let's dance!" Wanda exclaimed, turning on the music and grabbing Damian by the hand, pulling him away from Lacey and Vivienne, who glowered at her behind her back.

"She didn't waste any time sinking her claws into him," Carmela commented, handing Mindy a bowl of potato chips and pretzels. "Take these out-side to your guests."

Mindy walked onto the patio and put the bowls down on a table, watching as Wanda draped her body against Damian's while she danced.

"I thought she had a boyfriend," Carmela said, coming out with a bucket of ice and cans of soda.

"She does. Rick."

"Then what's she doing with him?"

"It's spring break," Mindy explained. "Wanda says she's taking a break from Rick this week."

Carmela rolled her eyes. "She can call it what-ever she wants, but that girl is cheating on her boyfriend!"

"You could also say that," Mindy agreed just as she heard the doorbell ring. "I'll get it. It's probably Ava and the girls."

Mindy went to the front door and opened it, expecting to find Ava. But when she saw who was on the other side, her mouth dropped open. It was the last person she ever expected to see.

Rick Cho.

Wanda's boyfriend.

He gave her a smile, his backpack tossed over one shoulder. "Hey, Mindy!"

She struggled to find her voice. "Rick! What are you doing here?"

"Why do you seem so surprised?"

Uh, maybe because you're not supposed to be here. You're supposed to be back home! Oh, and your girlfriend is busy cheating on you with another guy only a few feet away from us!

Mindy's mind scrambled for an answer, but all she could think was: *Danger! Danger! Wanda is wrapped around Damian tighter than a boa constrictor! If Rick gets a peek at that, there's going to be a major explosion! Must prevent that from happening. If I don't, I'm dead! Dead! Dead! Dead! Courtesy of Wanda Wong!*

"We didn't know you were coming," she said.

"My dad had to fly down for business and I asked if I could tag along." Rick looked puzzled. "I called yesterday and left a message. Didn't you get it?"

"You did?" Could Carmela have forgotten to give them Rick's message? But Carmela never forgot to give messages. She never forgot to do anything. "With who?"

"Lacey."

Aha!

Now everything made *perfect* sense!

Lacey hadn't told Wanda that Rick had called because she wanted her to get caught with Damian!

273

"Aren't you going to let me in?" Rick asked.

Mindy laughed nervously. "Of course!" She held the door open so Rick could walk into the house, trying to figure out a way to buy more time. She had to warn Wanda that Rick was here.

If she didn't . . .

She shuddered.

She didn't even want to think about it!

"What's going on?" Rick asked. "I hear music."

"We're having a pool party."

"Where's Wanda?" Rick asked. "I want to see her."

"Wanda's in the pool." Mindy steered Rick in the direction of the stairs leading to the second floor. "Why don't you change into a pair of swim trunks and then join us? There's a guest room at the end of the hall with extra swim stuff."

"Sounds good," Rick said.

Mindy waited until she saw Rick reach the top of the stairs. Then she ran out into the backyard. She needed to do *major* damage control. She had to warn Wanda that Rick was here.

As soon as she saw Wanda, who was still dancing with Damian, she grabbed her by the arm, pulling her off to one side.

"Hey!" Wanda complained, trying to shake off Mindy's grip. "What are you doing?"

"I need to talk to you," Mindy whispered. "It's important."

"Later," Wanda hissed. "I'm busy with Damian."

"Now!" Mindy insisted, yanking Wanda into the kitchen.

"This better be important," Wanda warned, snatching her arm away from Mindy.

"It is."

Wanda sighed. "What's the crisis?"

"Rick."

"What about him?"

"He's here."

Wanda stared at Mindy in disbelief. "What do you mean he's here?"

Mindy pointed a finger up in the air. "He's *here*. He's upstairs changing into a pair of swim trunks."

Wanda's eyes widened with horror. "What's Rick doing here?"

"I don't know! He said he called yesterday and left a message."

"I didn't get any message," Wanda growled. "Did your stupid housekeeper forget to give it to me?"

"Carmela's not stupid!" Mindy exclaimed.

"Then why didn't I know Rick was coming?"

It was on the tip of Mindy's tongue to tell Wanda

275

that Lacey, her so-called *friend*, hadn't given her the message. But if she did that, she would be pulled into whatever feud was going on between Wanda and Lacey. And Lacey would think she had stabbed her in the back. After all, wasn't she also supposed to be Lacey's friend? The best thing to do would be to keep her mouth shut for now.

Mindy shrugged. "I don't know!"

"Someone messed up," Wanda hissed, staring at Mindy.

The message was clear. *Mindy* had messed up. And *Mindy* would pay the price if Wanda wound up in hot water with Rick.

The sound of footsteps could be heard coming down the stairs. Seconds later, Rick, wearing a pair of yellow boxer-cut swim trunks with a black stripe down the side, was in the kitchen, pulling Wanda into a hug.

"Miss me?" he asked, giving her a kiss.

Wanda kissed him back. "You don't know how much!"

"Glad to see me? You seem kind of stunned."

"Actually, I wasn't expecting you," Wanda confessed.

"Didn't Lacey give you my message?"

Mindy sagged with relief against the kitchen counter. The secret was out! And it hadn't come from her lips!

Wanda's eyes narrowed dangerously, sending chills down Mindy's spine. "You gave a message to Lacey?"

"Yesterday morning," Rick said.

"She didn't give it to me."

"No big deal. Why don't we go join the party?"

"Let's," Wanda said.

Mindy followed Wanda and Rick back outside, wondering what was going to happen next. Whatever it was, it was *not* going to be good.

When they reached the pool, Wanda pointed out Ethan and Cooper, who were swimming. Vivienne was sunbathing on a chaise lounge while a smug Lacey was sitting on Damian's lap, running her fingers through his hair.

"Look who's here," Wanda said to Lacey, giving her an icy glare. "It seems you forgot to tell me something yesterday."

Lacey shook her head. "I didn't forget."

Wanda's eyes widened in shock, and Mindy couldn't believe what she was hearing. Did Lacey have a death wish?

"You *didn't* forget?"

Lacey gave Wanda a sweet smile. "I knew how much you were missing Rick, so I wanted his visit to be a surprise. That's why I didn't tell you he was coming. So, surprise!" Lacey glanced over at Rick. "Was she surprised?"

"You should have seen the look on her face."

"I would have loved to have seen it."

"I bet you would," Wanda muttered.

"I didn't know you had a boyfriend," Rick said to Lacey.

Wanda laughed and gave Lacey her own smug smile. "She doesn't. That's *Mindy's* boyfriend, Damian. Lacey just doesn't know how to keep her hands to herself!"

What?!

Mindy couldn't believe what she was hearing. This day just kept getting crazier and crazier!

"You've kept Damian's lap warm enough for Mindy. Time to let her take over," Wanda said, grabbing Lacey by the arm and pulling her away from Damian. "Go on, Mindy," Wanda urged, giving her a little shove. "Go sit on your boyfriend's lap."

Damian held his arms out to Mindy, his green eyes sparkling with mischief. Oooh, he was enjoying this! "I missed you," he said. "Did you miss me?"

Mindy's gut told her to play along. Wanda wanted Rick to think Damian was her boyfriend, so that was what she was going to do.

Mindy slid onto Damian's lap, wrapping her arms around his neck.

"You know what I really want to do?" he whispered in her ear.

"What?" she asked, looking down at him.

"Kiss you!"

And before Mindy could say or do anything else, Damian gave her a kiss in front of everyone.

An hour later, Mindy was still remembering Damian's kiss.

As she had suspected, he was an excellent kisser.

Well, that had been no surprise.

He probably got plenty of practice at South Ridge High.

Mindy had been kissed before, but Damian's kiss had been unlike any other kiss she'd ever had.

She had melted into it.

Melted!

As soon as his lips had touched hers, she'd gotten all warm and soft inside. Like a Hershey's Kiss that had been left outside in the sun too long.

Unfortunately, there had only been one kiss. Damian's kiss had ended just as Ava, Danielle, Lindsey, Jade, and Crystal had arrived, along with Steve and Howie, and Mindy had thrown herself into the role of hostess, making sure everyone had something to eat and drink.

Now Mindy was in the kitchen, getting some more ice, when Wanda came inside.

"I wanted to talk to you," Wanda said, making sure no one was around.

"About what?"

"Damian."

"What about him?"

"I wouldn't get too used to his kisses. He was playing along."

"I know that."

"Do you?" Wanda asked. "Because it seemed like you were enjoying his kiss a little bit too much. Remember, you're not really his girlfriend."

Mindy couldn't believe what she was hearing! Where did Wanda come off telling her how she should feel about Damian's kiss? She was acting like a jealous girlfriend, and Damian wasn't even her boyfriend. Rick was! And why was she getting all this heat? She wasn't the one who had tried to expose Wanda! Lacey was!

"I know I'm not really his girlfriend," Mindy said. *I don't need you to remind me! I'm well aware of it! But you want to make sure I don't forget, don't you?*

"Good," Wanda said, filling her red cup with ice and heading back outside.

That doesn't mean I couldn't be his girlfriend if I really wanted to! Mindy felt like shouting at her.

Then she smashed a tray of ice on the counter and began filling an ice bucket, practically throwing the cubes in.

"Working out some issues?" Ava asked as she came into the kitchen.

"Sometimes Wanda makes me so angry!" Mindy exclaimed.

"What's the Wicked Witch done now?" Ava asked, popping a Cheez Doodle into her mouth.

Mindy needed to talk to someone, so she filled Ava in on what had happened before her arrival.

"Damian is fair game," Ava stated when Mindy had finished. "Wanda has no claim to him. If you want him, you should go after him."

"But I don't know if I want him," Mindy admitted. "What makes me so mad is that Wanda already has a boyfriend and it's like she's trying to have another one! That's not fair! If she wants to be with Damian, then she should break up with Rick. She shouldn't be trying to keep him from the rest of us."

"Do you like him?" Ava asked.

"Yes," Mindy answered. "I like him. And he's a nice guy, but I don't think he's looking to date just one girl."

"So? Who says you have to date just one guy? Go out with him. Have some fun."

"Would you do that?"

Ava sighed. "You'd think I'd follow my own advice, wouldn't you?" She gave her words some thought. "I think every situation is different. You have to do what feels right for you."

"Mindy!" Wanda called from outside. "Minnnnnndeeeeee!"

Mindy opened the sliding glass door leading onto the patio and stuck her head out. "Yes, Wanda?"

"Bring me some bug spray. The mosquitoes are driving me crazy."

"Right away."

"What are you, her slave?" Ava asked as Mindy started rummaging through the kitchen cabinets, searching for bug spray. "Has she never heard of the word *please*?"

Mindy found the bottle of bug spray and emptied half its contents.

"What are you doing?" Ava asked.

Mindy chuckled as she refilled the bottle with water and sugar, shaking it up. "Wanda needs to find out what it's like to be sweet, don't you think?"

Ava laughed. "Remind me to never get on your bad side!"

"Here you go, Wanda!" Mindy sang out as she walked out onto the patio and gave her the bottle. "Spray away!"

Thirty minutes later, a mosquito-bitten Wanda ran into the house, vowing not to go back outside for the rest of the day. "Those bugs are eating me alive!" she shrieked as she ran up to her bedroom.

"Looks like the coast is clear for you and Damian," Ava told Mindy.

"At least for a little while," Mindy said. "I'm sure Wanda will make a reappearance at some point. Or get all of us to come inside."

"Then I say take advantage of her absence. Go!"

Mindy found Damian in the pool doing laps. When he saw her sitting on the side with her feet in the water, he swam over.

"My girlfriend returns," he said.

"I'm not your girlfriend."

"Shhh!" Damian whispered, pressing a finger to his lips. "We're pretending, remember?"

"Was that kiss pretend?" she asked, wondering if Damian had felt what she had.

"That kiss was real," Damian said. "And you know it."

"It was also the kiss that I owed you," she pointed out. "I guess that means our debt is settled."

"Paid in full," Damian agreed.

Mindy splashed Damian with her foot. "Of course, if you wanted to kiss me again, I wouldn't have a problem with that." She was wondering if that first kiss had been a fluke. There was only one way to find out. "After all, we are supposed to be boyfriend and girlfriend."

"We do have to make it look real for Rick, don't we?"

"We do."

"Then I guess I have no choice. I'll have to do what any guy would do when his girlfriend is sitting by the side of a swimming pool."

It took Mindy a second to realize what Damian's next move was going to be. When she did, she tried to jump up and run away, but she was too late. Damian grabbed her by the legs and pulled her into the pool.

"You rat!" she cried as she broke the surface of the water after she had been dunked, pushing her wet hair away from her face.

Before she could say anything else, Damian swam over to Mindy and pressed his lips against hers, giving her another kiss.

Once again, Mindy found herself melting. . . .

Cooper watched as Damian kissed Mindy in the pool. He wouldn't say he was *jealous*. More like envious. He wished he could be kissing Ava the way Damian was kissing Mindy.

Or the way Ava had kissed him that morning.

He still couldn't believe that Ava had kissed him. *She* had made the first move and taken him totally by surprise.

But it was a nice surprise.

At least for him.

As for Ava . . .

Cooper sighed. He knew she regretted what she had done. Not only because she'd frantically apologized but also because she was keeping her distance. Since she'd arrived at the party, he'd barely seen her, and now she was hiding inside.

He didn't want to go searching for her. If he did, it would only freak her out. Eventually, she'd come back outside. But even then, he would keep his distance and wait for Ava to come to him. She was probably trying to figure things out.

He knew the kiss had been unexpected. He didn't think Ava had *planned* it. It had just happened. And then *he* had kissed her and she *hadn't* pushed him away.

That had to mean something.

Didn't it?

Of course it did!

What Cooper really wanted to do was talk with Ava. Tell her what he was feeling. But he could tell she had been caught off guard not only by what had happened this morning but the entire week. As much as she didn't want to admit it to herself, she was falling for him.

The last thing Cooper wanted to do was pressure Ava, but there was something going on between them. Something was developing. He knew it. Ava knew it.

Only one question remained.

What were they going to do about it?

Chapter Twenty-One

"I don't believe it!" Danielle gasped the following morning as she walked into the kitchen.

Ava, who was right behind her, asked, "What don't you believe?"

"Take a look around!"

Ava pushed past Danielle and studied the quiet kitchen. "What am I missing?"

"There's no mess!" Danielle pointed out. "The kitchen is spotless. It's just the way we left it before going to bed last night."

Ava took a container of orange juice out of the refrigerator and then went over to a cabinet to get a glass. "You're right!"

"I guess Lindsey taught Howie not to tangle with us!"

"What did I do?" Lindsey asked as she walked through the kitchen's swinging door.

Danielle couldn't help but notice the way Lindsey was dressed. While she and Ava had just rolled out of bed — and looked it with their messy hair, unwashed faces, and oversize sleep shirts — Lindsey was dressed to perfection, wearing a white halter top, pink short shorts, and cork wedge sandals. Hmmm. What was up with that?

"You taught Howie a lesson!" Ava declared.

"Howie's not here?" Lindsey asked.

Was that a note of disappointment in Lindsey's voice? Danielle wondered. Things were getting more interesting by the second. . . .

Ava peered closely at Lindsey's face. "Are you wearing makeup?"

"Just a little lip gloss and mascara."

"And blush!" Danielle pointed out.

"And blush," Lindsey admitted.

"So early in the morning?" Ava asked as she poured herself a glass of orange juice. "Why would you do that?"

"Because she was hoping Howie would be here!" Danielle exclaimed.

Ava sputtered on the orange juice she was sipping. "What?!" She stared at Lindsey in disbelief. "You *like* him? I thought you couldn't stand him!"

"I don't like him!" Lindsey quickly stated.

"Then why do you look the way you do?" Danielle shot back. For once, Lindsey was going to be the one who got grilled!

"A girl can't fix herself up? Spring break is almost over. Why should the two of you have all the fun? Maybe I want a spring fling of my own. Maybe I want a little romance, too!"

"With Howie?" Danielle teased.

"Not with Howie!" Lindsey exclaimed.

"I wouldn't say I'm having a little romance," Ava said, sitting down at the kitchen table. "More like making a big mess!"

"You're being too hard on yourself," Danielle said, taking the seat next to Ava. She knew Ava had kept her distance from Cooper at Mindy's pool party, making sure she was never alone with him and always in a group. "Cooper knows you're trying to figure things out."

"I've been trying to figure things out all week and I still haven't!"

"Maybe today's the day that you'll have your breakthrough," Lindsey suggested as she poured some orange juice for herself.

"Maybe." Ava sighed. "I need to decide what to do. It's not fair of me to keep Cooper dangling."

"Are you hanging out with him today?" Danielle asked.

Ava shook her head. "No. I need to be alone so I can try to sort things out."

"But you're coming to the Miss Spring Break contest, right?" Danielle asked, a note of panic in her voice. "You, too, Linds?"

"I wouldn't miss it!" Ava promised.

"I'll be there," Lindsey said, sipping her juice.

Danielle sighed with relief. "Thanks, guys. I need all the support I can get. Jade and Crystal are coming, too. They're giving me a ride."

"What time do you have to get to the beach?" Ava asked.

"Twelve o'clock."

"Are you nervous?" Lindsey asked.

"Of course I'm nervous! I'm petrified! I'm going to be parading in a bathing suit in front of a bunch of guys!"

"You love the attention!" Ava teased. "Don't deny it!"

"It's been a fun few days," Danielle admitted. "But it's going to be over soon, and then it's back to the books."

Lindsey groaned. "Haven't you learned anything while we've been away? You're allowed to have some fun. You don't always have to have your nose to the grindstone! Besides, aren't you going to be busy with Ethan once we get back home?"

Danielle shrugged. "I don't know. Am I?"

"He likes you!"

"And I like him. But we haven't talked about what's going to happen after spring break. For all I know, I've just been a spring fling to him."

"It didn't look that way last night!"

Danielle blushed. She and Ethan had been joined at the hip throughout Mindy's party. When they weren't swimming and splashing each other in the pool, they were in adjoining lounge chairs, hands intertwined as they talked or just laid in the sun. After the party had ended, Ethan had driven her home and then walked her to the front door, giving her a good-night kiss that had lasted a bit longer than most good-night kisses did! He'd still been kissing her when Jade, Crystal, Ava, and Lindsey had gotten home and found them on the front porch. The kiss had instantly ended, Ethan left, and she'd been subjected to endless teasing once they'd gotten inside.

"That was last night," Danielle said.

"Ethan will kiss you like that every night if you let him!" Lindsey vowed. "Come on, Danielle! Loosen up!"

"I'll worry about Ethan and loosening up later," Danielle said, rising from the table and heading back upstairs to start getting ready. "Right now

I'm too busy worrying about the Miss Spring Break contest!"

Three hours later, Danielle was waiting to walk down the runway.

There were twenty girls competing for Miss Spring Break. They had been arranged in height order, from shortest to tallest. Danielle was standing toward the tall end of the line. She was wearing her red bikini — everyone said it made her look fab, so why not wear it? She was going to need all the help she could get! — and had slicked her hair back with gel so it looked wet and sleek, adding only a pair of silver hoop earrings.

A week ago, if any of her friends had told her she'd be in a beauty contest, she would have laughed at them. Danielle Hollis never worried about her hair and makeup; she never worried about how she dressed. The only thing she worried about was her grades.

Now here she was, getting ready to strut her stuff!

And worrying about it!

Danielle checked out her competition and once again wondered what she was doing here. She had to be crazy. The girls surrounding her were gorgeous. She didn't stand a chance against any of them! She should just leave. There was still time.

"We're ready to start!" a guy called out.

And then, before Danielle could step out of the line, she was hustled along with the other girls through a gauzy white curtain leading out to a runway set up on the beach.

As she walked out into the sun, Danielle could see there were rows and rows of guys. They were hooting and hollering. Laughing and whistling.

And they were all staring at her!

She tried not to look out at the audience, but it was hard. Instead, she focused on the high-heeled sandals she was wearing. She hated heels, but they *did* make her legs look good!

Out of the corner of her eye, she could see Ava and Lindsey rooting for her. Standing next to them was Jade, who had a huge smile on her face and was proudly pointing her out to Crystal, who gave her a wave.

But there was one person she was specifically looking for.

One person whose face she wanted to find in the crowd.

Where was he?

She tried not to be obvious as she searched for him.

And then, at the back of the crowd, she spotted him.

Ethan.

As soon as she saw him, she felt less nervous. Because she knew, to him, she was the prettiest girl there.

And that meant a lot.

She could feel his eyes following her every move as she reached the end of the runway, paused for a moment, gave some attitude the way Tyra Banks advised her wannabe models on *America's Next Top Model*, then turned and walked back the way she came.

Seeing him had given her the boost of confidence she'd needed.

After all the girls had walked down the runway, they waited in line before being broken into groups of five. The emcee of the contest explained to the audience that one girl would be picked from each group. Whichever girl in each group got the most applause would make it to the next round. Those four remaining girls would then be competing for third place, second place, first place, and Miss Spring Break.

Danielle was in the last group of girls. She watched from backstage as the audience applauded for each girl until the first three were picked.

Then it was Danielle's group's turn.

The first girl to walk down the runway was a leggy brunette wearing a one-piece gold swimsuit. She got a nice round of applause. The second girl was a redhead wearing a black bikini. She got as much applause as the brunette.

Then Danielle walked back down the runway.

When she did, the applause was thundering. For almost a second, she wanted to point a finger at herself and ask, "Who? Me?"

She couldn't believe what she was hearing!

After that, it was all over for the rest of her group. The level of their applause didn't come anywhere near Danielle's. She was named the winner and joined the other three girls who had already been chosen by the audience.

Now one of them would be voted Miss Spring Break.

The rest of the contest passed by in a blur for Danielle. Each girl walked down the runway one last time and the audience once again voted by applauding. A brunette with a short pixie cut won third place, and an African American girl with blond corkscrew curls won second place.

That left Danielle and another girl to find out who would win first place and who would win Miss Spring Break.

Danielle still couldn't believe she had made it as far as she had.

The emcee pointed to Danielle's competition, a petite blonde wearing a sky blue bikini. She got a loud round of applause. Then the emcee pointed to Danielle, who received an even louder round of applause.

"We have a winner!" the emcee announced, taking Danielle by the hand and raising it up in the air.

The competition was over.

A shocked Danielle was Miss Spring Break!

"I can't believe it!" Danielle said when she got off the stage and was surrounded by Ava and Lindsey, who instantly hugged her. She was wearing a sash that said MISS SPRING BREAK, and a plastic tiara had been slipped onto her head. In her arms was a bouquet of red roses.

"I knew you were going to win!" Lindsey gushed. "I just knew it!"

"I didn't!" Danielle laughed. "Thanks for the applause."

"Don't thank just us," Lindsey said, pointing over her shoulder. "You had a little help from a friend."

Danielle turned around with a smile, expecting to see Ethan.

Instead, she saw Rory.

"Hey, gorgeous!" he said. "Congrats!"

"Thanks," she said, surprised to see him.

"You didn't think I was going to miss this, did you?" he asked. "Didn't I say you were a shoo-in?"

Danielle felt herself blushing. "Yes, you were the one who told me to enter the contest," she admitted.

"And you didn't want to! See, I was right."

"You were right," Danielle agreed. "I owe my tiara to you."

"It looks good on you."

"It makes me feel special. I'm going to wear it until I get back home. That way everyone at North Ridge High can see that I was voted Miss Spring Break!"

"You should," Rory said.

"Where were you? I didn't see you."

"I was busy working up the crowd," he explained. "I've got a lot of friends. And they've got friends."

"You made them applaud for me?"

"I didn't make them do anything," Rory said. "If they applauded for you, it was because they liked what they saw. Just like I do."

Danielle blushed again. Before she could say anything, Jade came running backstage. "Li'l sis! You won! You won!" Jade wrapped her arms around Danielle in a huge hug, squeezing tight. "I'm so proud of you!"

"Me, too!" Crystal said, joining in with a hug of her own.

"I can't breathe!" Danielle laughed.

Jade broke the hug first. "This calls for a celebration!"

"What kind of a celebration?" Danielle asked.

"A party!"

"Where?"

Crystal's eyes lit up. "Back at the house!"

"Is Sharla going to be okay with that?" Ava asked.

"Aunt Sharla's going to be out late tonight," Crystal said. "*Very* late. She's got some sort of charity benefit. She's not going to be home until three o'clock in the morning."

Jade snapped her fingers in the air and bumped her hip against Crystal's. "Which means that we can *par-tay*!"

Crystal checked the time on her cell phone and then turned to Jade. "Come on! We need to go shopping. We've got tons to do!"

"Ava and I will help," Lindsey offered, hurrying after Crystal and Jade.

"Can you get back to the house okay?" Ava asked Danielle.

"I'll give her a ride," Rory offered.

"Thanks, but *I'll* be giving her a ride home," Ethan said as he walked up to Danielle's side and gave her a hug. "Congratulations."

At the sight of Ethan, Danielle's face lit up with a smile. "Hey! Where have you been?"

"Trying to make my way through the crowd. You've got a lot of admirers out there."

Not to mention the two back here, Danielle thought, picking up on the tension between Ethan and Rory. Why did guys have to be this way? Why couldn't they play nice?

"I have to pose for some pictures for the local paper," Danielle told Ethan. "Are you sure you don't mind hanging around?"

"Take all the time you need," Ethan said. "I'm not going anywhere."

Danielle noted that Ethan's last comment was aimed directly at Rory.

"So you're having a party tonight," Rory said. "Mind if I come?"

"You have to come!" Danielle exclaimed, ignoring the scowl that suddenly appeared on Ethan's face. How could she *not* invite Rory? "If it wasn't for you, we wouldn't be having a party," she said, hoping Ethan was listening to her words. "I wouldn't even be Miss Spring Break if you hadn't made me fill out an entry form. You have to be there."

"Then I'll be there," Rory promised. "Is it okay if I bring some friends?"

Danielle turned away from the mirror where she was checking her tiara, making sure it sat *just right* on her head. "Why not?" What were a couple more people? It was a party. "The more, the merrier!"

Chapter Twenty-Two

The party was out of control.

It had started out small and then it had kept growing.

And growing.

And growing.

Every room of the beach house was filled. Danielle had never seen so many people before. Everywhere she looked, there were guys and girls. In the bedrooms, the living room, the dining room and kitchen. They were also in the bathrooms, sitting on the stairs leading to the second floor, and lining the front porch. Music was blaring, couples were dancing, and everyone was having a good time.

Everyone except Danielle, Ava, and Lindsey.

"Where's everyone coming from?" a panicked

Danielle asked Ava as another two cars parked in front of the house and more couples spilled out.

"I don't know, but it's not letting up!" Ava exclaimed, turning away from the living room window.

"What are we going to do?" a worried Lindsey asked. "Even if everyone leaves by midnight, this place is going to be a mess. There's no way we'll get it all cleaned up by the time Sharla gets home. We're going to be in *big* trouble."

"Jade and Crystal are going to be in big trouble," Ava pointed out. "They're the ones who kept inviting everyone they crossed paths with at the supermarket! And those people probably invited their friends, who did the same thing!"

"This is my big sister we're talking about!" Danielle reminded them. "When have you ever known her *not* to drag me into things when she gets into trouble?"

"We should try to find them," Lindsey said, darting her head around the crowd.

"And then what?" Ava asked.

"Have them tell everyone that the party is over!" Lindsey stated.

"It just started!" Ava shot back. "No one's going to leave."

"Well, we have to do something!"

"Come on," Danielle said. "Let's see if they're in the kitchen."

It took them a while to make their way through the crowd, but they finally reached the kitchen. There they found Jade and Crystal opening bags of chips and jars of salsa, pouring them into bowls.

"Isn't this party a blast!" Jade howled when she caught sight of Danielle.

"There are *soooo* many cute guys out there," Crystal giggled.

"There are too many people!" Danielle exclaimed. "This house isn't big enough for everyone."

Jade waved a hand dismissively. "It's a spring break party! It's supposed to be big!"

"Massive!" Crystal added.

"You're not back at North Ridge High!" Jade added. "This is how the big kids party!"

"But when everyone leaves, the house is going to be a mess," Danielle said. "Sharla is going to flip out!"

"Don't worry about Aunt Sharla," Crystal said. "I know how to handle her."

"I hope so," Danielle worriedly stated.

Jade shoved bowls of chips and salsa at Danielle. "Here, take these into the dining room. Then relax. Have a good time! You're Miss Spring Break!"

"Maybe she's right," Lindsey said as she and Ava followed Danielle out of the kitchen. "Maybe we should just have a good time."

"I guess," Danielle murmured. "Things can't get any worse, right?"

An hour later, things had gotten worse.

Danielle was walking out of the dining room when Rory stepped in front of her.

"There you are!" he exclaimed, giving her a smile. "I've been looking all over for you. From the size of this crowd, it wasn't easy."

"The party's gotten a little bit out of control."

"But it's a blast!"

"I'm glad you're having fun." Danielle wished she could say the same thing, but she was too busy cleaning up spilled drinks, tossing out paper plates and plastic cups, and trying to make sure the house stayed in one piece. She and Ava and Lindsey had already collected all of Sharla's fragile belongings and hidden them away in closets so they wouldn't break.

"I see you're still wearing your tiara," Rory said.

"Of course I'm still wearing it! I told you, I'm not taking it off until I get back home."

"I never got a chance to congratulate you today," Rory said.

"Yes, you did."

"I mean *really* congratulate you. In a personal way."

"Personal way?" Danielle asked, confused.

Rory nodded, giving Danielle a smile. "I've been wanting to do this all week. Since the first time I saw you."

"Do what?"

"This!"

And then Rory caught Danielle off guard, pressing her against the wall and giving her a kiss.

Danielle wasn't going to lie to herself. She had wondered what it would be like to kiss Rory and now she was finding out.

His kiss was nice.

He definitely knew what to do with his lips.

But it wasn't anything special.

His kiss wasn't like Ethan's.

Ethan!

Oh, no!

NO!

Luckily, Rory's kiss ended and Danielle frantically searched the party crowd, but she didn't see

Ethan anywhere. In fact, she hadn't seen him all night. Maybe he hadn't arrived yet. Could she be that lucky?

She desperately hoped so.

She knew when it came to Rory that Ethan was jealous.

She didn't want to imagine what might happen if he saw Rory kissing her.

Ethan couldn't believe what he was seeing.

He had just walked through the front door and was making his way to the dining room for a soda when he saw Rory kissing Danielle.

Ethan didn't even think of what he was going to do next. Instinctively, he stormed his way through the party crowd and grabbed Rory by the arm, pulling him off Danielle just as he was getting ready to give her a second kiss.

Rory stared at Ethan's hand on his arm. "Let go," he said, his voice a steely whisper.

"What are you going to do if I don't?"

"This!" Rory shouted, throwing a punch.

Within seconds, Rory and Ethan were punching and shoving each other while the partygoers surrounding them started cheering them on, chanting, "Fight! Fight! Fight! Fight!"

"Stop it!" a horrified Danielle cried. "Stop it!"

But Ethan and Rory wouldn't listen. They kept fighting until Danielle tossed the contents of an ice bucket over their heads. As soon as they were splashed with water, the fighting stopped.

"What did you do that for?" Rory asked, wiping his face with the bottom of his T-shirt.

"I had to do something to break things up!" Danielle shouted.

"He started it!" Ethan accused.

"No, *you* started it!" Rory threw back.

"Who said you could kiss Danielle?"

"Hey, I might have made the first move, but Danielle didn't push me away from her. You've got two eyes. You saw what was going on. She let me kiss her!"

Listening to Rory's words, Ethan replayed the scene he had walked in on. It was true. Rory might have been kissing Danielle, but Danielle hadn't been doing anything to stop him. Suddenly, he felt like an idiot.

"I'm out of here," Rory told Danielle. "I don't have time for these games."

Danielle didn't say anything to Rory as he walked away. Instead, she turned to Ethan. "Let me look at your face," she offered, reaching out to gently touch a bruised cheek.

Ethan pushed her hand away. "Leave me alone!" he snarled.

Danielle stared at him in shock. "Ethan! I know you're mad, but I didn't ask him to kiss me!"

"Maybe you didn't ask him," Ethan accused, "but he's not solely to blame. You've been flirting with him all week. Admit it, Danielle! You wanted him to kiss you!"

Danielle didn't say anything, which for Ethan was all the answer he needed.

"I thought so," he whispered.

"Ethan! Wait!" Danielle pleaded. "Let me explain!"

Ethan didn't want to hear Danielle's explanation. Instead, he said exactly the same thing as Rory. "I'm out of here."

Then he turned his back on Danielle and left the party.

Mindy loved arriving late to parties. It meant she could make an entrance. Why show up early when no one was there? If no one was there, they couldn't see how fabulous you looked.

And tonight Mindy looked fabulous!

She was wearing a ruffled silk chiffon halter dress in purple with strappy sandals and dangling gold earrings.

Across the room, Vivienne waved at her. Mindy knew she and Lacey had come to the party on their own, while Wanda had been picked up earlier in the evening by Rick, who had taken her out to dinner.

"Love the outfit!" Vivienne raved, seeing it for the first time.

Mindy wished she could say the same about what Vivienne was wearing. It was a navy-and-white-zigzag minidress that made Mindy dizzy just looking at it. Lacey's outfit was just as bad. She was in a silver strapless bustier minidress that made it look like she was wearing aluminum foil! Both dresses had been chosen by Wanda during a shopping spree that afternoon. When Ava had texted Mindy to invite them to the party, Wanda had insisted they all buy new outfits. But once they'd gotten to the mall, instead of letting everyone buy what they wanted, Wanda had weighed in with her own opinion and *strongly* urged everyone to buy the dresses she suggested.

Everyone had.

But that didn't mean they had to wear them.

At least Mindy hadn't.

The lime green ruched rayon jersey dress Wanda had chosen for Mindy was back in her closet. And hidden *waaaay* in the back! Originally, she was going to wear the dress — *because that was what*

Wanda wanted — but she hated everything about it. The color, the fit, the fabric.

That night, before leaving for the party, she had been wearing the dress and studying herself in her bedroom mirror when Carmela walked by the open doorway. When she saw Mindy in the dress, she did a double take, rubbing her eyes.

"That is one ugly dress!" she exclaimed. "Have you suddenly gone blind?"

"It's not that bad," Mindy said, turning away from her image.

"It's *bad*!"

"At the store, Wanda said it looked good on me."

Carmela raised an eyebrow. "And you believed her?"

"Why would she lie?"

Carmela walked over to Mindy and had her face the mirror, pointing to her image. "That's why! You're a pretty girl. Much prettier than she is! She doesn't want you to outshine her."

"But if I don't wear the dress, she'll get mad."

"Do you want Damian to see you in this dress?"

"No!" Mindy instantly answered although she hadn't heard from Damian all day. Not that she was surprised. He'd collected his kiss (as well as a second one!) so all interest in her was probably gone.

Still, that didn't mean she couldn't look hot. Let him see what he'd be missing!

Carmela walked over to Mindy's closet and slid the door back. "You've got a ton of gorgeous dresses in there. Pick one that *you* like that's going to make Damian notice *you*."

"You really think I should?"

Carmela shook her head. "I'm not going to tell you what to do, Mindy. But there's a time when you realize you have to stand up for yourself. Sure, you can do what Wanda says and she'll probably let you into her group. But is that what you really want? Is that what's *really* going to make you happy? Think about it."

After Carmela left, Mindy turned back to her image in the mirror. Blech! She was a huge Fashion Don't! She couldn't wear this! She turned away from the mirror and reached back into her closet, pulling out another dress. The purple chiffon had been a recent purchase and she was dying to wear it. That afternoon, after they'd come home from shopping, she'd been going through her closet when Lacey had walked into her bedroom and seen it.

"Fierce!" she had declared. "I bet you wish you were wearing that tonight! You'd look sensational in it!"

"You think?"

"Without a doubt!"

In the end, Mindy decided to wear the dress that she wanted. After all, how could she *not* look sensational? Wanda might get pissed off at her, but it was a small price to pay. Besides, she had done everything else Wanda wanted this week. She'd definitely paid her dues.

"So you decided to wear that dress," Lacey said as she sipped from a red plastic cup. "I didn't know you were such a rebel. Wanda's not going to be too happy."

"Stop scaring her!" Vivienne said.

"I'm not scaring her! I'm telling her the truth." Lacey lifted her cup, pointing it at herself and Vivienne. "The only reason Wanda picked these hideous dresses for us is because she doesn't want us to look better than she does."

"They're not *that* bad," Vivienne said.

"It's why she picked that lime green dress for you," Lacey told Mindy. "But you're not wearing it. And when Wanda finds out, she's going to be *pissed.*"

"Where is Wanda?" Vivienne asked. "I haven't seen her all night."

"Stick around," Lacey said. "She's going to flip out *big-time* when she sees what Mindy is wearing."

Mindy found herself getting nervous. "She's not going to be *that* mad, is she?"

312

Lacey shrugged, giving Mindy the same secret smile as the other day. "Wait and see."

Okay, now it was official. Mindy was panicking. Lacey's smile was what did it. It meant trouble. Maybe she should leave the party and go home and change before Wanda saw her. Maybe . . .

"Mindy!"

She turned around and saw Damian headed her way.

"You look hot!" he exclaimed.

Maybe she *wasn't* going to go home and change.

Maybe she was going to keep wearing this dress!

"Did you just get here?" he asked.

"Five minutes ago."

"Want something to drink?"

"Coke is fine."

"Be right back."

Mindy turned back to Vivienne and Lacey, but both were gone. That was strange.

And then she heard another voice behind her.

A voice that made her blood turn cold.

"That's not the dress I picked out for you."

Mindy whirled around, swallowing the lump of fear in her throat. No wonder Lacey and Vivienne had disappeared. Standing behind her, with fury in her eyes, was Wanda.

Wearing the exact same dress as Mindy!

"Is this your idea of a joke?" Wanda hissed, poking a finger in Mindy's chest. "To show up wearing the same dress as me?"

"Th-th-that wasn't the dress you bought this afternoon!" Mindy pointed out, trying not to sound nervous, and failing. "Where did you get it?"

"As if you didn't know!"

"I don't!"

"Lacey bought it for me. It was an early birthday present. She gave it to me late this afternoon. She told me that you helped her pick it out."

Lacey! Even though she couldn't have known for sure that Mindy would wear the purple chiffon, she'd taken a chance that Mindy would and bought the exact same dress for Wanda. She'd set her up and Mindy had fallen right into her trap!

"And that isn't the dress you bought, either!" Wanda shot back. "I picked out the dress you were supposed to be wearing tonight, remember?"

"I changed my mind and decided to go with something else."

"Obviously you made the wrong choice," Wanda said, folding her arms over her chest. "So what are you going to do about it?"

Mindy knew what she had to say. "Go home and change."

"Change into what?"

There was only one answer. Mindy had no choice. She had already defied Wanda and couldn't do it again.

"The dress you picked out for me."

Wanda smiled smugly. "That's right. Who do you think you are, Mindy? Here I am trying to be your friend, giving you advice, and you ignore it! Are you stupid?" She didn't give Mindy a chance to answer. "That must be it. You're stupid! No wonder you don't have any friends at North Ridge High! You think you're smarter and better than everyone else."

Mindy could feel tears forming in the corners of her eyes. She did *not* think she was better than everyone else! And she would never humiliate a friend the way Wanda was humiliating her in front of everyone. She knew people were staring. Listening. Whispering.

Before she could say anything, Damian came to her rescue.

"If anyone should go home and change, it's you, Wanda," he said, handing Mindy her Coke. "That dress looks way better on Mindy than it does on you. She's got the bod for it. You don't."

Hearing those words, Mindy gasped, almost dropping the red plastic cup that Damian had given her.

Oh, no!

315

No!

What had Damian done?

Behind her, she could hear people snickering and laughing.

But not at her.

At Wanda.

Mindy stole a peek at Wanda's face and saw what she expected.

Hatred.

And it was aimed directly at her. She'd embarrassed Wanda, and Wanda would never forget that.

Mindy knew it was all over.

There was no way she'd be getting into the Princess Posse now.

Danielle felt awful. Awful! The fight between Rory and Ethan was all her fault, and now Ethan thought she was cheating on him!

Jade found her sitting on the steps of the back porch and sat down next to her. "What are you doing hiding out here when there's a party in your honor going on inside?"

"I messed things up." Danielle sighed, resting her head against Jade's shoulder.

Jade wrapped a reassuring arm around Danielle. "How'd you mess up?"

Danielle told Jade how she'd been flirting with Rory for most of the week, how he'd kissed her at the party, and Ethan's reaction.

"That's what you're so upset about?" Jade laughed. "That happens to me almost every week!"

"Stuff like that might happen to you, but you know how to handle it!" a frustrated Danielle cried. "I don't! I'm not the pretty Hollis sister. I'm the smart one! I've only been the pretty sister for a few days. I'm not used to it!"

"You're smart *and* pretty," Jade told Danielle, looking into her tear-filled eyes. "You always have been. You just didn't know it. Don't be so hard on yourself. Nobody's perfect, Danielle. Okay, so you got a little bit out of control this week with your makeover, but you didn't do anything wrong. It's not like you were dating Rory behind Ethan's back or lying to them. Both guys knew about the other one. It's not your fault that Ethan got jealous. In fact, I think you still have a chance with him."

Danielle sniffed, wiping away her tears. "I do?"

"The fact that Ethan lost his temper means something."

"It does?"

"Yes! He likes you!"

"Then why wouldn't he let me explain?"

"Duh! He's a guy. Guys have huge egos."

"What should I do?"

"I think you should find Ethan and make him listen. Any idea where he might have gone?"

Danielle stared at the house next door. "I think so."

"Then what are you waiting for?"

"I just need to go inside and get something," Danielle said, heading back into the house. "Thanks for the advice, Jade."

"That's what big sisters are for!"

"Why did you do that?" Mindy hissed at Damian once Wanda had stormed off. She didn't care who was watching. She was too angry! "Why? You ruined everything! All I had to do was go home and change my dress. Everything would have been fine!"

Damian stared at Mindy in disbelief. "Did you not hear a word she said? She called you stupid. She was insulting you!"

"That's the way Wanda is."

"I can't believe you're defending her!"

"I'm not defending her!"

"So you *like* being treated like that?"

"Of course not!"

"Then why do you want to put up with it?"

"I already told you!"

"Yeah, yeah, yeah," Damian said, rolling his eyes. "So you can be part of her group."

"It might not matter to you, but it matters to me!"

"Is that witch the best you can do for a friend?" Damian asked. "If no one at your high school wants to be friends with you, then they're nuts! I'll be friends with you."

Mindy snorted. "Why would you want to be friends with me?"

"Why not? You're funny and smart and you know how to go after what you want. You're also a knockout and you know how to wear a smoking hot dress!"

Mindy had never gotten so many compliments at once from a guy. But she was still mad at him! He'd ruined things with Wanda!

"Maybe I don't want to be friends with you!" Mindy shouted.

"Oh, you don't?" Damian asked, leaning into Mindy's space and pressing his face close to hers . . . so close that she could look into his green eyes . . . so close that she could smell his cologne . . . so close that she could reach out and trace his lips with a finger. "What do you want?"

"Maybe I want to be more than friends!"

Damian gave Mindy a wicked smile. "I wouldn't

have a problem with that. Maybe I need to see what it's like to go out with just one girl."

"Think you're up to the challenge? Think you can handle me?"

"Oh, I can handle you. The question is, can *you* handle *me*?"

"I'm willing to give it a shot if you are," Mindy said, her heart pounding madly as she waited for Damian's answer.

"Then what are we waiting for?" he asked. "Let's make this official!"

And then, before Mindy even knew it was happening, Damian was kissing her . . . and she was kissing him right back!

Danielle rang the doorbell of Ethan's beach house. Seconds later, he came to the door.

"What you do you want?" he asked.

"I brought you something," she said, holding up a dish towel filled with ice cubes. "I thought you could use it."

Ethan unlocked the screen door and walked back into the house. Danielle followed him into the living room, where the TV was on. He plopped back down on the couch, picking up the remote control as Danielle sat next to him.

"What are you watching?" she asked.

"I'm just channel surfing."

"Is it okay if I press this against your cheek?" she asked, holding up the dish towel.

Ethan shrugged. "If you want."

Danielle moved closer to him, pressing the dish towel against his cheek. Already it was starting to bruise. "Does that hurt?"

"It's fine," he said, even though he flinched.

"Ethan, I'm sorry," she said. "I didn't know Rory was going to kiss me tonight. It just happened."

"You liked kissing him," Ethan accused.

"Actually, I didn't."

"You didn't?" Ethan skeptically asked. "Could have fooled me."

"I will admit that I wondered what it would be like to kiss Rory, but I *never* encouraged him," she clarified. "Besides, I liked your kisses better."

Ethan perked up. "Really?"

"Uh-huh." Danielle pressed the dish towel back against Ethan's cheek. "What can I do to make things up to you?"

Ethan thought about it. Then he said, "A kiss would be nice."

Danielle leaned over and removed the dish towel, kissing Ethan's bruised cheek. "Better?"

Ethan shook his head. "I was hoping you'd kiss me someplace else."

Danielle kissed his other cheek. "Better?"

Ethan shook his head again.

Danielle pretended to think. "Hmmm. Where else can I kiss you?" And then she leaned down and kissed Ethan on the lips. "Better?"

Ethan smiled. "*Much* better!"

"Hey!" Damian exclaimed from the doorway, Mindy by his side. "You won the bet!"

Danielle stared from Damian to Ethan. "Bet? What bet?"

"Oops!" a red-faced Damian exclaimed, pressing a hand to his mouth.

Mindy sighed. "What did you do *now*?"

Ethan glared at Damian. "Thanks a lot, bigmouth!"

Damian took Mindy by the hand, pulling her into the kitchen. "I think I'll let Ethan explain."

"So what's this about a bet?" Danielle asked after Damian and Mindy were gone. "Tell me."

"Cooper and I made a bet on the first day of spring break," Ethan explained. "To see who could get kissed first by one of the girls next door. Cooper suggested we switch places so I could see what it was like to be a rich guy and he'd be an average guy. He seemed to think girls were only interested in him for his money. The Mercedes didn't come with the beach house. It's Coop's."

"So the credit cards were his, too?"

"Cut off by his father."

"I'll bet you were pissed off at Cooper that day we went to the restaurant."

"I was mad because you had to wash those dishes."

"I've washed dishes lots of times. It was no big deal."

"It was to me," Ethan said. "I wanted to treat you like a princess, Danielle."

"You did? Why?"

"Because I like you." A blushing Ethan stared down at the remote control in his hands. "A lot."

Danielle placed a finger under Ethan's chin, lifting his head up. "I like you, too." She paused and then said, "A lot."

"Anyway," Ethan continued, "as Cooper and I got to know you and Ava, we decided to call off the bet."

"How come?"

"We liked both of you and we didn't want the first time one of us kissed you to be connected to the bet."

Danielle was silent for a moment. Then she said, "Okay."

"That's it?" Ethan asked. "Aren't you going to say anything else?"

"What's there to say?"

"You're not mad?"

"What's there to be mad about? You might have been pretending to be someone else, but on the inside, you were still the same Ethan. The same sweet guy I fell for," she said softly.

"You fell for me?" Ethan asked.

"Yes." Danielle pressed the dish towel back against Ethan's cheek. "Besides, I'm just as guilty as you."

"Guilty? What do you mean?"

"I've been pretending this week, too," she confessed. "Back home in North Ridge, I'm not the hot spring break babe you've been around all week." Danielle pulled off her tiara and tossed it onto the coffee table. "I'm as fake as this plastic crown."

"What do you mean?"

"This isn't me. Until this week, I was never into the way I looked. Clothes and hair and makeup never mattered to me. My sister and my friends gave me a spring break makeover on our first day and, well, it kind of went to my head. All of a sudden, I was getting all this attention from guys and I wasn't used to it. I'm usually a bookworm who *doesn't* flirt with guys. I've always been a one-guy girl."

"How about if we both start over?" Ethan asked. "We go back to just being ourselves. Ethan and Danielle."

"I'd like that," Danielle agreed with a smile. "But on one condition."

"What?"

"You get to be my one guy."

"Only if you get to be my one girl."

"I'd like that," Danielle whispered as she gave Ethan a kiss. "I'd like that a lot!"

Chapter Twenty-Three

Cooper usually loved to party, but he wasn't in the mood tonight. All around him, couples were laughing and dancing, having a good time, but he was oblivious to it. All he wanted to do was talk to Ava, but he couldn't find her anywhere. He'd arrived more than an hour ago and they hadn't crossed paths yet. It was almost like she was avoiding him. And he knew why. Ava was scared . . . scared that she was developing feelings for him.

That kiss she had given him yesterday was proof that she felt something for him.

But she didn't want to admit it.

Instead, she wanted to hide.

Well, Ava could hide for now, Cooper thought as he scoped the party crowd, but eventually he was going to find her.

And when he did, he was going to tell her how he felt.

He liked her. A lot. And he wanted to keep seeing her once they got back home to North Ridge.

Hopefully, she'd want to keep seeing him.

Hopefully, she'd want to be his girlfriend.

Because he wanted to be her boyfriend.

Ava made him feel special. She didn't make him feel like he was a prize that was being competed for the way most of his dates did. She didn't care about his family's money. Heck, she didn't even know about it! She just liked him for who he was.

Finally, Cooper caught sight of Ava heading into the kitchen with a stack of empty red cups. He hurried after her and found her trying to reach a bag of potato chips perched on the top shelf of a cupboard.

"Let me do that," he said, reaching above her.

She whirled around. "Cooper!"

"Surprised to see me?" he asked, handing her the potato chips.

"Of course not! You were invited."

"First time I've seen you all night," he pointed out.

"As you can see, it's a zoo out there," Ava explained as she ripped open the bag of potato chips and poured them into a bowl. "Plus, I've been running around playing hostess."

"And avoiding me," Cooper stated.

Ava bit into a potato chip. "Why would I be avoiding you?"

"Because you don't want to talk to me."

Ava shoved another potato chip into her mouth. "That's silly! Of course I want to talk to you."

"Really?" Cooper leaned against the refrigerator, crossing his arms over his chest as he watched Ava nervously eat another potato chip. "Then why haven't I seen you all day?"

"I needed some time to myself," she admitted. "I've been thinking."

"About?"

"Us."

Hearing that word, Cooper's heart nearly stopped. "There's an us?" he dared to ask.

"Yes, there's an us. You know there is."

Cooper shrugged, trying to remain calm. Trying not to get his hopes up. "How would I know that? Like I said, you've been avoiding me. You need two people to make an us. Just like you need two people to make a couple. Do you see us as a couple, Ava? Because I do."

Ava sighed, abandoning the potato chips. "Cooper, I like you. I really do. You're a great guy and I've loved every minute I've spent with you."

"I sense a *but* coming," Cooper said, hoping he was wrong but knowing he wasn't. "That's never a good sign."

"But I'm not ready to be in a relationship," she finished. "I just ended things with Josh and it's too soon for me to start dating again. I'm still nursing a broken heart and I need to put the pieces back together before I'm ready to give my heart to someone else. I do have feelings for you; I'm not going to deny that I do. It's been great feeling all nervous and excited again. Butterflies in my stomach and tingles down my spine. The magic of kissing someone new and wanting to kiss them again. You know what I'm talking about, right?"

"I sure do," Cooper whispered.

"It's all been wonderful, but before I start dating another guy, I need some time to myself."

"How much time?"

"I don't know."

"And then? Once you've had that time?"

"There might be a chance for us," Ava said. "But I don't know when that will be and I don't want you waiting for me. It wouldn't be right. Can't we just be friends? Or have I broken the Smooth Operator's heart?"

Cooper stared at Ava in shock. "Where did you hear that nickname?"

"Smooth Operator?"

"Yeah."

"From my cousin Amelia," Ava said. "She goes to South Ridge High. She's a junior. The last time I was over at her house, I was flipping through a copy of the *South Ridge High Gazette* and I saw your photo. You had won some sort of academic award. Anyway, when Amelia saw me looking at your photo, she told me all about you. She says all the girls at South Ridge High are *crayzeee* about you."

Crazy about me or crazy about my family's money? Cooper wondered.

"You're *quite* the catch," Ava teased. "Every girl at South Ridge High wants to go out with you."

"Except you," Cooper said, trying not to feel rejected, and failing. It hurt that Ava didn't want to go out with him. That she didn't want to take a chance on them. Wasn't that what life was all about? Taking chances? Risks?

"I don't go to South Ridge High," Ava pointed out. "So you didn't answer my question." She touched Cooper on the arm. "I know what I've said isn't what you wanted to hear, but right now, it's the best I can do. And I really do mean it. I want to be friends with you, but if you can't handle it, I understand."

Cooper thought about what he wanted to say. He was still reeling over the fact that Ava knew all about him. That she knew he was rich. He wasn't upset, because it hadn't made a difference with her. Ava liked him for who he was. And if it was possible with Ava, maybe it was possible with another girl. A girl who was just as nice as Ava. The thing was, he didn't want another girl. He wanted Ava. But just because he was rich, it didn't mean he could always get what he wanted. It was like they said. Money couldn't buy happiness.

And then he realized something else. There had been no reason for the bet. It had been pointless because all along, Ava had known who he really was. He started laughing.

"What's so funny?" Ava asked.

Cooper decided he would tell Ava about the bet later tonight. He didn't think she would be upset. She'd probably even understand. But right now, they had something more important to discuss.

"I'd love to be friends," he said, watching as Ava smiled. He could see from the relief on her face that she'd been hoping he'd say those words.

"Friends hug," she said. "Can I give you a hug?"

"I'd love one."

As Ava gave him a hug, Cooper held her close. She felt so good in his arms. He didn't want to let go, but knew he'd eventually have to.

Holding Ava, Cooper made a decision. If she needed time for herself, then he was going to give her all the time she needed.

Like they said, some things were worth the wait.

And when it came to Ava, he was willing to wait.

"Do you think anyone noticed we were gone?" Mindy asked Damian when they returned to the party.

"Nah. Lots of couples have been sneaking off, trying to have their last bit of fun before spring break ends."

Damian had taken her next door because he'd wanted them to be alone so they could talk and maybe even kiss a little bit more, but the house hadn't been empty. First they'd walked in on Danielle and Ethan; then Steve had shown up with a bunch of girls, followed by Howie and a bunch of guys. In the end, they decided to come back to the party.

"I'm glad Danielle and Ethan patched things up," Mindy said. "They make a cute couple. Although you nearly ruined things with your big mouth!"

"It just slipped out! Besides, all's well that ends well."

"Don't say anything to Cooper!" Mindy warned. "Let him tell Ava in his own way."

"My lips are sealed," Damian vowed.

Mindy laughed. "Yeah, right! You're worse than me when it comes to keeping a secret! I'll bet you're the biggest gossip at South Ridge High."

"Speaking of gossip, what do you think the grapevine's going to say once we get back home?"

Mindy sighed. "Everyone's going to love dishing the dirt about Wanda and me."

"Actually, I think they're going to be talking about something else."

"What could top our catfight?"

"How about Wanda getting caught cheating on her boyfriend?"

"What?!" Mindy exclaimed in shock.

"Take a look," Damian said, pointing with a finger. "Or rather, take a listen!"

Mindy stared across the room at the staircase leading from the second floor. Rick was racing down the stairs, followed by a pleading Wanda, who was begging him to let her explain why she was with another guy. She'd never seen Wanda so upset before. She was practically on the verge of tears. She reached an arm out to Rick, but he shoved her away, telling her not to touch him. A motionless Wanda stared at him, almost as if she was expecting him to come back to her. When he didn't, Wanda turned around and ran out of the house.

"I wonder what happened," Mindy murmured.

Ava raced over to Mindy. "Where have you been? You missed all the excitement!"

"What are you talking about?"

"Rick caught Wanda making out with a guy in one of the spare bedrooms! He was looking for the upstairs bathroom and opened the wrong door!"

"Who told him which door to open?" a suspicious Mindy asked.

"I saw him talking to Lacey before heading upstairs," Ava said knowingly. "I think you can connect the dots."

"She set Wanda up!" Damian exclaimed.

"Big-time!" Ava agreed.

"What are you all whispering about?" Cooper asked as he joined them. Damian quickly filled him in.

Mindy stared across the living room and saw Lacey "consoling" an upset Rick, giving him a hug and whispering in his ear. Mindy noticed that Lacey's hug lasted a bit longer than necessary. It was definitely more than friendly.

Mindy couldn't believe it. Lacey and Wanda were supposed to be best friends, yet Lacey was making a move on her best friend's boyfriend. She wasn't trying to patch things up. She was making a move on Rick!

It was then that Mindy realized Lacey had been scheming against Wanda the entire week. She might have expressed an interest in Damian, but the guy she'd really been after had been Rick! Wanda had avoided the first trap that Lacey had set for her, but she'd fallen into the second.

Now Wanda had lost Rick.

Tonight, Mindy had seen how awful both Wanda and Lacey could be. She'd experienced it firsthand. And she didn't want to be friends with them. Not anymore. They were mean and selfish, caring only about themselves. Vivienne wasn't so bad. At times, she was even kind of nice. Maybe they could be friends.

But Wanda and Lacey?

Forget it!

She would much rather be friends with someone like Ava.

Hopefully, once they were back in North Ridge, they would be. Mindy felt like the beginning of a friendship with Ava had been started this week.

Ava pulled Mindy off to the side. "So I see that

you and Damian disappeared for a little bit. I want the dirt!"

Mindy pretended to be shocked. "I thought I was North Ridge High's Queen of Gossip."

Ava gave Mindy a smile. "You are! That's why I came straight to the source! So spill! I want *all* the details. Don't leave anything out!"

Mindy spilled!

Chapter Twenty-Four

The airport was a madhouse.

"I can't believe spring break is already over!" Danielle exclaimed as she hurried through the crowd of travelers with Ava and Lindsey. They'd already said good-bye to Jade and Crystal, who had gone off to their gate. "Doesn't it seem like we just got here?"

"I don't know about you two," Lindsey said, "but I can't wait to get back home. I'm all partied out!"

"Don't mention the word *party* to me," Ava groaned. "Not after the one we just had!"

"We're lucky Sharla was too tired to drive back and called to tell us she was staying at a hotel," Danielle said. "Can you imagine if she'd come home that night?"

Ava shuddered. "Our party definitely got out of control."

After getting everyone to leave at two A.M., it had taken the girls the rest of the night to clean the house and get it back in order before they'd crawled into bed at six A.M. They'd slept late yesterday and then gone to the beach, barely moving from their spots in the sand before heading back to the house for a final barbecue. Like their first night, they'd invited the guys next door, as well as Mindy, who came only with Vivienne since Wanda had changed her plane reservation and flown home a day earlier, while Lacey had gone out with Rick.

"What do you think's going to happen at school next week with the Princess Posse?" Lindsey asked as they arrived at their gate and found seats.

"Lacey's definitely out," Ava said.

"After stealing Wanda's boyfriend, I would think so!" Danielle stated.

"Does that mean Mindy's in?" Lacey asked.

Ava shook her head. "Wanda's mad at her, too, but I don't think Mindy cares. She's over wanting to hang out with Wanda."

"It looks like she's going be hanging out with Damian," Danielle said. "They were joined at the hip last night."

"Damian already asked her to the South Ridge

338

High junior prom," Ava said. "She and I are going to go to the mall and look at prom dresses one day after school next week."

"Mindy's not so bad once you get to know her," Danielle said. "Is it okay if I come?"

"Mindy would love it!"

"Count me in, too," Lindsey said as her cell phone buzzed and she checked a text message. Seconds later, she sent a text back, then raised an eyebrow when she saw Danielle reach into her shoulder bag and pull out a copy of *People*. "What are you doing reading that?"

"I got addicted to it, all right?" Danielle grumbled. "And it's all your fault!"

"That's not the only thing you got addicted to!" Lindsey teased. "I thought we were going to have to tear you out of Ethan's arms this morning."

Ethan, Cooper, and Damian had stopped by the house early that morning to say good-bye before beginning their drive back home to North Ridge. "Can I help it if I was already starting to miss him? I didn't want him to go!"

"Hopefully, Damian won't get Cooper and Ethan to agree to any more bets on the drive home!" Lindsey exclaimed.

"If it hadn't been for that bet, we might never have met Cooper and Ethan," Ava pointed out.

"And they did confess to what they did," Danielle added. "In a way, it was kind of romantic."

"So when are you going to see Ethan again?" Ava asked.

"We're getting together on Tuesday night," Danielle said. "It's going to be our first date on home turf. How about you and Cooper? Are you guys going to hang out together?"

"We talked about catching a movie next weekend."

"Is he okay with just being friends?" Lindsey asked as her phone buzzed again.

"He's cool with it," Ava said. "And who knows? Maybe down the road we'll be more than friends."

"I hope so," Lindsey said as her phone buzzed a third and then a fourth time.

"Who *is* that?" Danielle asked, trying not to sound annoyed.

"No one," Lindsey answered a little too quickly.

"*No one* has been texting you most of the morning," Ava said, snatching Lindsey's phone out of her hands and checking the text on the screen. When she saw the name of the sender, she gasped. "I don't believe it!"

"Who's been texting her?" Danielle asked. "Don't keep me in suspense! Tell me!"

"Howie!" Ava announced.

"I knew it!" Danielle exclaimed. "I knew you liked him!"

Lindsey snatched her phone back from Ava. "Did you ever stop to think that maybe *he* had a thing for *me* and that's why he kept crashing our kitchen?"

Danielle laughed. "He crashed our kitchen because he was always hungry!"

"When did this romance begin?" Ava asked.

"It's not a romance!" Lindsey insisted. "We hung out a little bit during the party. That's all."

"Did you kiss him?" Danielle asked.

Lindsey blushed, causing Ava and Danielle to screech.

"You've been holding back!" Danielle accused.

"I can't believe you didn't tell us!" Ava declared.

"It was only a kiss good night. Hardly worth mentioning!"

"A kiss is still a kiss!" Danielle pointed out, giving Lindsey a hug. "And kisses sometimes lead to love! Don't be mad, Linds! We're happy for you! After all, it wouldn't be spring break without a spring fling. And now we've all had one!"

For more North Ridge High romance, don't miss

Be Mine

By Sabrina James

Jennifer couldn't believe how smug Claudia was being. What made her think she was going to win? There were lots of other couples at North Ridge High. Maybe one of them would be voted Most Romantic. There was no guarantee that Claudia and Chase were going to win.

Listening to Claudia go on and on, Jennifer wanted nothing more than to knock her down a few pegs. She couldn't stand listening to her anymore!

Before Jennifer could stop herself, the words came tumbling out of her mouth.

"I wouldn't be too sure about winning," she said.

Take another trip to North Ridge High in

Secret Santa

By Sabrina James

Noelle focused her attention on the red velvet bag Mindy was holding. Then she dipped her hand inside, swirling it around the many slips of paper.

Somewhere inside was Charlie's name.

Unless it had already been picked.

Think positive! Noelle scolded herself. *Positive. Positive. Positive. Charlie's name is in this bag. It is! It is! It is! And I will pull it out. I will! I will! I will!*

Holding her breath, Noelle closed her eyes and reached into the very bottom of the bag, wrapped her fingers around a slip of paper, and pulled it out.

Point
www.thisispoint.com